WITHDRAWN
AND DISCARDED

CENTRAL
AVENUE

Author Note

When I first visited Ireland, I was struck by the raw beauty of the Emerald Isle. The friendliness of the people, the love of stories and the rich traditions made me fall in love with the country. While walking amid the castle ruins, I could sense the ghosts of the medieval folk who dwelled within the walls. It was there that the stories of my MacEgan Irish warriors were born.

This past summer I visited the archaeological remains of several Irish ring forts and Norman ring works. These fortresses were the sites where legendary chieftains and kings fought, lived and loved. I hope you'll enjoy the stories of the MacEgan brothers and the women who captured their hearts. I love to hear from readers, and I invite you to visit my Web site at www.michellewillingham.com. There you'll find some "behind the scenes" photographs.

Her
Irish
Warrior

MICHELLE WILLINGHAM

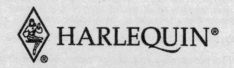

HARLEQUIN®

TORONTO • NEW YORK • LONDON
AMSTERDAM • PARIS • SYDNEY • HAMBURG
STOCKHOLM • ATHENS • TOKYO • MILAN • MADRID
PRAGUE • WARSAW • BUDAPEST • AUCKLAND

ISBN-13: 978-0-373-29450-3
ISBN-10:   0-373-29450-6

HER IRISH WARRIOR

I would like to thank archaeologist Patrick Neary
for teaching me the differences between
Irish ring forts and Norman ring works, and for
answering numerous questions about medieval Ireland.
To MLFF, Tabbwriters, Fiona Lowe, Michelle Styles,
Anna Campbell, Larissa Ione, Jillian Hart and Subcare at
eHarlequin—I deeply appreciate your support during this
journey. Special thanks to Allison Littlehales who helped
me see the manuscript with fresh eyes and to my agent
Carolyn Grayson for her patience. All of you helped me
in many ways you didn't realize.

And most of all, thank you to my editor, Joanne,
for seeing potential and for helping me
to become a better writer.

Dedication

To my family and my husband, for always believing
in me over the years and for your unfailing support.

Chapter One

The island of Erin, 1171 AD

Genevieve de Renalt's breath burned in her lungs as she ran. Every muscle in her body cried out with exhaustion, but she refused to stop. With every step, freedom came a little closer. In the distance she heard hoofbeats approaching. He was coming for her.

I am such a fool, she thought. She needed a horse, supplies, and coins if she had any hope of success. But there had been no time. She had seen the opportunity to flee and seized it. Even if her flight was doomed to failure, she had to try.

This was her only chance to escape her betrothed. The thought of Sir Hugh Marstowe was like a dull knife against an open wound. For she had loved him once. And now she would do anything to escape him.

Hugh kept his horse at an easy trot. He was playing with her, like a falcon circling its prey. He knew he could catch her with no effort at all. Instead, he wanted her to anticipate him. To fear him.

He had controlled her for the past moon, deciding how she

should behave as his future wife. She'd felt like a dog, cowering beneath his orders. Nothing she said or did was ever good enough for him. Her nerves tightened at the memory of his fists.

Loathing surged through her. By the saints, even if her strength failed her she had to leave. She stumbled through the forest, her sides aching, her body's energy waning. Soon she would have to stop running. She prayed to God for a miracle, for a way to save herself from this nightmare. If she stayed any longer she feared she would become a shell of a woman, with no courage, no life left in her at all.

A patch of blackberry thorns slashed at her hands, the briars catching her cloak. The afternoon light had begun to fade, the twilight creeping steadily closer. Genevieve fought back tears of exhaustion, pulling at the briars until her hands were bloody.

'Genevieve!' Hugh called out. His voice sent a coil of dread inside her. He had drawn his horse to a stop at the edge of the woods. The sight of him made her stomach clench.

I won't go back. Stubbornly, she pushed her way through the gnarled walnut trees until she reached the clearing. Frost coated the grasses, and she stumbled to her knees while climbing the slippery hillside.

A strange silence permeated the meadow. From her vantage point atop the hill, she caught a glimpse of movement. The dying winter grass revealed the presence of a man.

No—*men,* she realised. Irishmen, dressed in colours to blend in with their surroundings. Behind them, at the bottom of the hill, she saw a single rider. The warrior sat astride his horse, his cloak pinned with an iron brooch the size of her palm. He did not reach for the sword at his side, but his stance grew alert. A hood concealed his face, and a quiet confidence radiated from him.

Tall and broad-shouldered, he watched her. She could not tell if he was a nobleman or a soldier, but he carried himself like a king. With a silent gesture to his men, they scattered and disappeared behind another hill.

Her heart pounded, for he could strike her down with his sword. Nonetheless, she squared her shoulders and stared at the man. She walked towards him slowly, even as her brain warned her that warriors such as he did not treat women with mercy.

But he had a horse. A horse she needed if there was any chance of escaping Hugh.

The man's gaze locked with hers. If she screamed, it would alert Hugh to their presence. Precious seconds remained, and soon Hugh would overtake her.

'Please,' she implored him. 'I need your help.' Her ragged voice sounded just above a whisper, and for a moment she wondered if the soldier had heard her. Upon his cloak she noticed a Celtic design. This time she repeated her request in Irish. The man's posture changed, and after a moment that stretched into eternity he turned his horse away. Within seconds he disappeared behind a hill, along with Genevieve's hope.

Bevan MacEgan cursed himself for his weakness. From the moment she spoke he had recognised the woman as a Norman. The familiar hatred had risen within him, only to be startled by the desire to help her.

She had awakened the ghost of a memory. With her face and dark hair, the first vision of her had evoked a nightmare he'd tried to forget for two long years. He closed his eyes, willing himself to block her out.

He'd seen her fleeing, long before he had given the order for his soldiers to hide among the hills. Her attacker did not intend to kill her. Were that the case, he could have done so already. No, the Norman's intent was to capture the woman.

And by turning away he'd let it happen.

He'd been forced to choose between the safety of his men and a woman he didn't know. And, though he knew he'd made the right decision, his sense of honour cringed. He was supposed to protect women, not let them come to harm.

But if he interfered now, his battle plans could go awry. He dared not risk the lives of his men by giving away their position. Their attack depended upon the element of surprise. He needed to watch and wait for the right moment.

He found himself issuing orders. 'I want five men to accompany me inside the fortress. Take the others and surround the outer palisade. At sunset, light the fires.'

'You're going after her, aren't you?' the captain of his men remarked.

'I am.'

'You cannot save them all. She is only a woman.'

'Do as I command.' *Tá*, it was an unnecessary risk. But in the woman's eyes he had seen pure terror—the same terror as in his wife's eyes just before the enemy had taken her captive.

And he felt the same helplessness now.

Bevan chose the men who would accompany him and led them towards the fortress of Rionallís. It was his land, stolen by the invaders. With the help of his men, he meant to take it back.

Rionallís was not a *rath*, like the other fortresses, but slightly larger. Within it he'd built an earth and timber castle, similar to the Norman style. He knew every inch of it, and exactly how to penetrate its defences.

At his command, the men moved into position. Bevan waited until they were ready, and pushed away the brambles hiding the entrance to the *souterrain*. The secret tunnel led beneath the fortress, into the chambers used for storage.

He glanced up at the *donjon*, silhouetted by a blood-red sunset. Inwardly, he prayed for victory.

The chill of the *souterrain* passage surrounded him as he entered. He had not been here for the past year and a half, and he noted the emptiness of the storage chambers. They should have been filled with bags of grain and clay-sealed containers of food. His people would suffer this winter unless he did something to help them.

Though he hadn't known about the conquest of his lands until now, he blamed himself. He had allowed his grief to consume him while he hired his sword as a mercenary to other tribes. And last spring the Normans had descended upon Rionallís like locusts, feeding off the labour of his people and desecrating his home. His small army was outnumbered, but he knew the territory well. He would stop at nothing to drive out his enemy.

When he reached the ladder leading into one of the stone beehive-shaped cottages, he paused. He wished he had not seen the Norman woman, her eyes filled with fear as she pleaded for help. It would have been easy to simply hate them all and kill them, spilling their blood for vengeance. But the woman complicated matters.

She was a pretty *cailín*, with a sweet face and deep blue eyes. An innocent, who deserved his protection. He had been unable to save his wife from her attackers. But he could save this woman.

It should have made him feel better. Instead, it added a further element of risk to an already dangerous attack. And yet his mind grasped the possibilities. She would make a good hostage, providing him with the means to regain the fortress. Afterwards he would grant her the freedom she so desired.

Bevan climbed the ladder, surprising the inhabitants of the cottage. He held a finger to his lips, knowing his people would never betray him. The blacksmith moved towards his hammer, in an unspoken promise to give aid if needed.

At the entrance to the hut, Bevan counted the number of enemy soldiers in the courtyard. He would enter the fortress tonight, he decided. And Rionallís would be his once more.

'Genevieve, I am glad to see you safe.' Sir Hugh embraced her while Genevieve fought to breathe. Her strength had given out, and he had caught her at last. She held back tears of frustration, her skin freezing cold.

Dark memories assaulted her. She knew what he would do. She closed off her mind from her body, for it was the only way she could bear the pain.

There was no one left to help her. Her father had sent close friends of his, Sir Peter of Harborough and his wife, to act as guardians until his arrival. He might as well not have sent anyone at all. Both were blind to Hugh's deeds. They saw only a strong leader, a man respected by his soldiers.

When she'd complained of Hugh's punishments, Sir Peter had only shrugged. 'A man has the right to discipline his wife,' he'd said. But she was not Hugh's wife. Not yet. And nothing she said would convince them of any wrongdoing.

Her father's men refused to interfere. The last man who had tried to shield her from a beating had been discovered dead a few days later. The soldiers obeyed Hugh without question, emptiness in their eyes. They were afraid of him, and he knew it.

'I feared for you, out here alone.' Hugh pressed a kiss upon her temple. The gesture felt like a brand, burning into her skin. His words mocked her attempt to escape, seemingly gentle. But she recognised the hardened edge to his voice, the promise of punishment.

Possession dominated his blue eyes. She had once thought him handsome with his dark gold hair cut short. But his heart was as cold as the chain-mail covering his strong form.

She steadied herself. 'Let me go home to my family, Hugh. I am not the wife you need.'

He cupped her chin, his fingers tightening over her flesh. 'You will learn to be the wife I need.'

'There are other women, wealthier than I.' She could not meet his gaze when his hand moved lower, to her waist.

'None of such high rank.' His palm spanned her back, his thumb brushing against a bruise that had not healed. 'None with land such as Rionallís.' His voice grew tinged with ambition. 'Here I can become a king. These Irishmen are primitive, with no knowledge of what it means to fight.' His mouth curved upward. 'And you will reign at my side. The King has commanded it.'

She said nothing. Hugh's prowess on the battlefield had earned him King Henry's favour. When he had offered for her, and received the King's blessing, Genevieve had fallen prey to his flattery. Believing his false courtship, she'd begged her reluctant father for a betrothal. Now she wished she had remained silent.

Hugh lifted her upon his horse, mounting behind her. At the contact of his body against hers, she shuddered with revulsion. He spurred the horse onward, his harsh embrace imprisoning her. When the fortress came into view, the last vestiges of her courage died.

Denial and panic warred within her. Was there anything else she could do to stop this wedding? More than anything, she needed her father's help. Each day she prayed to see his colours flying, heralding the arrival of his entourage. And still he did not come.

They rode beneath the gate, and she did not miss the pitying looks upon the faces of the Irish. Hugh dismounted and forced her to accompany him. 'You must be weary,' he said. 'I will escort you to your chamber.'

Genevieve knew what would happen as soon as they reached the chamber. Closing her eyes, she searched for an excuse—any means to delay the inevitable punishment.

'I am hungry,' she said. 'Might I have something to eat beforehand?'

'I will have food sent above stairs. After we discuss your…journey.' Hugh gripped Genevieve's arm with a strength that reminded her of the retribution to come. Her eyes filled with unshed tears. She would not grant him the satisfaction of making her weep.

She concentrated on the pain of Hugh squeezing her arm as he directed her up the stairs and towards her chamber. He bolted the door behind them with a heavy wooden bar. Alone, he stood and watched her.

'Why did you run from me?'

She didn't answer. What could she say?

'Don't you know I will always come for you? You are mine to protect.' He caressed her hair, tangling the strands in his fingers. She stood motionless, trying not to look at him.

'The King has summoned us to Tara,' Hugh said, releasing her suddenly. 'We will be married there within a few days.' Pride swelled within him. 'He may grant me more land, as a wedding gift to both of us.'

Leaning down, he brushed a kiss upon her closed mouth. 'Do not look so glum. It will not be long now.'

His claim was not at all reassuring. She had been thankful that King Henry had delayed Hugh's earlier requests to come. Political alliances with the Irish kings took precedence. Now her time had run out.

'I will not marry without my father.'

'Thomas de Renalt will come.' His expression tightened. 'He should have arrived by now.'

'He was ill,' Genevieve argued. Her father had ordered her to continue on to Rionallís without him. With an escort of soldiers and her guardians, Papa had believed her to be safe. Genevieve had bribed a priest to send missives, pleading with her father to end the betrothal. She had sent the last one only a sennight ago. But Thomas de Renalt had given no reply, and she feared Hugh might have intercepted the messages.

'I will not wait on him any longer.' Hugh shook his head. 'I know not what the Earl's intentions are, but the betrothal documents are signed. With or without him, I will wed you.'

'I will never wed you,' she swore. 'I care not what the King says.'

His fist struck the back of her head. Pain exploded, ringing in her ears, but Genevieve refused to cry out.

'You have not lost your spirit, have you?' Hugh remarked.

She swallowed hard, wishing she had not provoked him. She knew better than to fight him, for his strength was far greater than hers. If she offered her obedience, he was often more lenient in the punishment. She struggled to force back the words of defiance.

Then he smiled, the cruel smile she had grown to despise.

'Remove your garments.'

Bile rose in her throat at the thought of him holding her down. For the past few weeks he had gloried in humiliating her. If she refused his commands, he beat her until she could no longer stand. Though he had not breached her maidenhead yet, she knew it was but a matter of time. Fear pulsed through her at the thought.

When she did not obey, Hugh struck her stomach, causing her to double over. She clutched her side, unable to stop the moan of agony from her lips. Was this what her life would become? Would she surrender everything to this man, letting him dominate her?

She closed her eyes, afraid it would be so. Though another woman might consider ending her life, Genevieve did not want to risk eternal damnation. She'd not let him take possession of her soul as well.

He unsheathed his dagger, and her heart nearly stopped when she saw the blade. In a swift slice, he cut the laces until her kirtle pooled at her feet. Clad only in her shift, Genevieve tried to cover herself.

'You belong to me, Genevieve.' He set the dagger upon a table, moving towards her. Genevieve's glance darted to the weapon. She avoided another blow and let herself fall against the table. The dagger clattered to the floor.

'Please,' she whispered. 'I am sorry.' It was not true, but the apology might slow his fists. Her head ached; blood was trickling down her cheek.

He began to strip his own clothes away, revealing a muscle-hardened body. 'No. You are not sorry. But you will be.'

He closed the distance between them. 'It's time you learned how to be an obedient wife.' His fingers closed around her nape in a gesture of control. 'Soon, Genevieve,' he promised. He kissed her roughly, bruising her lips until she tasted blood. 'You have no idea of the pleasure I can bring you.'

'No,' she whispered.

'I do not wish to force you,' he said, his fingers suddenly gentle. 'I could have taken you at any time, were that my intention. But I am a patient and forgiving man. Give yourself to me willingly, and I shall teach you the rewards of obedience.' His hand curled beneath her jaw. 'I know you better than you know yourself. You want my touch, though you fight me.'

Never. At the thought of his hands upon her, nausea pooled in her stomach. She lifted her chin and stared into his ruthless blue eyes. His handsome face repulsed her, and she spat at him. 'I hate you.'

Hugh's hands curled up with rage. Fury flashed in his expression, and he struck her cheek. She turned at the last second, falling to her knees. She shut out the pain, her hand closing around the fallen dagger. Before Hugh could see what she had done, she'd hidden the weapon behind her in the folds of her shift.

Genevieve tightened her grip upon the dagger. The hilt felt cold in her palm, its unfamiliar weight awkward. She didn't know if she had the courage to use it. A thousand doubts filled her mind. But she clung to the thread of survival.

A furious pounding sounded upon the door. Genevieve's glance darted towards it.

Hugh cursed, and donned his tunic before opening the door. 'What is it?'

'An attack, my lord,' the servant informed him. 'Irish invaders have set fire to the outer palisade.'

'Stay here,' Hugh snarled to Genevieve. Within seconds, she was alone. Fate had granted her a reprieve. Genevieve laid her cheek against the wall. It felt as though she might blend in with the wood and plaster, so cold was she. Her fingers clutched the linen of her shift, as though the thin fabric could somehow shield her from Hugh's return. No relief filled her, for he would come back. And then his punishment would start anew.

She could feel the old fears coming back to taunt her. She let go of the dagger, the opportunity to defend herself gone. Her hair hung down around her face. Blood matted the back

of her scalp, so she removed her veil. Her dark hair would
hide the injury.

Below, she could hear the men shouting commands. She
rested her forehead on her knees, trying to gather her strength.
If they were under siege, she'd have another chance to get
away. But she could not remain idle.

Wearily, she rose to her feet. Her body ached, and she wondered if Hugh had broken her ribs this time. It hurt to breathe.
Her kirtle lay on the floor, where it had fallen. Genevieve
winced as she leaned over to pick it up. The stabbing pain
eased when she straightened and slipped the gown over her
shift. The laces were destroyed, but it would keep her warm
for now.

You must leave, she told herself. Now was her opportunity,
and she could not let it go.

A strange noise caught her attention. She turned towards
a large tapestry hanging upon the wall. It rippled for an instant. Genevieve backed away, not knowing what the movement was. Instinct told her to be on guard. She took the
dagger in her hand once more.

A man emerged from behind the tapestry, fully armed, with
a sword at his side. He wore trews and a moss-coloured belted
tunic that fell in folds to his knees. She recognised the large
iron brooch pinning his cloak. It was the soldier from the hillside. A quiet authority resonated from his stance, but her anger
remained. He had not helped her when she'd needed him most.

'Who are you?' she asked, holding the dagger steady. His
hair, black as the devil's soul, flowed across his shoulders. A
thin scar, long ago healed, marred one cheek.

'I am Bevan MacEgan.'

Beneath his tunic she saw the outline of heavy muscle.
It occurred to her that he might be a more dangerous threat
than Hugh.

'And what is your name, *a chara?*' He crossed his arms, waiting for her answer. Deep green eyes regarded her as though judging her worth.

Her mouth went dry. 'I am Genevieve de Renalt.'

MacEgan stared at her for a moment, his gaze noting her injuries. 'What happened to you?'

Genevieve suddenly remembered her torn kirtle, and she shielded her body as best she could. 'I was punished for running away.'

'By whom?'

Genevieve hesitated, but answered truthfully. 'Sir Hugh Marstowe.'

'And why was he hunting you?'

'Because I refused to give myself to him.'

His eyes turned cold, like the frost-laced granite stones that lined the hills. 'I could kill him for you, should that be your desire.'

'You missed your opportunity.' Heat rose in her cheeks, along with anger that threatened to break loose. 'I could have been safely away from him by now. But you stood by and did nothing.'

'It's not over yet,' he said quietly. 'And I am here now.'

He was nothing more than an intruder, a man who had abandoned her. But she saw something in his expression when he spoke, something unexpected: sincerity. He might be a rugged barbarian, intent upon conquering Rionallís, but the timbre of his voice and the brutal honesty in his face made her reconsider.

It was better than waiting for Hugh to return, she decided. Given the choice between staying here or going with a stranger, she would rather take her chances with Bevan MacEgan.

'If you will see me to safety, that will be enough,' she said crisply, lowering the dagger. 'How did you get inside?'

He pulled the tapestry aside, revealing a narrow space. A single rope hung down the passageway inside the wall. 'You don't expect me to go down that way?' she said, her throat tightening at the thought of the sheer drop.

'No. I will take you another way.' His expression changed into a mask of determination. 'Come.'

'Where?'

'Below stairs. I have a condition before I grant your request.'

'What condition?'

'You will be my hostage.'

For a moment, she hesitated. She knew nothing about this man, and there was a chance he could harm her.

But he had come back, answering her earlier plea. It seemed she had little choice. 'You won't deliver me into his hands, will you?'

'No. But you may help to grant us more time.'

'Why are you attacking the fortress?' she asked.

'I am the rightful owner of Rionallís.'

She decided that now was not the time to inform him that Rionallís was part of her dowry. Especially when she relied upon him for her freedom. He would learn it soon enough.

Her hands closed on the wooden bar, but MacEgan grasped her waist and pulled her aside. At his touch, she gasped with pain. She bit her lip until she had control of herself.

'I will go first,' he said. 'Then you.'

He opened the door and she clutched at her torn kirtle, reluctant to face Hugh. A dark side of her wished fervently that Hugh would fall to MacEgan's blade. Without him, life would go back to the way it had been before.

After noting that it was safe, MacEgan pulled her into the hallway. Genevieve saw other men, armed and ready. He gave a sharp command in Irish, an order to follow him and guard their backs. With his hand upon her neck, he guided Genevieve down the winding stairs until they reached the Great Chamber. He positioned a knife at her throat. 'Do not flinch. I would not have my blade slice your skin.'

It seemed strange that she should feel safe with him. A sense of calm descended upon her, because he was giving her a second chance at escape.

When the Norman guards caught sight of them, they moved to defend her.

'Come no closer,' MacEgan said, and they held their weapons steady. Genevieve searched the Great Chamber for Hugh, but saw no sign of him. It made her uneasy.

'Tell Sir Hugh I wish to speak with him,' MacEgan commanded. One of the soldiers departed, and he guided Genevieve in front of him. She waited agonising moments for Hugh to appear. The blade had warmed beneath her skin, and she dared not move. At the touch of MacEgan's hand upon her nape, her skin prickled.

The soldiers held their weapons in readiness, but she could tell from their expressions that they would not act until Hugh gave the command.

But Hugh did not come. Instead, Sir Peter Harborough came forward. His greying hair was dishevelled, his armour stained with sweat and blood. 'Release her,' he commanded. He reached to draw his sword.

'Sir Peter, wait!' Genevieve cried out.

MacEgan held the knife at her throat. 'If you do not wish her to die, I would suggest you call off the men. And I want to see Sir Hugh.'

Genevieve watched the soldiers, wondering when her betrothed would emerge from the shadows. No doubt he was near.

Sir Peter's expression held a combination of fury and hesitation. After a moment, he sheathed his weapon. 'Damned Irish. Haven't the sense to know when they're conquered.' He caught the glance of another soldier and ordered, 'Bring in the prisoner.'

MacEgan grew alert. Genevieve had not known of a captive. When the prisoner was brought in, she saw a lad of hardly more than four and ten. He was skinny, with reddish-gold hair and a stubble of fuzz covering his cheeks. His head hung down, as though he were ashamed of himself.

MacEgan exploded with anger. He spoke in Irish, likely to keep the others from understanding him.

'What were you thinking, Ewan? I told you to stay at Laochre.'

The boy drew back. 'I am sorry, brother. I thought—'

'You thought you could join in our fight? And how long did it take for them to capture you?'

The boy's face reddened.

Genevieve could hold her silence no longer. 'Leave him be. He is only a boy.'

'Who may not live to be a man if he behaves in such a fashion.' MacEgan's grip tightened upon her, and his tension became palpable.

Sir Peter revealed a smile of victory. 'And so we come to the terms, MacEgan. You shall call off your men, return the Lady Genevieve unharmed, and in exchange we release the boy.'

'What if I refuse?'

'That is your choice, of course. But you are outnumbered.' Sir Peter gave a nod towards the opposite wall, where archers waited with bows drawn. 'We could kill you before your men could release their weapons.'

Although Sir Peter was trying to protect her, Genevieve

wanted to curse the man. He had spent nearly each day of the past two moons drinking ale and eating. Not a finger had he lifted to guard her from Hugh. But the moment an Irishman tried to rescue her, he decided to play the role of saviour.

'This fortress was mine long before the Normans took it,' MacEgan said. 'The people are loyal to me. It would not be long before a dagger would slide between your ribs one night.'

Sir Peter shrugged. 'That is Marstowe's concern, not mine. My purpose is to guard the Lady Genevieve until her marriage.'

'You seem to be doing a poor job of it.'

Rage exploded upon the man's face, and Bevan's grip tightened around her. She held her breath, afraid of the knife at her throat. Though she didn't believe he would hurt her, the slightest pressure could make the blade slip.

Where was Hugh? Genevieve did not trust him to stay out of this. Had he run? Or was he plotting against them?

She caught a slight movement from the shadows. The gleam of an arrow-tip reflected in the firelight. Out of instinct, she pushed backwards against MacEgan with all her strength, just as the arrow was fired. The shaft grazed MacEgan's shoulder, and would have struck her had she not moved in time.

The knife left her throat for an instant, and strong arms dragged her away.

'Seize him!' a voice commanded.

Five guards took hold of MacEgan. He fought back, slashing with his dagger, but there were too many of them. Genevieve tried to free herself from Sir Peter's grasp, but he held firm. After a fierce struggle, they disarmed him. Seconds later, Hugh emerged from the shadows. At the sight of him, Genevieve's blood ran cold. The expression on his face appeared tender, loving. Genevieve knew the act well.

He took her in his arms and touched the soft part of her throat where the blade had rested. 'I will kill him for touching you.' Unsheathing his dagger, he stared at MacEgan. 'Perhaps I shall slit his throat now.'

Genevieve closed her eyes, knowing that none of the prisoners would be released.

Hugh traced a finger down her jaw. The gesture made her skin crawl. 'But I would rather have him suffer for what he has done. On the morrow, I will have him executed, so that all will know not to attack Rionallís. He can watch the younger one hang first.'

Genevieve turned to him, unable to hide her hatred. 'I thought you would let the boy go.'

'I let no one escape who attacks what is mine. Return to your chamber and bolt the door.' He clapped Sir Peter on the shoulder. 'Thank you for defending her.'

'It was no trouble.' Sir Peter's hand returned to his sword. 'Shall we rid ourselves of the rest of them?'

Hugh inclined his head. To his soldiers, he ordered, 'Secure the outer bailey. Spare no one.' With those words, Hugh donned his helm and left.

Genevieve forced herself to go above stairs, each step heavier than the last. She could not allow MacEgan to die, not after he had tried to save her. She cradled her arms against her sore ribs, remembering the hungry look in Hugh's eyes. He had enjoyed hurting her. Her hands moved down to her hips, and she trembled in fear, knowing exactly how he intended to hurt her this time.

She had one last chance. She would find a way to save MacEgan and his brother, even if it meant risking her death.

Chapter Two

Genevieve hid in a chamber used for storing food and herbs until the sounds of battle faded into the distance. The thickness of smoke tainted the air, and she tried not to think of the number of men who were now dead. There were two she could save, and save them she would.

She studied the dried roots and stalks until she found the ones she was looking for. Mixed with ale, their bitterness would not be tasted by the guards, and the herbs would cause sleep.

Hugh had sent the captives to an underground cellar. As Genevieve had anticipated, MacEgan was heavily guarded. She balanced the pitcher of ale and tankards while climbing down the ladder. The cool air raised gooseflesh on her arms, but she squared her shoulders and put on a false smile.

As soon as the guard saw her, he frowned. 'Lady Genevieve, you should not be here.'

'I thought you and your men deserved a reward for your bravery this eve,' she said, holding out the pitcher.

The guard brightened at her offering, allowing her to fill his cup. He lifted his tankard in a toast, then drank heartily.

Genevieve poured ale for the other soldiers, and soon they relaxed with a game of dice. For a moment she waited, to see if anyone responded to the drugged mixture, but nothing happened.

Had she added enough? Or, worse, would the herbs take effect at all? Tonight was her only chance to help the MacEgans escape, while Hugh was occupied with the Irish invaders. She glanced towards the prisoners, shrinking back at the sight of Bevan MacEgan's suspicious glare.

He rested on his haunches, both wrists chained. Though outwardly he appeared calm, she sensed he was biding his time. He exuded strength, a caged wolf prepared to tear out the throat of his enemy, given an opportunity.

Was it the right decision to free them? If it were only the young boy, Ewan, she'd not hesitate. But she knew nothing about Bevan MacEgan, nor whether he was an honest man.

She moved towards the ladder as if about to leave. Another soldier raised his hand in farewell, and she pretended to step upon the ladder. When their attention was firmly on the game, she slipped into the shadows. She leaned back against the cool stones, her pulse thrumming in anticipation.

In the darkness, she saw MacEgan staring at her. His penetrating gaze made her shiver, though he said nothing to reveal her presence.

It was taking far too long for the herbs to take effect. Genevieve did not know what she would do if the guards did not succumb to sleep.

The younger boy struggled with his chains, fighting to gain release. MacEgan settled back against the wall, not a trace of emotion upon his scarred face. He waited with the patience of a man who had known captivity before. Genevieve prayed she had not been mistaken about trusting him.

Before long she heard footsteps approaching. Hugh's

voice echoed off the stones as he descended the ladder. 'I want to speak with the prisoners alone.'

At the sound of his voice, she tried to shrink back further. She found a small niche behind one of the barrels, pulling her body into a tight ball. The guards climbed the ladder, but none seemed aware of her. She clenched her hands together, every muscle tensed.

Hugh withdrew a dagger and fingered the edge of the blade. The steel flashed silver in the torch light. He stood before MacEgan, a grim expression lining his mouth.

'You should not have touched her. She belongs to me. Any man who threatens her will die.'

The boy paled, but MacEgan met his adversary's gaze evenly. 'Then you must be ready to face death yourself. It was you who beat her, was it not?'

A murderous rage darkened Hugh's face. He unsheathed his dagger and slashed it at MacEgan's cheek, carving a wound that mirrored the scar on his opposite cheek.

Though a flash of pain dimmed the Irish warrior's eyes, he did not move. He stared at Hugh in a silent challenge. Genevieve held her breath, her hand moving towards her bruised ribs.

Then Hugh plunged the dagger into MacEgan's shoulder, where the arrow had skimmed it earlier. Genevieve expected MacEgan to cry out, but he made not a sound. Instead, he met Hugh's gaze, his features tight with pain.

She had seen enough. If she didn't act now, Hugh would slit MacEgan's throat next. She emerged from her hiding place, grabbing the pitcher of ale. The fragile pottery shattered across Hugh's head, but he remained standing. Genevieve tried to move away, but he caught her.

He struck her across the face, and a fierce pain blasted through her cheek. She couldn't stop the cry that slipped from her mouth at the terrible agony. His fist collided with her bruised ribs, expelling the air from her lungs. For the first time she glimpsed the face of death. She had crossed the boundary past fear and anger, slipping into the need to survive. Her knees buckled, for she could not breathe. Darkness hovered at the edge of her periphery.

Bevan seized the opportunity and wrapped his chains around the man's throat. He tasted blood, but ignored the fiery pain in his shoulder. A clear sense of focus sharpened the anger rising within.

When the Norman knight had struck Genevieve, it had been as though he were seeing a vision of his wife. Past and present had blurred, and the images of a battlefield had filled his mind. He saw his wife, Fiona, crying out for help while the Normans chased her on horseback. He had fought against the hordes of enemy soldiers, trying with all his strength to reach her.

His failure had haunted him ever since.

Though it was Genevieve who had fallen beneath Sir Hugh's fists, it was his wife he was seeing as he tightened the metal chain around the man's throat, strangling him. The chains strained and the knight's face grew slack, his body slipping into unconsciousness.

Motion caught his eye, and soldiers began descending the ladder, swords drawn. He was forced to release Hugh, though he wished he'd had time to twist the life from him. Any man who struck a woman was not worth the dust beneath his feet. He risked a glance at Genevieve, and saw her cradling her ribs. She was alive, but it unnerved him, having a woman try to rescue him.

A blade arced towards him, and Bevan caught the blow with his chains. Years of training made it easy to defend himself, and he waited for an opportunity to disarm his opponent.

Strangely, the soldiers were unsteady on their feet, behaving as though they had drunk too much ale. One of the men aimed for Ewan, and Bevan twisted to take the blade's impact upon his chains. He breathed easier when the men left his brother alone.

Ewan dropped to the ground, using his feet to trip one of the guards. Bevan evaded more slashes while fighting to remain on his feet. Energy surged through him when one stumbled, and Bevan seized the sword. Seconds later, the man lay dead upon the ground.

The second guard stumbled forward, his expression vacant. A dagger lay embedded in his back. Behind him stood Genevieve, her face ghostly pale. Bevan had seen that expression before. The first time she'd killed a man, he'd wager. And she looked as though she expected God to strike her down for the sin.

Bevan no longer cared about his soul. He'd lived through everlasting damnation during the past two years. He seized the third guard, wrapping his chains tightly around the man's throat and aiming the sword at his belly. 'Unlock our manacles.'

The guard glanced towards the ladder. Bevan's patience disappeared. 'You will be dead before they get here unless you unlock these.'

The man fumbled for the heavy iron ring of keys at his waist, and unlocked the chains.

'Now my brother.'

When the last chain fell free, the guard tried to bolt towards the ladder. Bevan swung his sword towards the man's head, striking him with the hilt. The guard crumpled to the ground, unconscious.

'You didn't kill him,' Genevieve murmured.

'I keep my word.' To his brother he said, 'Get our weapons and free the men. Tell them to alert the others and return to Laochre.'

Ewan scurried to the far end of the storage chamber to do his bidding.

Bevan helped Genevieve stand, though she was still guarding her ribs. 'You're hurt.'

'Not as badly as you,' she managed. 'Let me tend your wounds. Your shoulder is bleeding badly.'

'There is no time.' His injury was not a mortal wound, though the pain staggered him.

'You have to leave. They'll kill you.'

He knew it, just as surely as he knew that he had to take her with him. It was the only way to keep her safe. 'Are you coming with us?'

Genevieve's eyes glimmered with tears, and she stared at the fallen body of Hugh. 'He's still alive?'

Bevan shrugged. 'For now.'

'I can't stay here. Not any more.'

Ewan returned, carrying a bow and arrows, as well as two swords. The blade was easily more than half the boy's height, but Ewan clutched it with fervour. 'The men have left. Through the *souterrain* passage, as you ordered.'

'Good.' Bevan sheathed his sword and held out his hand to Genevieve. 'Go or stay. It is your choice, *a chara*.'

With a fearful look back at the man who had beaten her, she put her hand in his. 'I'll go.'

They escaped through the narrow passageway, the scent of wet soil and clay surrounding them. Bevan led them to a secondary tunnel that opened out into the forest. The night had grown cold, its chilled air biting their faces as the harsh wind swept by.

Genevieve clutched her side, her face tight with suffering, but she made no complaint.

A kind of madness had overcome him, to bring a woman

along. It was his weakness that he could not stand to see a woman beaten. He suspected that Sir Hugh was someone close to Genevieve—a relative, or her betrothed.

Bevan knew he had to find shelter for the three of them. The journey back to his brother's fortress would take days, and there had been no time to retrieve the horses. The voice of doubt sank its teeth into his confidence. He didn't know if they would make it.

And he had seen no sign of his men. It bothered him, for he knew not if they had escaped detection. In the blackness of the forest, he paused to look back at Rionallís. Fiery torches blazed in the darkness amid the glinting of chain-mail armour. They needed more distance, and he increased their pace.

The slickness beneath his tunic reminded him that he would have to stanch the bleeding. The pain had become a vicious reality, but he had no choice except to move onward. If they stopped now, they were dead.

His brother was keeping up, but Genevieve had started to fall behind. She leaned up against a tree, her arm wrapped around her ribs. 'Grant me a moment,' she pleaded, catching her breath.

'We can't. They're following us.' He studied her, assessing her injuries. Lowering his voice, he asked, 'Would you rather stay here? Return to them?'

'No.' Rebellion blazed in her eyes, and she straightened her shoulders. 'I'll never go back to him.' She steadied herself, then began walking once more.

'Who is he? Your husband?'

'My betrothed.' She increased her pace until they cleared the forest. 'But no longer. Not if I am free of him.'

They traversed the open field, instinct guiding him upon the right path. Shrouded in darkness, he used the dim glow of light coming from the church. With each step he felt his strength ebbing.

Genevieve must have sensed it, for she stopped him. 'You need to bind your wounds.'

'It's too dangerous.'

'She's right, Bevan.' Ewan gripped his hand. 'You would not make it much further.'

He didn't like admitting a weakness, particularly when both of them depended upon him for their survival. Yet he would be no good to them were he to stumble and fall. His gaze fixed upon the lights in the distance. At last he said, 'I know a place where we can stay. But if there is any sign of Sir Hugh's men, we must leave.'

When they reached the outskirts of the tenants' lands, Genevieve motioned towards a beehive-shaped cottage. Bevan shook his head. 'I'll not endanger my people.'

There was only one possibility for shelter. He pointed to a round stone tower in the distance that rested beside the church. 'Stay behind me.'

As they approached they saw that the church was small, but the tower would provide the greatest protection for the night. Bevan spied a candle lit in the window and raised his fist to the door. A tall, thin priest answered his knock. He recognised Father Ó Brian, a quiet man, who had been known to wield a sword in his younger days. He respected the priest, and the man's strength of faith.

'We seek a place to stay,' Bevan said.

The priest glanced at the three of them, his attention caught by the bloodstained tunic. 'Bevan MacEgan.' He rubbed the brown beard on his chin and opened the door wider for them to enter. 'It has been a long time. Almost a year and a half it's been since you were at Rionallís.' The priest gestured for them to enter. 'I am glad to see you. We have prayed for your return since the invaders came.'

Bevan caught the silent censure. But, after Fiona's death,

the emptiness of Rionallís had made it unbearable to stay. For that first year he'd travelled from one tribe to another, hiring his sword. Then, last spring, his people had endured attack and conquest.

He clasped the priest's arm. 'We will return again. I swear it.' His younger brother Ewan's face flushed with embarrassment. The boy blamed himself for the failed invasion.

'Good.' Father Ó Brian gestured towards the small chapel. 'What can I do to assist you?'

'We need shelter for the night, and food. Horses on the morrow, if that is possible.'

The priest nodded. 'I believe the round tower would be best.' He led them back outside, behind the church. The stone tower stood high against the shadows of the landscape, narrow in diameter. The priest brought a ladder for them to ascend to the entrance, leading the way. Once inside, he closed the door and lowered a rope ladder to the next level.

'What is this place?' Genevieve asked.

'We use it for storage,' Father Ó Brian replied. 'But we can also detect our enemies from a distance. It has been here for hundreds of years. Some say the priests used to hide religious treasures in these towers.'

Using a torch for light, he led them up several levels, but did not take them to the top. High above them was the bell used to sound the hours. Six windows surrounded the topmost level. Bevan intended to use them to sight their enemies.

'There is no fire, but you should be warm enough on this level. There is a pallet, should you wish to sleep.' Father Ó Brian gestured towards Bevan's wound. 'I'll bring a basin of water to tend your injury—'

'I'll tend it,' Genevieve interrupted. 'Have you a needle and thread? Some of his wounds are deep.'

The priest inclined his head, and left his torch inside an iron sconce before he departed. After he had gone, Genevieve stared up at the interior of the round tower, past each level to the top.

Wind howled against the stones, a shrieking sound that made Bevan think of evil spirits. Though he was not a superstitious man, he crossed himself. He did not deceive himself by believing they were safe this night.

It took a while until the priest returned, but Father Ó Brian brought bread and mead, along with water and clean strips of linen. He handed Genevieve a small cloth packet containing the needle and thread. Then he left them alone. Ewan lifted the first ladder away, sealing the main entrance, then busied himself with the food.

With Genevieve's help, Bevan removed his tunic, gingerly avoiding his wounded shoulder as much as possible. She cleansed the wound, her eyes never meeting his. Though she performed the duty with calm efficiency, he sensed a greater discomfort. She was afraid of him, even after everything that had happened.

Her own cheek had swollen up, a bruise beginning to form. Caked blood marred her temple, tangling the dark hair. He was glad he'd taken her from Rionallís. And yet he did not know what to do with her now.

'Do you have other family here?'

She shook her head, threading the needle. 'My father was supposed to come. He grew ill and could not journey with me to Rionallís. Instead he sent Sir Peter and his wife as my guardians.' She held the edges of his shoulder wound together, and Bevan tensed. 'I was supposed to marry Sir Hugh upon our arrival.'

'Why didn't you?' He gritted his teeth through the pain of her stitching. He felt foolish that such a small needle should cause dizziness, while he had endured the stabbing wound without flinching.

'The King wanted to witness the marriage.' A wry expression tilted at her mouth. 'I suspect Hugh wanted the King there. He overestimated his importance to King Henry. I was glad for the delay.' She tied off the thread and Bevan expelled a sigh of relief.

'Your guardians…they were supposed to look after you?' He gazed pointedly at her bruise, then down to her ribs. The torn kirtle reminded him of Sir Hugh, and the brutal beating he'd witnessed.

Genevieve reddened. 'Yes. Sir Peter believed I was disobedient, and that Hugh was right to punish me.'

Her hands moved to the cut upon his face, and Bevan steadied himself for the needle once more. 'What of Sir Peter's wife?'

'She hardly ever spoke to me,' Genevieve admitted. 'She complained about Ireland and wanted to return to England. Most of the time she stayed in the solarium, weeping.' She frowned in distaste.

Her needle moved swiftly, stitching the wound closed. Thanks be, she had finished. He breathed easier now that it was done.

She bound the wound tightly with linen strips. With a cloth, she sponged at the slash on his cheek. She finished treating his wounds and poured him a cup of mead.

Bevan drank the fermented beverage and pointed towards the bruise on her cheek. 'Where do you want me to take you on the morrow?'

'Away from Hugh. It matters not where.' She rose and crossed the room, to sit upon the pallet.

Bevan reminded himself that he should not concern himself with Genevieve's problems. She was the daughter of an enemy, nothing more. He had repaid his debt to her, and the sooner their ways parted the better. Yet her presence disconcerted him.

Her hair was dark, like his wife Fiona's. Her eyes were a deep blue, the colour of the sea. She was tall, the top of her head reaching to his chin. Though she turned away from him, he saw the way she cradled her ribs. Tonight had not been the first time Sir Hugh had harmed her. What he could not understand was why anyone would allow it to happen.

Bevan brought the basin over and sat beside her. The faint scent of lavender emanated from her skin. Without thinking, he washed away the blood upon her temple.

What was he doing? Guilty thoughts invaded his mind with the intimate act, for it was the first time he'd touched a woman in a very long time. He held the cloth out to Genevieve, and she took it from him in silence. 'He hurt you.' It was not a question.

Genevieve soaked the cloth once more, wringing it out. Her hands brushed over her ribcage. 'I don't think he broke any bones, but, aye, it hurts.'

He regretted not killing Sir Hugh when he'd had the opportunity.

They ate the meagre meal provided by Father Ó Brian while outside the wind howled. Bevan climbed up the rope ladder to the level surrounded by windows. Wind blasted through the openings, but he peered into the darkness to see if the enemy approached. A flurry of white swirled into the room.

'Do you see anything?' Ewan called up.

'Snow.' He climbed down several levels, favouring his good shoulder. The change in weather lightened his worry, though he saw the confusion in Ewan's eyes. 'It will hide our tracks, should they try to pursue us. For tonight, so long as the snow continues, we are safe.'

An answering smile tipped at Genevieve's lips. The softness of her expression drew his attention, and Bevan took a step forward. She held his gaze for a moment before looking away.

What was it about her that bewitched him so? Her Norman kinsmen had slaughtered his people and stolen his home. The blood running through her veins was the same as his enemy's. And yet she remained an innocent, caught up in a battle that should not involve her.

'Sleep now,' he said, moving away from her. 'I'll keep watch for tonight.'

Genevieve curled up on the straw pallet, huddling to keep warm. Ewan slept against a sack of grain on the opposite side of the tower.

The night stretched in long moments, making Genevieve uneasy about leaving Rionallís. Hugh would come after her, hunting her until he possessed her once more. He would not stop until she returned to him. In many ways she wished she could become invisible—a serf who would attract no man's attention.

She remembered Bevan's eyes upon her, and the way he had tended her wound. Once she might have encouraged his attentions. She might have welcomed the feelings he could awaken within her as his hand warmed hers.

Now she knew better. Those days were over, and she no longer trusted her own judgement. She would let no man court her affections again, though Papa might arrange a different marriage. Her heart grew heavy as she closed her eyes, wishing she knew what the morning would bring.

In the darkness, Bevan watched Genevieve sleeping. She slept on her stomach, her palms atop the pallet, her breathing steady and even. Dark hair fell across her shoulders. He reached out and touched a strand of her hair. It curled around his finger, soft as a silken ribbon, before he released it.

Why had she helped them? Her desperation to escape Sir Hugh was genuine, and he knew her act of bravery had saved their lives. In return, he had sworn to protect her. And yet the promise meant bringing an enemy among his family.

Ewan had accepted their escape as a lucky twist of fate, but then, he was a boy. He did not stop to consider the repercussions of Genevieve's actions. Although she had fled willingly, Bevan knew Sir Hugh would come after them, seeking their deaths. He welcomed the prospect of killing him, but he could not allow Genevieve to stay with them. Her presence would endanger those he loved.

A soft sound broke his attention. Genevieve was awake. She sat up and brought her knees to her chest, keeping her gaze upon him. The wind battered the stone tower, moaning in the winter's darkness.

'I cannot sleep.'

He made no move, no sound, but stared at her. Genevieve's long hair flowed across her shoulders like a pool of water, haloed against the dying torchlight. The intense blue of her eyes regarded him in the stillness.

'I never thanked you for saving me,' she said. 'There are no words to express how grateful I am.'

'As soon as we reach my brother's fortress I'll arrange to send you away to a safe place,' he said gruffly.

'I want to go home to England.' Genevieve glanced at Ewan and added, 'But later, when you have brought your brother to safety. Your lives are at stake, after all.'

'I care not for my own life. Only his.' He had not meant to voice the thought aloud, but it was true. Death did not frighten him any more. Many times Patrick and Connor had chastised him for his recklessness in raids against other tribes.

Genevieve drew nearer, her scent rising to tempt him. She took another step closer, and he could scarcely breathe. Raising her palm to his cheek, she traced her fingers along the fresh scar upon his jaw. 'Your cheek is bleeding again.'

In the darkness, with her hair unbound around her shoulders, he could almost imagine she was a lover, reaching out to him.

He jerked backwards. 'Leave it be.'

Bevan tried to shut out the images in his mind. Before he lost his only thread of honour, he climbed to a higher level of the tower, seeking the cold iciness of the night.

Chapter Three

'It is time to leave,' Bevan said in the quiet morning darkness.

Genevieve opened her eyes, and a strange mixture of elation and hope overcame her. She had escaped Hugh. If she could return to England, she held faith that her father would help her end the betrothal.

'Where are we going?' She rubbed her arms, trying to bring warmth into them. Inside the tower, the stones held a chill. Her breath formed clouds in the morning air.

'To the Norman encampment at Tara. You can find an escort there.'

Genevieve was not so sure. If she went to Tara, Hugh would find her within days.

'It will be safe,' Bevan reassured her.

'No. The men there are loyal to Hugh.' She sensed irritation from Bevan. He did not like her questioning his authority. Though she was grateful to him for his help, she could not risk being left at Tara. Hugh's fighting reputation had earned him respect among his peers. They would not see her as anything but a hysterical female. She needed to find her father, the one person who could help.

Bevan's shoulder wound had begun to seep, in spite of the stitching. A dark stain spread across the linen of his tunic. 'We need to find a healer to care for your wound,' she said. She didn't like the tension etched upon his face, the silent pain he endured.

'My brother's healer will tend it.' He buckled his sword belt around his waist. Genevieve realised that he had slept against the wall on the floor—if he'd slept at all. He drew near, and she shrank back against the stone wall of the round tower.

'What about you?' he asked softly. 'Are your ribs broken?'

'They are only bruised.' The pain was more bearable now, though they were tender to the touch.

Bevan shook his younger brother awake. Ewan yawned, stretching his gangly frame. His fair hair was rumpled from sleep, and his tunic hung open. He reminded Genevieve of her own brothers when they were younger. She had idolised them, believing they could slay dragons for her. A pang of remorse curled within her. She hadn't seen her brothers in almost a year. Her eldest brother, James, had married, while the second-born, Michael, had gone to Scotland. She missed them, even though they had teased her mercilessly.

She had almost considered sending for one of them, but dismissed the idea. If Michael or James ever came to Ireland they would murder Hugh without a second thought. Her father was a better choice, for he could end the betrothal without any bloodshed.

'Come,' Bevan said, carefully adjusting his cloak. 'Father Ó Brian has arranged two horses for us.'

Genevieve sat up slowly, biting back a cry at the aching of her ribs. Everything hurt, even the back of her scalp.

They did not stop to break their fast, but said farewell to Father Ó Brian and departed. Outside, thick snowflakes continued to fall, covering the ground in a layer of pristine white. The sun had not yet dawned, but a faint light in the east turned the sky lavender against the grey shadow of morning.

Bevan lifted her astride a brown mare, swinging up behind her on the saddle while Ewan rode a black rouncy. Genevieve masked the pain of her ribs, refusing to show any sign of weakness. Nothing could be done for them, and she did not want to slow down their escape.

With his nicker to the mare, the animal broke into a trot across the fields. When the church was barely visible behind them Bevan increased their pace to a gallop. She gritted her teeth, fighting the vicious ache in her side.

Her eyes scanned the horizon, searching for a trace of Sir Hugh's men. She wished for a forest, or for some way to hide. Riding across open fields would make it easy for an archer to strike them down.

The snow continued to fall, covering their tracks. Behind her, she felt the warmth of Bevan's body heat. His rough demeanour and wiry strength intimidated her. Though she understood the necessity of sharing a horse, she inched forward, trying not to let his body touch hers. The position made her ribs burn from the effort, but his injuries were far worse. She did not want to cause him further discomfort.

After a brief interval he shifted their direction. Ewan followed, bringing his horse alongside theirs.

'This isn't the closest way,' he protested.

'Be silent.' Bevan glanced behind them, and urged the horse faster. Genevieve saw that they were moving towards the coastline, slightly south of Rionallís.

Her fingers dug into the mane of the horse as she wondered what Bevan was doing. He changed their pattern once more, heading downhill. Genevieve could now see Rionallís, further back from the sea. Below them, small fishing boats bobbed in the water. Bevan led them towards the boats and dismounted.

In the early morning, the sea reflected the cloudy sky above. A pungent, salty aroma filled her nostrils as they approached. The screech of seagulls echoed in the morning silence as the birds swooped in search of fish.

The rocky coastline held a hint of frost, but no snow covered the sands. Fishermen loaded their nets onto the small water crafts, talking in hushed voices. Bevan dismounted and approached one of the fishermen, pointing towards the boat.

After a lengthy discussion, Bevan exchanged silver with him. The fisherman gathered his things and left the tiny boat, muttering beneath his breath.

She couldn't understand why he wanted a boat. It was much faster to travel on horseback. Where did he plan to go?

Bevan beckoned, and she followed, taking his hand to board the small wooden vessel. The fisherman led the two horses away.

'Stay down.' Bevan pressed her shoulders back so she lay against the bottom of the boat. Genevieve obeyed, but the rocking motion made her stomach churn.

'Where are we going?' she asked. Neither answered at first, so she held her tongue. She glanced behind, wondering if he had seen anyone following them. Although the falling snow continued to cover their tracks, she didn't for a moment believe that Hugh would let her go. Somewhere, men were looking for her.

She laid her head against the damp wood, watching the men. Bevan's arm muscles strained as he rowed, and she did not miss the subtle flash of pain. He pulled the oars through the water effortlessly, though it cost him. After a short while they unfurled a sail and set their course.

She watched him row, snowflakes catching upon his lashes and face. His green eyes met hers for a moment, and within them she saw emptiness. His gaze returned to the landscape, as though searching for something.

'What is it?' she whispered.

'My men. I don't think they made it past the Normans.'

'You don't know that for certain,' she offered, but he shook his head.

'We would have found them by now.'

Genevieve risked a look back at the mainland. Clouds of snow obscured the coast, and the sea surrounded their tiny boat. The water was a deep grey colour, almost black. She wanted to reassure him that he could go back for his men, that he could rescue them. But if he did, more of her father's soldiers would die.

Instead, she changed the subject. 'You never said where we're going.'

Ewan adjusted one of the sails, tying the rope while the wind made it billow. 'Ennisleigh,' he replied. The look on his face showed pride.

'Where is that?'

'It's an island fortress that belongs to our older brother, Patrick. They can't track us by water,' was all Bevan said.

A slight smile curved her lips. At this time of morning no one would look for them along the coast. The snow made the small boat nearly invisible, cloaked in the foggy mist.

She settled back against the swaying boat, watching the snow drift along the breath of the wind. After nearly an hour she saw gulls gliding in the air. They pulled in the sail, and soon the boat scraped bottom. Ewan jumped from the boat onto the rocks, avoiding the water. Bevan stepped directly into the sea, lifting Genevieve into his arms so her feet would not touch the water. He set her down upon the shoreline, seemingly unaware of the cold. His feet had to be freezing. He and Ewan pulled the boat onto the sand.

She took a moment to look at her surroundings. They had arrived at a small island off the coast, with an imposing ring fort. 'Is this where you live?'

Bevan shook his head. 'But we will stop here to rest. I'll leave you here until an escort can be arranged.'

Genevieve held her tongue, not at all pleased with the idea of being left alone. 'What about you?'

'I will gather more soldiers and renew the attack on Rionallís. I have to go back for my men.'

'Why did you leave Rionallís at all?' she asked. 'When my father's men arrived last spring, no one held claim to it.' The fortress had been all but abandoned when she'd arrived. The Great Chamber had not been cleaned in months, and layers of rotten food and dirt had covered the rushes. None of the people living within the palisade had set foot inside the dwelling.

Bevan's expression was stony, unreadable. 'I gave orders for no one to enter my home. My people obeyed. They knew I would come back to protect that which belongs to me. Especially from the *Gaillabh*.'

'I am one of those foreigners,' she pointed out. 'And Rionallís now belongs to my father. It is part of my dowry.'

'A stolen dowry.'

She didn't know what to say. Even if she held the power to give him back the land, a part of her didn't want to let it go. She had spent day after day cleaning the fortress, helping the soldiers repair the palisade. And in that time she had come to think of it as her own. Sometimes, at night, she would climb up to the gatehouse and watch the moon spill over the fields.

'It is a beautiful place,' she said at last. 'My father has sworn to keep the land safe for King Henry.'

Bevan's eyes turned dark as he climbed up the pathway

leading to the fortress. In his visage she saw a man prepared to wage war upon her family. And, worse, she understood why.

'Perhaps we can seek a compromise?' she offered.

'There will be no compromise. The land belongs to me.'

'I set both of you free,' she argued. 'Are your lives not worth peace between us?'

'I will grant you an escort to take you back to England,' he said. 'Then my debt will be repaid. After that, I owe you nothing more.'

The cool tone of his voice silenced her. She glanced back at the grey water below them. Her fears rose up at the thought of Bevan fighting against her father. It would happen—unless she found a way to stop it.

Her shoes did little to protect her from the craggy rocks at the base of the island, but she climbed, ignoring the ache in her ribs. Bevan made no complaint, though once he stumbled and touched a hand to his shoulder.

What sort of man was he? He did not dress as a nobleman, but his skill with a sword and his unquestioned leadership made it a possibility. And yet his plain clothing and stoic demeanour could easily allow him to pass for a commoner. A warrior, she decided. A fierce man, with a strong sense of justice.

The snow swirled harder, but in time they reached the entrance. The men there greeted Bevan by name, acknowledging him with a respectful nod. Genevieve tried to count the number of tribe members, but there were too many. It made her uneasy, knowing that so many were on hand to attack Rionallís and her family.

She followed Bevan inside, to a room with a bright fire burning in the hearth. Genevieve neared it, warming her hands. A servant brought them food and drink, and she ate hungrily. Ewan did the same, but she noticed Bevan did not partake of the meat and bread.

He removed his cloak and sat down, closing his eyes for a moment. His posture stayed erect, but Genevieve could see the signs of exhaustion. She picked up a piece of bread and brought it over to him. 'You should eat something.'

'I require nothing.'

His voice sounded sharp, and his face was haggard in appearance. A dark lock of hair fell across his eyes, which were glazed with pain.

'You need to lie down and rest. Your wound must be hurting. And you need to warm your feet from the sea water.'

'I am fine.'

On impulse, she reached out and touched his forehead. His skin felt hot and feverish.

'Leave me, Genevieve,' he said.

Stubborn man. Like as not his wound had become poisoned. She could see all the signs. And yet he would be the sort of soldier who refused to admit a hint of vulnerability.

'You saved my life,' she said, her voice barely above a whisper. 'And I saved yours. But were it not for me you would not have this wound. Let me tend it. I'll not say anything to your brother or your men. Tell them you are showing me to a chamber where I may rest.'

He took her wrist, stopping her. 'I need no nursemaid, nor do I require your help.'

She ignored him. In a loud voice, she said, 'Well? Is there no place in this fortress where I may rest?'

Ewan looked uncomfortable, but a middle-aged bearded man moved forward. A steward of some sort, she guessed, from the large ring of keys tied to his waist. He nodded to Genevieve. 'With your permission, Bevan, I will show her to a chamber.'

'I will show the lady her place,' Bevan said, rising to his feet. He sent Genevieve an angry look, but she ignored it.

'I would like some warm water and clean linen to wash,' she told the steward. 'Please have them sent up.'

The steward inclined his head. Genevieve found a winding staircase leading to an upper level, and Bevan followed her. The fortress was not a large one, and it showed recent signs of repair to the roof. All along the walls she saw weapons of every kind. Some appeared decorative, while others revealed nicks and the evidence of battle.

'Why do you defy me?' he asked in a low tone.

'You are being foolish. The wound may be poisoned with bad blood.'

He stepped in front of her, crossing his arms. 'I do not intend to give up the attack on Rionallís, if that is what you are thinking.'

'No. Such would show more wisdom than you have,' she shot back.

'What you are doing is far more foolish,' he warned. 'I have said that I do not want your aid.'

Genevieve entered a small chamber containing a bed. The hearth held nothing but cold ashes. A chair and table stood by one wall.

'Sit,' she commanded, while she bent to build the fire. At the motion, her ribs ached. Genevieve pushed away the pain, focusing on her task. Within minutes she had a small blaze going.

Glancing behind, she saw him watching her. He tried to keep his expression neutral, but she could see the underlying strain. It reminded her of her older brothers, when they did not want to admit an injury from the practise field.

A knock at the door sounded, and when she answered she saw the steward, bearing a basin of water and fresh linen. Genevieve thanked him and closed the door.

Bevan remained standing, even as she laid out the water and linen to change his bandages. The fierce glare upon his face intimidated her. The new scar on his cheek twitched.

He moved towards her so swiftly Genevieve flinched, covering her face instinctively. A moment later, she lowered her arms, her face flooded with shame.

'I do not strike women,' he said, his tone softer. She stiffened, hating herself for the moment of weakness.

'I know.' She busied herself with the linen, trying to regain her composure. 'I—you—you startled me.'

He reached out to her with deliberate slowness, his fingers grazing the bruised side of her cheek. 'Only a coward would use his fists upon a woman. Only one with the need to prove himself.'

She swallowed and nodded. 'Aye.' The whisper of his touch made her cheeks flush. All at once she wanted to fade away, to disappear from his penetrating gaze.

'Sit and let me change your bandage,' she said. To her surprise, he obeyed.

Bevan's hands gripped the arms of the chair as Genevieve brought the basin over to the table. Tension lined every muscle in his body, and she feared she would cause him pain, no matter her desire to be gentle.

She saw that she would have to unfasten the buckle at his waist. His fists clenched before she lifted the bloodstained tunic over his head, but he made no sound.

Though she had seen his chest the night before, the intimacy of touching his bare skin made her shiver. Hardened muscles, formed from years of training, tensed beneath her palms. His heated skin held its bronzed colour from the summer sun, and she imagined him upon a practise field without his tunic. Deep ridges outlined his stomach muscles.

The wound in his shoulder was swollen, and she saw a

dark purple bruise forming over the torn flesh. Gently, she touched the edge of the wound and he flinched. By the saints, she did not know how he had managed to go as far as he had without collapsing. But her stitches had held, in spite of the journey.

She washed the dried blood away with the linen, trying not to cause him discomfort. With a quick glance around the room, Genevieve saw large cobwebs, their threads glinting in the low light of the fire. She went to the corner, reached up, and grabbed handfuls of the sticky material.

She held a cloth to the wound, to wipe away the excess blood, before packing his shoulder with the cobwebs. She had seen evidence of their healing powers, and knew they would help mend his flesh. Last, she bound his shoulder with clean linen.

'This needs a poultice,' she said. 'I'll ask the steward for the herbs I need.'

He said nothing, his face tense with pain. Genevieve knelt down and removed his boots, baring his feet. She lifted them into her lap and massaged his cold skin.

She had never touched a man's feet before. The gesture felt strangely intimate. His feet were rough, and she smoothed her fingers over his skin, trying to bring feeling back into them. She rubbed firm, muscled calves, continuing the motion until the colour returned to them.

'I am sorry you had to suffer for my sake,' she whispered.

'Pain is a part of battle. I am accustomed to it.'

His face tightened, and she guessed that some of her ministrations were beginning to work.

'Come.' Genevieve helped him over to the bed. 'Lie down and rest.' She pulled back the coverlet on the bed and eased his head onto a pillow. Bevan's skin still felt fiery hot to the touch, and she worried about his fever.

'My thanks,' he said, and then closed his eyes.

Genevieve touched the back of her palm to his forehead. 'Sleep now.'

She studied his bare torso, checking for any other wounds. She did not see any. She found herself comparing him to her betrothed. Unlike Bevan, Hugh's skin was pale, the colour of rising dough. She shuddered at the thought.

She sat before the fire, staring into the flickering warmth. Her eyes caught sight of the old bandage lying on the table, stained with blood.

There was no going back now. She would never let Hugh Marstowe near her again.

Genevieve stayed near Bevan all night, though she confided in the steward about Bevan's wounds. The man was helpful, and provided the herbs Genevieve requested. She made a poultice of comfrey and other roots to help heal Bevan's torn flesh.

The sky had grown darker, and Genevieve pulled the shutters closed. The fire upon the hearth brought a little warmth inside the small chamber, but still she shivered. She sat upon the bed beside Bevan, trying to make him drink tea made from willow bark. He tossed and turned in his sleep, his skin burning to the touch. She sponged his brow with cool cloths, but often had to hold him down to restrain his struggles.

Once, he caught Genevieve's waist and pulled her close. She struggled, but his strength overpowered her, even with his injury. It was only when she lay beside him that he calmed. His hands threaded through her hair, and he slept.

Genevieve could not extricate herself without more fighting, and after a time she gave up. If her presence brought him comfort, so be it. It was a small price to pay for escaping Hugh.

The night hours stretched out, the freezing winter air enveloping them. The meagre fire did little to warm her, so she curled up against Bevan's length. At long last she succumbed to sleep.

Bevan dreamed of Fiona, of her milky white skin, soft as the first spring flowers. Her raven hair tangled in his fingers as he traced the lines of her face. Downward his hands skimmed, until they cupped her breasts. They seemed fuller than he remembered, but it felt good to have her in his arms once more.

His body hardened as he pulled her bottom against him. By the god Lug, how he had missed her. He wanted to roll her beneath him and sink inside her, loving her until they both trembled with ecstasy.

A harsh aching burned in his shoulder, but he refused to dwell on it, giving his full attention to his wife. He pulled her closer and captured her lips with his own.

Dark and sweet, just as he'd remembered. He heard her give a muted cry, and he stroked the softness of her nape, tasting her mouth as though it were the first time.

'*A chroí,*' he whispered, for she was his heart, his soul. At the edge of his memory he sensed something was wrong, but he forgot it when his lips met hers again. 'Don't leave,' he whispered.

He pulled her into his arms and heard the sound of her weeping. He reached out a thumb to brush her tears away.

'Bevan—stop,' she whispered. Her hands pushed at him, pushing him away. Why? He tasted her lips again.

'Let me love you, Fiona. Let me give you another child.'

'No!' She was fighting harder this time, struggling to move away from him. 'Let me go.'

His hands stilled, and in the dim fog of his dream he saw his wife leaving him. She didn't love him. She didn't want his touch. He rolled away, releasing her while a tightness filled his throat.

'You were dreaming. Hush, now.' A cool cloth touched his forehead and he closed his eyes. 'Sleep.'

Genevieve pulled her chair near the fire, her body shaking with fear. She had known Bevan was dreaming—known he was thinking of a woman.

But when his hand had stroked her breast feelings had come alive within her. They had been terrifying feelings, unlike the pain Hugh had caused. Bevan's touch had made her relive those moments, and yet she had felt pleasure, too. She had been about to push him away when he'd kissed her.

Dear God, she had not known what to do. He had murmured endearments, words of love, making her feel desire such as she'd never known. Hugh had never kissed her with love or compassion. There had been only degradation in his embrace.

But this…

Bevan had used his tongue, worshipping her mouth. Her hand moved to her breast, where the tip was still hard and pebbled. The enormity of her desire had made it the hardest thing in the world to push him away.

But he wasn't dreaming of her. He wasn't touching her or calling her name. It was someone else. The fever had caused him to lose sight of where he was.

And yet she wished she could have known such a love. There had been a time when Hugh had brought her ribbons and flowers. Her heart had leapt whenever he'd smiled at her. She had thought it was love.

What did she know of love anyway? Her own parents' marriage was a rarity. She should not use their match as a comparison for her own.

She began to straighten up the room—anything to occupy her hands—and spied something small and white on the floor, near Bevan's discarded tunic. The tiny scrap of linen was hardly as large as her palm. She wondered where it had come from. At the bottom, a tiny row of embroidered flowers covered its hem.

It was too small to be a lady's handkerchief. She frowned. It must belong to Bevan. For all she knew it had no value whatsoever.

Then, on a whim, she placed it upon the table, folding it. She sensed that it meant something to him and should be guarded carefully. What kind of man kept a token such as this?

He slept, his breathing harsh with pain. But she believed he would heal. When he did, she would try to convince him to let the matter of Rionallís rest.

As the sun rose along the waters, turning the sea from darkness into a silvery reflection of the sky, Genevieve prayed that more blood would not be shed on her behalf.

Hugh Marstowe rubbed at his neck. Red lines marred his skin where the prisoner had dared to strangle him.

Genevieve had helped the man—helped both of the prisoners escape. And now the bastard had his betrothed. Hugh's skin itched at the thought of any man touching her. Even now Genevieve might be sharing his bed, the whore. Hadn't he shown restraint? Holding back his lust when she pushed him away? He was a patient man.

But now she had run from him, keeping company with an Irishman. His hand tightened upon the metal links of the chain.

He'd learned more of the prisoner—Bevan MacEgan— from a wench in the village. It had taken hardly any convincing at all for the girl to tell him where the MacEgan family holdings were.

He remembered the look of fear in the maid's eyes when he'd strangled her, leaving her body in the woods. He had used the same chain that had been used on himself. He'd kept the heavy iron chain, for he meant to tighten it around the Irishman's neck, watching until the life faded from his enemy's eyes.

But not yet. No. He needed to learn more about MacEgan. If Genevieve's father learned what had happened, Hugh risked losing her and the dowry. He would not let anything threaten this opportunity to own Rionallís and to become lord of his own demesne. The land was his foothold—a stepping stone for becoming a powerful lord. He had no doubt King Henry would bestow a title upon him one day. Rionallís would be one property among many.

But first he had to regain his bride. There was no question Genevieve was in the company of MacEgan. Hugh had sent men to follow them, and they had tracked the prisoners to the coast. Now was not the time to rush into battle, but rather to plan carefully.

The MacEgan holdings were among the strongest fortresses in Erin. He did not have enough men to launch an attack—not without alerting Genevieve's father. Hugh selected a sword from the armoury, testing its sharpness with his thumb until a thin line of blood appeared.

He refused to admit weakness of any kind. He would bring Genevieve back without the Earl ever learning the truth.

He chose a mace as a second weapon and swung it, letting the heavy spiked ball smash into a wooden table. He imagined it was MacEgan's face.

Soon, my sweet Genevieve, he thought. *I'll come for you soon.*

'I am leaving for Laochre tonight,' Bevan said. Days had passed since Genevieve had first tended his wound. Though the skin remained raw, no longer did it seep poisoned blood. In a few more weeks she believed he would have full use of his shoulder.

She refused to look at him, focusing her concentration on his wound while cutting away the old bandage. Bevan had removed the tunic so she could better reach the injury. The sight of his bare skin made her uncomfortable.

'You will stay here,' he added. 'It will be safe until I can arrange for your escort.'

'If you say so.' Not for a moment did she believe Hugh had given up. The longer she stayed, the greater the chance he would find her.

'There are over sixty men here,' Bevan pointed out. 'And no one has tracked you here thus far.'

Genevieve tied fresh linen around his shoulder. 'For now, that is true. But Hugh will come after me.'

A grim expression settled over his face. 'You are safer upon Ennisleigh than out there alone.'

She tied the bandage and folded her hands in her lap. 'That may be so. But I've no wish to be caught in the middle of your war against my people.'

'This battle was begun long before you came to Éireann,' he said. 'Rionallís belongs to me, and I'll not let it fall into Norman hands.'

'I am a Norman,' she said, a hardened edge rising in her voice. He was beginning to distance himself, placing her along with the enemies he despised. She didn't like it.

'I know.' His gaze locked with hers, with no intent of retreat. She understood suddenly that whatever peace lay between them would vanish once she returned home. Bevan would regard her as an enemy.

In her heart she knew the property rightfully belonged to Bevan. But her father had conquered the land and would defend it. She could not allow Bevan to endanger her family.

Genevieve chose her next words carefully. 'The land is part of my dowry, meant to be given over to my husband when I wed.' Her voice dropped to a whisper. 'Would you shed my blood to get it back?'

Bevan stood, his shadow looming over her. Taut muscles, scarred from battle, flexed as he leaned in close. Genevieve tried to retreat, but he caught her nape and held her fast. 'My men will take you to England. And I would suggest that you stay there.'

Her pulse quickened, even as she tried not to be afraid of him. 'Your escort cannot protect me,' she said. 'Hugh will kill your men and take me captive once more. The only person whom I trust to take me home is my father,' she said. 'Send word to him and you need not inconvenience yourself.'

'And bring the Norman enemy upon us? No.' His tone was sharp, menacing. He sat, donning his tunic and hooded mantle.

'He will come for me,' she said softly. She believed it in her heart, even though Thomas de Renalt had not answered a single one of her missives. More than anything she had come to believe Hugh had intercepted them. 'I know he will.'

'I'll ask nothing of a Norman.' Bevan stood and turned to leave. He had seen the hurt in her eyes, the wounded spirit. He hadn't meant to speak so harshly, but he could not let himself befriend an enemy.

Genevieve moved towards him suddenly, taking his hand in hers. Before he could react, she laid something against his palm. 'You would not want to leave this behind,' she said.

He recognised the token and curled his fingers around it. 'Where did you get this?'

'You brought it with you.' She had not moved her hand away from his, and the soft innocence of her palm sent a flare of desire through him.

No woman had touched him since Fiona. No one had dared to. Outside, the bitter winter wind sliced through his garments, but he could still feel the heat of Genevieve's impulsive gesture.

It meant nothing. He would not dwell upon it. He pushed the uncertainties from his mind, tucked the scrap of fabric away and gathered his cloak around him.

Bevan muttered a farewell to her, not waiting to hear a response. He climbed down to the shoreline and boarded one of the boats. As he crossed the waters, Bevan turned his gaze to the horizon. Two years ago enemy torches had cast their reddish glow upon the sea. Norman swords had dripped the blood of his kinsmen upon the earth.

He fingered the familiar piece of fabric Genevieve had given him. The tiny bit of linen was a reminder of his purpose—revenge against the Norman invaders who had taken Rionallís.

In the evening twilight a gull circled the sea, sweeping lower towards its prey. The sun drenched the horizon in a bronze glow, a benediction of light. He watched from the shoreline until the rosy hues dimmed into a rich purple.

It reminded him of the evenings he and Fiona had spent together, waiting until the stars emerged. He had shared with her his hopes for the future, his dreams yet to be fulfilled. His hand had rested upon the swelling at her waist, his greatest hope of all.

He pushed the despair aside and forced his mind upon the present. He would find another mercenary battle to fight, using mindless bloodlust as a means to forget.

And he would leave Genevieve behind, try not to think of the feelings she had stirred within him.

Chapter Four

When he first laid eyes upon his sister-in-law Isabel, Bevan felt as though a hand had choked off the air in his lungs. She held her newborn son in her arms, her face as serene as the Madonna. At a closer glimpse he saw the wrinkled infant face, the grey-blue eyes, and the tiny mouth working in search of a warm breast.

'His name is Liam,' Isabel said softly. 'For the uncle he never knew.'

Bevan saw the look of pride upon his brother's face, and managed to mutter his congratulations. Isabel lifted the baby to her shoulder, and he thought of the time years ago when his own daughter had nuzzled into his neck. He forced his gaze away.

'We've missed you, Bevan,' Isabel said, giving him a light hug.

'You look well,' he responded.

'Will you be staying with us longer this time?' she asked, cradling the child in her arms.

'*Níl.* Lionel Ó Riordan has asked for my sword against Strongbow's army. His men are fighting in Kilkenny. I'll be joining them after I've resolved the matter of Rionallís.'

Isabel's face showed her disappointment, but his brother Patrick offered support. 'If that is your wish. Tell me what happened. I gather Ewan got himself into trouble again?'

Tension edged upon him. Bevan inclined his head, and began to relate the story. At that moment his younger brother entered the Great Chamber.

'What are you doing here?' Ewan demanded. 'I thought you were with Genevieve.'

At the mention of the name, Bevan saw his sister-in-law brighten with curiosity. 'Who is Genevieve?'

Bevan sent a warning look to Ewan, but his brother ignored it. 'She's—'

'Stay out of this, boy—'Bevan threatened.

'—the woman we rescued,' Ewan finished with a cocky grin. 'In truth, she rescued us first.'

He dodged before Bevan could grab him, standing behind Patrick.

'Really?' Patrick mused. 'Now, this is interesting.'

'Very,' Isabel agreed. 'Who is she? And why isn't she here?'

'It was a temporary arrangement,' Bevan said. 'I've left her at Ennisleigh.'

He could tell Isabel was itching to ask more questions, but her husband silenced her with a warning look.

'She's a Norman,' Ewan piped in.

'A hostage?' Patrick asked. His expression turned serious. 'Not a wise move, Bevan.'

'She's not a hostage. She saved our lives. All she wanted in return was to escape her betrothed.' Bevan shrugged, acting as if it were of no matter. He was going to cut off Ewan's meddling tongue if the boy didn't stop his chatter. To Ewan he said, 'Meet me on the training field tomorrow morn, and we'll see if your sword is as good as your mouth.'

Ewan's grin widened, and Bevan wished he had not risen to his brother's bait. He knew Ewan longed for more lessons in swordplay. Bevan loathed the training, for no matter how much he tried, Ewan never improved. His skills with a sword would get him killed one day, and all knew it. He would be better off serving the Church.

After they departed, Isabel turned to her husband. 'Bevan hates the Normans. There's more he's not telling us.'

'He must have been forced to it,' Patrick said grimly. 'He would never have brought her otherwise.'

'I wonder what kind of woman she is?' Isabel mused, putting her son to her breast to nurse. The infant latched on, making soft sighs as the milk flowed. 'Why would she leave her home?'

Patrick shot her a suspicious look. 'You're not planning anything?'

'Not yet,' Isabel promised. 'But I would like to know more about her. I think I may pay a visit to Ennisleigh.'

'Do not interfere, Isabel.'

She lifted the babe to her shoulder for a burp. 'I wonder if she's pretty? Bevan has been alone for a long time.'

Patrick put his arm around his wife's shoulders. 'Let him be, *a chroí*. He grieves for her still.'

Isabel raised her gaze to her husband. 'Then 'tis high time he started living again. I shall find out what I can about this woman.'

The following morning, Bevan's sword sliced through the air, nicking his brother's arm. 'Are you trying to let me kill you?' he demanded. 'Raise your shield!'

Ewan dodged another blow and stumbled, catching the tip of Bevan's sword. Bevan turned at the last second to keep his brother from skewering himself.

In disgust, he sheathed the weapon. 'That's enough. Face the truth, brother. You were not meant to be a soldier.'

Ewan coughed, his head bowed towards the frozen earth. Bevan could see the frustration in his stance.

'I could be,' Ewan insisted. 'I need more training.'

'You've been training all your life,' Bevan said quietly. 'And I can't protect you forever.'

'I never asked you to,' Ewan said, his voice hoarse. He rose to his feet, picking up his fallen sword. 'I can look after myself.'

Bevan nearly said, *No, you can't,* but he kept his mouth shut. 'Go back inside.'

His brother raised his chin, and in his eyes Bevan saw rage, not acceptance. 'I'll prove to you that I can be a warrior. I swear it. I never meant for the Normans to capture me.'

'No one ever intends to be caught,' Bevan remarked. 'But you were. You could have been killed.'

'I am sorry.' Ewan sheathed his own sword. 'For all of it.'

Bevan knew he referred to the failed conquest of Rionall-lís, but he did not acknowledge his brother's apology. Instead, he calmed his tone of voice. 'You should find another skill. Not every man has to be a soldier.'

'I am a MacEgan. That's who we are.' Ewan stared hard at Bevan, and in that moment Bevan feared that his brother would never accept reality. The fierce determination on Ewan's face made it evident that he would die before choosing another path.

At the thought of another brother dying to the sword, a lump caught in his throat. His eldest brother, Liam, had died in the fight against the Normans—the same battle that had claimed the life of Fiona.

He reached out and tousled Ewan's hair. 'One day, perhaps,' he said. The acknowledgement earned him a smile.

'Are we going to see Genevieve again today?' Ewan asked, his mood suddenly brighter. 'I like her.'

Bevan made a noncommittal sound. '*We* are not going anywhere. I may arrange for her to return to England on the morrow. Or the next day. But you will remain here.'

'Sir Hugh won't let her go,' Ewan reminded him. 'Even now he might be raising an army.'

'He does not have enough men to fight us. And Genevieve is safe at Ennisleigh.'

Ewan shrugged. 'Possibly.'

'What do you mean?'

'He could come at night, alone. 'Tisn't hard.'

'No one can get through our guards.'

'I can,' Ewan said. 'Many times have I gone to Ennisleigh. I like to sleep beneath the stars.'

'The guards know you.'

'They did not know I was there,' Ewan insisted. 'But if you send Genevieve with an escort to England he will find her. And kill any man with her.'

The boy's assertion infuriated him, because it was exactly what Genevieve had said. He wanted to groan with frustration. For the only way to ensure Genevieve's safety and prevent Sir Hugh from capturing her was to escort her himself.

Bevan cursed when he set foot on the island. He hadn't intended to come back to Ennisleigh, but not only had he returned, he'd brought Ewan with him. Ewan had begged to come along, since he'd had to endure teasing after his failure at Rionallís.

Bevan had gone over Ewan's arguments many times, and he had no desire to be Genevieve's escort. Yet he hadn't forgotten the beating Marstowe had given her, nor the fear in her eyes when she'd cowered beneath his fists.

Again, he wished he'd had time to kill the man.

Ewan was right. Sir Hugh would come sooner or later to

claim his betrothed, or he would intercept them on their journey to Dun Laoghaire.

Bevan reached up to touch his shoulder wound, which
had begun to heal. It would take weeks yet, but thankfully he
had been wounded on the left side, which had not affected
his sword-fighting.

He strode into the inner bailey, towards a section set aside
for training. His tribesmen were engaged in their daily exercises, overseen by their captain. Ever since the invasions, all
men were expected to defend the ring fort. It was the only
way to survive.

Ewan joined them, practising his swordplay. The clang of
metal rang out over the stones, and the breath of the men hung
in clouds in the icy air.

Genevieve stood nearby, watching. She wore a hooded
black cloak, and when she saw him approaching, her face
brightened. ''Tis good to see you again, Lord MacEgan.'

'Bevan,' he corrected. 'We do not use titles here—unlike
your people.'

'Bevan, then.' She turned back to watch the men. 'Do they
do this every day?'

'*Tá.* Our soldiers are among the best-trained in Éireann.'

She shivered in the cold air, and a light drifting of snow
began. 'Do you think they could train me?'

'What do you mean?'

She stared at the soldiers. 'Not sword-fighting. Hand-to-
hand combat.'

'Why?'

'So that a man like Hugh will never touch me again.' Her
words were brittle, like the icicles that hung from the turrets.

'Come inside. It's cold.' He led her away from the men,
but she stopped him.

'I want to learn to fight,' she insisted.

'You're safe here. There is no need.' The bruise on her cheek had deepened to a purple hue, he noted. A protective instinct rose within him to guard her from Marstowe.

'I don't want to feel that way ever again. Helpless. I was not strong enough to defend myself.'

He laid a hand on her arm, and she jerked. Tears glistened in her eyes, but they were tears of anger, not sorrow. 'I will learn to take care of myself. With or without your help.'

If his wife had known how to defend herself, would she still have been taken by the invaders?

'I'll teach you,' he said finally. One day more would not matter. It was too late in the day to start their journey to Dun Laoghaire, he reasoned. On the morrow would be soon enough.

He was rewarded with a faint smile. Mayhap this was his second chance to atone for his sins. He had not been able to protect his wife.

But he could teach Genevieve to protect herself.

Their first lesson began in the Great Chamber. Bevan faced Genevieve, and tilted her chin up to meet his gaze. 'Never take your eyes off your enemy.'

She obeyed, watching him. The scars on his face only accentuated the strong planes, the firm mouth, and those fierce green eyes.

'Don't fight fair. Aim for the soft spots. A man's eyes. His throat. His groin.'

Her glance flickered downwards as she remembered the feeling of his skin against hers. His warm touch, his hands moving over her. Her body tightened in response to the memory. She did not like the way he made her feel. Strange longings conjured up fears she didn't want to face.

Bevan stepped behind her, gripping her across her shoulders. Though the gesture meant nothing, a tremor of unwanted desire kindled within her veins. She forced it away, along with her discomfort at being held so closely.

'If a man attacks you this way, use the back of your head to smash his nose. With any luck you'll break it, and his concentration.'

Her concentration had already wandered away, but she managed a nod. 'You had a knife,' she said. 'What should I do then?'

'You can still fight off your opponent.' He switched places, standing in front of her. 'Pretend as though you have a knife at my throat.'

Genevieve reached up, but her arms would barely surround his broad shoulders. She stood on her tiptoes to reach him, an imaginary knife in her hands.

The posture reminded her of an embrace, and she lost her courage for a moment.

Do not be a fool. You must learn this. She took a deep breath and adjusted her position.

'First, I would tuck my chin down and take a good grip on the man's knife arm.' He covered her hands with his own.

The closeness of him made her uncomfortable once more. He smelled clean, of woodsmoke and the wintry forest.

'Now you step back.' He pressed his leg backwards, against hers, twisting his body to the right. Genevieve lost her balance and had to grab him. Within seconds he had her on the ground beneath him.

She could not stop the trembling, the blind fear that hit her. Hugh had tried to hold her down like that once before. Though a part of her was dimly aware that Bevan had no intention of harming her, she closed her eyes tightly.

'If you fall on top of him, 'twill knock the breath out of his lungs,' Bevan instructed. 'And then you have the knife against his throat.'

She opened her eyes, but could not mask her terror.

'What is it?' Bevan sat beside her on the ground, lifting her to a seated position. 'Did I harm you?'

She shook her head, trying to push away the sharp burst of fear that kept clouding her mind. He was not Hugh.

But Hugh would come for her. He would not stop hunting her. Not until he had her cowering beneath him again.

'He still frightens me,' she whispered.

'Every man is afraid in battle. The only man who isn't afraid is the man who is already dead.'

'You weren't afraid that night. I saw Hugh stab you. He would have killed you.'

'No. His intention was to harm me, not to kill me.'

'How? How could you know something like that?' She held her arms tightly, furious at herself for being unable to control the terror. 'He tried to make you fear him. But you faced him. As for me…' Her voice trailed off. 'I can't take away my fear.'

'Do not try to. Practise what I taught you until you no longer have to imagine any of the moves. You've no time to think when an enemy attacks. Why do you suppose our men train every day? So they never have to think. Their training causes them to act.'

He sounded so sure of himself. She wanted to believe it.

'But you're wrong,' he added. 'I did fear that night.'

'For your brother?' she said, thinking of Ewan and his lack of experience.

Bevan paused, and his gaze locked with hers. Genevieve waited for him to agree, but he held his silence a moment longer. With his knuckle, he touched the edge of her bruise, his expression unreadable.

He revealed nothing of his emotions, but she became more aware of him. The battle scars, the quiet, untamed power of this Irish warrior, both frightened her and drew her in. His dark hair and sea-green eyes watched her in a way that made her shiver.

'*Tá*,' he said. 'I feared that night.'

Bevan stood and held out a hand to help her up. Genevieve rose, but he did not release her hand. 'So long as you are with me, I swear I will not let him harm you. He'll not touch you.'

He squeezed her palm as if to seal the vow. Genevieve wanted so much to believe him, but whispers of doubt eroded her confidence.

'May it be so,' she managed to reply.

As the afternoon faded into evening, Bevan showed her other tactics, ways of fighting an enemy. Genevieve practised, determined to learn. Alone in her chamber, she committed every move to memory, fighting against an invisible foe.

From her window she spied Bevan, sparring with the soldiers in the bailey below. He moved with the ease of experience, blocking one blow while slashing hard with his sword arm. If she had not seen it for herself she would never have known he was injured, so swiftly did he move. Watching him, she couldn't help but admire his skills.

At the evening meal, she asked, 'Where did you learn to fight?'

'My father taught my brothers and myself.'

'You are skilled.' She took a sip of mead. 'Does your shoulder hurt?'

'*Tá*,' he admitted. 'But in time it will heal.' Bevan rose to his feet. 'Ready your belongings. At first light I will take you to Dun Laoghaire.'

'Why not take a ship from here?' she asked. 'If we do not travel by land, Hugh's men cannot touch us.'

'Strongbow's Norman armies are patrolling along the

coast. We have no choice but to make our crossing north of here.'

His reasoning was sound. She had heard the stories of Richard FitzGilbert de Clare, nicknamed Strongbow. Strongbow had come to Ireland two years ago, to help the deposed Irish King Diarmuid MacMurrough regain his kingdom. His soldiers had slaughtered hundreds of men, but they had succeeded in their quest.

In return, Strongbow had wed MacMurrough's daughter, planning to claim the kingdom for his own. King Henry had grown suspicious of Strongbow's territorial gains. He had ordered Genevieve's father to Ireland, along with other Norman lords, to keep a closer eye upon Strongbow.

Genevieve wholeheartedly agreed with Bevan's desire to avoid the southern coast. 'How many men will accompany us?'

'There are enough men.'

His answer did not please her. 'How many?' she repeated.

Bevan's face showed his displeasure at her question. 'Our soldiers are among the strongest fighters in Éireann. You need not fear Sir Hugh.'

'Strength matters not,' she argued. 'You did not have enough men to retake Rionallís. Did the other soldiers ever arrive?'

He remained silent.

'I thought not.' She shook her head. 'If you cannot spare enough men for an escort, I prefer to remain here and let my father's men come for me.'

'I can defend you against Sir Hugh,' Bevan said.

'I have no doubt that you are a skilled fighter. But you've been injured.'

Bevan rose from the table, his hand resting upon the hilt of his sword. 'You do not think I can protect you?'

She hesitated. 'You helped me escape, and for that I am grateful.' She did not mention that the only man she trusted to see her safely home was her father. Sir Hugh held no power over Thomas de Renalt.

His expression turned as hard as the ice covering the earth outside. She straightened her shoulders, refusing to back down. There was something else in his expression, behind the wounded pride. A haunted look—one that dissipated in moments.

'Do not worry about protecting me,' she said. 'At least here we can see our enemy. I would be safe until my father's arrival.'

'I have already said that I'll not bring more Normans here.'

'My father would not harm your men. He would reward you for your aid.'

'How? By returning Rionallís to me?' he mocked gently. Genevieve shook her head. 'It is not possible.'

'You would bring my vengeance upon your family?' he asked, his voice like a thread of steel. 'You would have me take up the sword against those you love for a piece of land?'

She folded her arms across her chest. 'I do not believe you would do such a thing.'

He moved forward until only a breath hung between them. Though he did not touch her, she could feel the unspoken threat. Her lungs seized, cold fear racing within her veins.

'Believe it. I let no one endanger what is mine.'

Genevieve knew he wanted to frighten her, to force her into surrendering the land. But, though she did fear him, an underlying thrill heated her skin. The sweet ache he had awakened rushed through her. Darkness and desire warred within, and her body remembered his forbidden touch.

'Rionallís belongs to my family,' he added. 'Patrick's son, Liam, will inherit the land when he comes of age. Or Ewan.'

'What of you? Surely you will wed and have sons of your own?' It seemed strange that he would fight for something he did not want for himself.

'I have sworn never to wed again,' he said.

She heard the anger and pain in his voice and asked, 'Is it something to do with Fiona?'

He stiffened. 'Where did you hear that name?'

'You called out for her when the fever was upon you.' Genevieve caught a glimpse of his pain, though he masked it with anger. 'Was she your wife?'

'She was.'

'What happened to her?'

'She was murdered by the Normans.'

His voice remained steady, but Genevieve heard the razor edge of fury in his tone. Though he had cast her people as the enemy, she saw through his rage. Instead of a warrior bent upon vengeance, she recognised a grieving husband. And yet not a trace of emotion could she see upon his face. It was as though he had an invisible shield guarding his feelings.

Genevieve longed to ask him more, but she fell silent. Beneath the scarred face of a warrior lay a man who had not yet defeated the ghosts of his past. Her heart ached for his loss.

She did not want to ask more of him than he'd already given. 'Send a message to my father,' she urged. 'Why would you endanger your men for my sake? You know as well as I the risk to them.'

He did not respond, and she pressed further. 'My father intended to travel for my wedding to Sir Hugh. It may be that he is already here in Erin.'

Bevan glanced towards the mainland and at last relented. 'If what you say is true, then on the morrow we will journey to my brother's home, Laochre. Should your father attempt an attack, his men will suffer at the hands of over three hundred soldiers.'

'I have already told you—he would not do such a thing.'

'I will not trust a Norman,' Bevan said. 'The sooner you leave us, the safer we will all be.'

She did not let her face show the hurt he had caused her. His blatant prejudice against all Normans included her, though she had done nothing wrong.

Her consolation lay in the fact that Hugh had made no attempt in these past few days to reclaim her. If nothing else, Bevan had kept her safe, as he'd promised.

In the firelit chamber of Rionallís, Hugh Marstowe paced. Genevieve remained with MacEgan, and he envisaged her soft skin marred by the Irishman's touch.

Bevan MacEgan would die for it.

Hugh stood, and held a polished mirror to study his appearance. The manservant had clipped his fair hair short, in the Norman fashion, and shaved his cheeks smooth. Hugh ran a hand across his jawline, ensuring that no stubble remained.

In his bed, a young maiden awaited him. Her hair was dark, like Genevieve's, but she was not nearly as slender or beautiful.

'Come, my lord,' she beckoned, opening her bare arms to him. Her breasts were inviting and plump, and he would take advantage of her offering. But it burned within his gut that Genevieve had left him.

He loved her. She was to be his wife, and jealousy snaked through his heart at the thought of her running from him. Why would she do it? He had punished her with a beating, aye, but it was for her own good. The sooner she learned how to be a proper wife, the better. He disliked having to discipline Genevieve, but during the weeks she had been alone with him he had seen a stubborn side to her.

She was like a wild mare that needed to be broken. He

would be the man to tame her spirits, and she would be grateful for it. When she sat beside him as his wife, his status would be complete.

His gaze fell upon the golden torque he had ordered. Made of finely beaten gold, and set with sapphires, it would match her eyes. He hoped the gift would help her to forgive him. If she had not run away, he would not have punished her.

He would teach Genevieve what she needed to know, and she would become the perfect wife—completely obedient to his every wish. And in return he would reward her with precious gifts. He fingered the delicate torque, imagining it against her skin.

There was little time left. His missive asking Genevieve's father to delay his journey had met with dismissal. Thomas de Renalt, the Earl of Longford, would arrive within a sennight. If he did not have Genevieve back by then, Hugh did not like to think of the Earl's wrath.

Discomfort grew like a worm in the pit of his stomach. Dismissing the girl from his bed, he summoned Sir Peter.

He dressed carefully, ensuring that no stains or dirt were visible upon his tunic or hose. He added a chain of gold to emphasise his appearance as lord of the fortress.

A knock sounded at his door. 'Enter,' Hugh said.

Sir Peter folded his arms across his chain-mail armour. 'My wife and I are returning to England at dawn.'

'You were supposed to bring Genevieve back.'

'We lost them in the snow. And there are too many Irishmen against our forces. We need the Earl's men.'

Hugh's temper snapped. 'I will not tolerate excuses. You were her guardian, responsible for her care.'

The knight's expression grew insolent. 'You are not my overlord. I have admitted my mistake to the Earl. He knows his daughter was taken by the Irish.' With a shrug, he added, 'And you were her betrothed, sworn to protect her. You may answer to the Earl's displeasure. We are leaving.'

With a disdainful bow, the knight closed the door. Hugh fought to control his rage. He barked an order to a passing servant to send in the commander of his troops.

Within minutes Robert Staunton, the leader of his men, entered. He bowed. 'My lord.'

The formal address soothed his anger somewhat. At least Staunton knew his place.

'Why have our men not brought her back?' Hugh demanded. 'Why have they failed in their duty?'

Staunton's expression grew strained. 'We have thirty men at our disposal,' he said. 'And the MacEgans have over three hundred. We will gladly give up our lives for your honour, my lord. But I would rather make the sacrifice knowing we have been successful at our task.'

Hugh detected a faint trace of sardonic humour from the commander. 'I'll not let my future wife perish at the hands of the Irish,' he reminded Staunton.

'I have a prisoner who might interest you,' Staunton replied. 'If you wish to accompany me below, I could show you my proposition.'

Hugh concealed his distaste at the thought of the filth, and accompanied Staunton below. When he saw the MacEgan soldiers, still chained, it returned his good spirits. At least he had managed to capture *them,* even if he could not reach Genevieve.

Staunton led him to the last prisoner—a woman.

'Where did you get this one?' Hugh asked. The woman was thin, her face streaked with dirt. He noticed that one of the soldiers stiffened, and the pair exchanged glances.

'We found her among the servants here. She was trying to

help the men escape. I would have executed her, but I thought she might be useful to us.'

Hugh could not see how, but he allowed Staunton to continue.

Staunton withdrew a dagger and the woman blanched. When the commander brought the blade to her throat, he added, 'I could kill her now, of course.'

'Don't,' came a voice. When Hugh turned to see the source of the sound, he saw one of the MacEgan soldiers. Short of stature, with hair the colour of fire, and square shoulders, the man seemed hardly fit to be a fighter.

'Your name?' Hugh demanded.

The soldier struggled against his chains and spat at Hugh's feet. 'Leave her alone.' Rage outlined the soldier's face, along with a hint of desperation.

The woman meant something to the man. It pleased Hugh to hold such power over another. He approached the woman, taking the dagger from Staunton. He fingered a lock of her fair hair. With a swift slice, he cut it off.

'Answer my question.'

The soldier stared at him, and Hugh saw hesitation. The woman was his weakness, and he pressed his advantage.

'The next thing I cut off will be one of her fingers.'

Hugh gripped the woman's hand, separating the fingers while she fought him. Again, he revelled in the feeling of overpowering her. She could do nothing against his strength.

'Do you know Bevan MacEgan?' Hugh asked the soldier.

The man gave a nod. '*Tá*. I know him.' Struggling against his chains, he begged, 'Let her go.'

Staunton stepped forward, lowering his voice to a whisper. 'We will use him to get to MacEgan. Let him bring back information to us, so that we may better plan our attack.'

'A traitor,' Hugh said softly.

'Aye.'

The idea took shape and metamorphosed. If this man wanted his woman to live, he would obey every dictate they asked of him.

Hugh smiled—a thin smile of gloating. And dreamed of vengeance.

Chapter Five

It took less than an hour to reach the fortress of Laochre upon the mainland. Though Genevieve felt foolish, glancing behind her every few moments on such a short journey, she did not breathe easily until the square towers of the gatehouse were within view. Ewan rode ahead of them, instructed to keep his eyes open for potential attackers.

Genevieve suspected Bevan wanted his younger brother out of the way, for Ewan had chattered without ceasing ever since they had left the island.

Her heart caught in her throat at the majesty of the donjon. Gleaming white in colour, a thick wall protected a fortress nearly three times the size of Rionallís. It stood atop a hillside, and she could see soldiers patrolling the upper battlements.

'I didn't realise it was made of stone,' Genevieve remarked. Many of the Norman castles in England were currently being converted to stone, but few were complete.

'It isn't,' Bevan said. As they drew nearer, Genevieve saw what he meant. The smooth white walls were plaster, covering a timber frame. 'But our enemies believe it is, and that is all that matters. Patrick is replacing it with stone.'

She marvelled at the ingenuity of the architecture. The guards let them pass inside the gates, and Genevieve was struck by the vast bustle of activity.

The heavy clang of a blacksmith's hammer mingled with the din of people working. Servants carried stacks of peat for burning, while one merchant brought a wagonload of goods to be inspected for purchase. Horses were led to the stables and children ran freely, laughing at a game.

The people greeted Bevan with smiles and hearty claps on the back. A tall fair-haired man greeted Bevan with a bear hug—another MacEgan brother named Connor. A smile softened Bevan's face from the rugged fierceness she had grown accustomed to.

When he wasn't glowering, he was actually rather handsome, she admitted. His deep green eyes, the colour of rough-hewn malachite, along with the black hair, were a striking combination. The scars along the planes of his face added an element of danger.

'I must meet with my brother Patrick,' Bevan said at last. To Ewan, he instructed, 'See that she has a place to sleep.'

Genevieve started to follow Ewan, but before she did she cast one look back at Bevan. She could not forget the look of determination on his face when she'd refused to relinquish Rionallís. How could she trust a man who wanted to conquer the land that was hers? But her fear of Hugh was stronger, and so she had little choice.

She did not feel safe here, not yet. Despite all the soldiers, and the proud Irish warrior who had sworn to protect her, she could not let down her guard. Her heart heavy, she accompanied Ewan inside the donjon.

Bevan strode in the direction of the donjon, greeting friends as he passed. He located Patrick, commanding a group of soldiers.

'You brought the woman, I see.' Patrick dismissed the men, greeting his brother with a nod.

'I told Ewan to find a place for her. She wishes to send word to her family, to return to England.'

'Why do you not escort her yourself to Dun Laoghaire?'

Patrick's query revived the anger he felt towards Genevieve. After her admonition that she did not believe him capable of protecting her, his first instinct had been to cast her out, to let her fend for herself against Marstowe. Or he could prove himself capable by escorting her to Dun Laoghaire, despite her desire to await her family.

Her doubts hardened his resolve to wash his hands of her. Let her remain here. Let her family come for her. She was no longer his responsibility, and his debt to her was paid.

'I intend to renew the attack upon Rionallís,' he said. 'Keeping the woman here may prove to our advantage.'

'You may be accused of kidnapping her,' Patrick pointed out. 'Their King Henry will demand compensation.'

'Henry will not risk warring against us. He's better off having us as allies.'

'The Norman armies have already invaded Meath and Breifne. Henry will set his sights on Laochre next, should you draw his wrath upon us.' Patrick met his gaze, and then he revealed what Bevan had already suspected. 'Your men did not return from Rionallís. If they are not already dead, Sir Hugh Marstowe holds them captive. He may try to use them against us.'

'If you grant me more fighters, I can free them.' Bevan would not rest until he had atoned for his defeat. He hated the thought of his men in Marstowe's custody.

'You are needed here,' Patrick said. 'I will send Connor to free them. The Norman King is visiting Tara, holding court there with the High King. It may be that we can work out an agreement to avoid war between our people.'

'What kind of agreement?'

Patrick changed his tack, not answering Bevan's question. 'Or we could exchange the lives of our men for Genevieve. You could return her to Rionallís and not trouble yourself with her further.'

'She was beaten, Patrick. If I'd left her there, Marstowe would have killed her eventually.'

Patrick sobered, and accepted a goblet of wine from a servant. He handed another to Bevan. 'And that is why you took her with you?'

'*Tá*. The bastard hurt her, far worse than you can imagine. If any man had laid a hand on Isabel, you'd have done the same.'

The words came out before he'd intended them. He had never thought to compare his feelings towards Genevieve to the feelings Patrick had for his wife. He wanted to protect her; that was all. And he didn't like seeing any woman in pain.

'Have a care, brother,' Patrick said. 'I've no wish for you to lose your life over a woman.'

'You needn't worry that I would ever let a woman interfere with my life.' Especially not one who stubbornly clung to the belief that Rionallís belonged to *her* family. It irritated him to think that Genevieve would continue to fight him for the land he had owned for years.

Bevan added, 'I will free the men, regardless of how long it takes. Rionallís will be ours again.'

'That may be,' Patrick acceded. 'Or the Norman King may agree to my offer of an exchange without bloodshed. I believe the prospect will please him. A bond between our family and Genevieve's.'

Bevan suddenly understood his brother's reasoning: an arranged marriage. 'No.'

'You are a fool if you believe Ríonallís is yours for the taking. The Norman King will only send more of his men to recapture the land,' Patrick said. 'And our men are likely already dead. If you hope to keep the fortress, your only recourse is to wed Genevieve.' His expression turned grim. 'A match between you may assuage their king's anger, for it will allow him to have a strong alliance with us.'

'You've no right to ask such a thing of me.' Bevan could not imagine the idea of taking another woman as his wife. He had sworn never to wed again, and he intended to keep that vow.

'As your king and overlord, I can command it,' Patrick said. The threat was thinly veiled.

Bevan refused to believe his brother would act upon it. 'She will return to her parents' home in England. In the meantime our men will go to Ríonallís.'

'If you will not wed her, perhaps Connor will.'

At the thought of another man laying hands on her, Bevan wanted to snarl. Genevieve had suffered enough. The best place for her was an abbey, where no man could touch her.

'You care for her, don't you?' Patrick said quietly.

'She risked her life for mine and Ewan's. That is all there is between us.'

'I have my doubts upon that, brother. Else you would not be so angry.'

Bevan took a long drink of wine, glaring at Patrick. 'I brought her to safety, nothing more.'

His mood blackened as he thought of Marstowe's abuse. It occurred to him that her family had arranged the betrothal. Even if Bevan sent her home, she might still be forced to wed Marstowe.

Though he did not want to wed Genevieve himself, he did not want to see her suffer again. He envisaged Fiona's beautiful face, hearing her screams as the Normans took her from him. The reddish haze of battle, the cry tearing from his throat as they struck him down. He hadn't been able to save her.

If he released Genevieve, her marriage with Sir Hugh would take place. Bevan was certain of it. She would endure suffering, and it would be his own fault.

Guilt and fury assailed him, for Patrick was right. The only way to protect Genevieve from Marstowe was to wed her himself.

As a few flakes of snow scattered across the wind, he lifted his face to the cold. The seeds of Genevieve's doubt had taken root within him.

How could he call himself a warrior when he could not defend the people he loved? Once he had fought with the confidence of experience, knowing his sword was stronger than his enemy's.

But the attack on Rionallís had failed. He could not blame Ewan for it. They had underestimated the Normans. And he had brought about the imprisonment of his men, if not their deaths.

The ripple of movement caught his attention, and he saw Genevieve standing, silhouetted against the battlements. Her face was lined with worry as she stared out onto the horizon.

Unbidden came the thought of her warming his feet, her fingers soothing heat within them. She had tended his wounds, stayed up at night to keep watch over him.

Bevan climbed the stairs to the battlements, drawing nearer until he could see her expression. Shadows lined her face, and a dark bruise covered one cheek. She had taken that blow while trying to rescue Ewan and himself.

They didn't speak, and he didn't have to ask what she was

thinking. The timorous expression on her face revealed all
to him.

Unable to stop himself, he reached out and touched the
bruise. Her hand cupped his, and the feeling of her warm
palm against his sent a jolt through him.

She closed her eyes, and a dark strand of her hair blew free
of the veil, against his hand. Though the icy breath of winter
reddened her cheeks, her skin felt soft. His thumb moved to
caress the bruise, as if to soothe it away.

She leaned into his palm, her lips brushing against his skin.
It was not a kiss, only the barest hint of a touch. His loins
tightened, and suddenly he found himself wanting to feel her
lips upon his. He wanted the softness of a woman, to quench
the thirst of two years of being alone.

He lifted her face up to his and stared into her cerulean
eyes—eyes that held a fear he could not silence.

He understood suddenly why a marriage could never happen between them. To wed Genevieve would be to face the
demons of his past. If he took her as his bride, he could not
ignore her and continue on the way he had lived his life.

Abruptly, he turned away. He could not accept Patrick's
suggestion. Nor could he let Genevieve go back to Marstowe.

He vowed to journey to Tara, to seek the help of the High
King. If need be, he would appeal to the Norman King as
well. For the sake of his pride, he would somehow see to it
that Genevieve and his men were safe.

Genevieve rose at dawn, having shared a room with two
other women. She donned her kirtle before the others awakened, wincing at its torn condition. With her fingers, she tried
to comb her hair, wishing she had a veil to hide it.

She left the chamber, going below stairs. A few servants
cast curious looks her way, but Genevieve ignored them. She

found her way to the Great Chamber, where people had gathered to break their fast.

A tall woman regarded her with an interested expression. From the way others deferred to her, Genevieve guessed she was the lady of the castle.

The woman wore a deep blue overdress and a white *léine*, an Irish gown that fell to her ankles in soft drapes. Her golden hair was braided across her forehead while the rest hung down to her waist.

'You are Genevieve?' The woman spoke the Norman language so fluently it surprised Genevieve to hear it.

'I am.' She extended her hands in greeting, and the woman took them.

'My name is Isabel MacEgan. My husband is Patrick MacEgan, King of Laochre.'

'A king?' Genevieve questioned.

'Not High King.' Isabel smiled in response. 'There are many petty kings in Ireland, just as we once had in England.' She added, 'But you needn't be intimidated by my husband or by me. I merely wanted to meet the woman who saved the lives of Ewan and Bevan. It isn't often that a lady can rescue one of Ireland's finest warriors.'

Genevieve reddened. 'Bevan helped me to escape the man I am betrothed to. Saving their lives was a way to save myself.'

'You have our gratitude,' Isabel replied. 'And I can see why Bevan was so taken with you.'

Genevieve did not respond to the compliment, not knowing what to say. 'You exaggerate, I fear, Queen Isabel.'

'You may call me Isabel. And, no, I do not stretch the truth. Bevan has not interacted with a woman since the death of his wife.'

'Our paths crossed, nothing more,' Genevieve argued. She

sensed that Isabel wanted to play the matchmaker, and she would have no part of it. She had trusted her heart to a man every bit as handsome as Bevan. And Hugh had nearly destroyed her.

'We are having a celebration feast this eventide, to welcome Bevan home,' Isabel said, changing the subject. 'He told me you would be travelling back to England soon, but I thought you could share in our festivities before you go.'

'I would love that.' Genevieve stood up. 'May I help with the arrangements?'

'So eager are you?' Isabel appeared amused.

'I would like to be more useful,' Genevieve admitted. ''Tis difficult to wait, and I do not wish to be idle.'

Isabel gestured towards the Chamber. 'You may have your choice of activities here. What do you enjoy most?'

Genevieve thought a moment. More than anything she loved music. She had played the psaltery at her father's house, entertaining the visitors with her voice. Hugh had destroyed the instrument when she'd driven him to another rage. He had called it a useless activity, and she had not sung again for fear of antagonising him.

She feared that the others would also regard music as foolishness, and so she replied, 'I am good with a needle.' With a glance down at her torn kirtle, she admitted, 'I've been trying to repair this, but I haven't the proper tools.'

'I will see to it that you have everything you need. And...' Isabel pondered a moment. 'If it doesn't offend you, you might wish to try the Irish style of dress later. 'Tis quite comfortable.'

Genevieve agreed, wanting to rid herself of the frayed gown as soon as possible.

'You speak my husband's language very well,' Isabel remarked. 'How did you learn it? No one speaks the Irish tongue in Normandy.'

'I am from England, not Normandy,' Genevieve corrected.

'But my father's lands are near the Welsh border. I was fostered in Wales, along with an Irish woman. We taught each other our languages as we grew up.'

Isabel brightened. 'My family was also from England.' She described the location of her father's lands, but they were far from Genevieve's parents'.

'How long has your family lived there?' Isabel asked.

'For three generations. My great-grandfather came over from Normandy. He married, and his bride brought him a great deal of property. She refused to wed him unless he allowed her to stay in England.'

'And you wish to go back?' Isabel asked.

Genevieve hesitated, but nodded. 'Until the matter of my betrothal is resolved, it is for the best. One day I hope to return here.'

Isabel smiled and led her outside. They walked past several outbuildings towards the inner bailey. The familiar sounds of activity were no different from those she had heard at home. Nearby, steam rose from a cauldron as a woman used a paddle to stir laundry. There was a sense of security here, of people who were at ease in their work despite the outside threats.

Next they entered a hut that contained weaving looms, and Isabel spoke to one of the women. She arranged to have lengths of wool and linen brought to her chamber later.

When they went back inside the donjon, Genevieve's respect for Isabel grew. She was obviously accustomed to hard work. A servant spreading fresh rushes was instructed to bring more, and Isabel herself joined in the activity of scattering the rushes.

Genevieve hung behind, not knowing what to do. She had never seen the lady of a castle engaged in the same menial tasks as the servants. She didn't know what to think of it, but she soon joined in the work. The women laughed and chattered as they performed their tasks.

As Isabel stood atop a bench, to correct a hanging tapestry, a man came up behind her. He resembled Bevan, with black hair and grey eyes, but he moved with a stealthy grace. The man embraced Isabel, catching her around the waist and letting her slide against him until her feet touched the ground. He kissed her, and Genevieve guessed that the man was Isabel's husband, Patrick.

The pair were completely absorbed in one another, and Genevieve looked away guiltily. Footsteps approached from behind her, and she turned to see Bevan.

His face had healed, but she could see a bandage beneath his tunic, covering his shoulder wound.

'Bevan,' Genevieve greeted him quietly. She held out her hands to him, meaning only a polite welcome.

He did not take them, and so she lowered them, her face flushed with embarrassment. He looked as though he wanted to say something to her, but the uncomfortable silence stretched on.

Masking her disappointment, Genevieve raised her glance to the ceiling and turned around. 'Laochre is the largest fortress I've ever seen. And yet Patrick is not your High King?'

'He was asked to compete for the honour,' Bevan said, 'but he turned down the invitation.'

'Why would he do such a thing?'

'He preferred to look after his own tribe,' Bevan replied.

Genevieve was surprised that any man would turn down such an opportunity for power, but she supposed it held great sacrifices with the position.

Bevan stood beside her, and they watched as Isabel and the servants arranged greenery around the chamber for the feast.

Several times she tried to ask Bevan questions, but he only mumbled a reply or spoke in single-word responses.

'Have you sent anyone to bring my father here?' she asked.

'No.' He did not look at her, his attention fixed upon a swag of greenery.

Genevieve tried again. 'What are your plans?'

'Patrick has agreed to handle the matter.'

More than anything, Genevieve wanted this awkwardness between them to end. She decided to be direct.

'You are avoiding me, I think.' Crossing her arms, she nodded, as if speaking to herself. 'You do not wish to speak to me because I am a dreadful Norman who devours newborn babes and breathes fire.'

His mouth twitched, but he did not respond.

'Or perhaps you are sulking like a child because I did not want you to escort me to Dun Laoghaire? Is that it?'

'That was your choice. I have other tasks to attend—ones that do not involve you.'

Bevan stepped in front of her, and she saw he was trying to intimidate her with his height. Looking up at his strong arms, his wide chest, she knew she should fear him. And yet part of her believed he would never harm her, despite his rough words.

'And I am not a child, Genevieve.'

She kept her chin up. 'Then stop behaving like one. My family will come for me, and you need not trouble yourself over me again.' Leaving him standing there, she went over to help Isabel with the preparations.

Bevan couldn't believe her accusation. At that moment he was itching for a sword fight—anything to relieve the tension growing within him. To Patrick, he called out, 'I am going to the training field. Send Ewan to me for another lesson, if he wants it.'

'Genevieve, come above stairs with me,' he heard Isabel say. 'I have a *léine* that I believe would fit you.'

Bevan barely heard Genevieve's reply as he returned outside. The air had grown colder, the clouds swelling with forthcoming snow. He needed to feel the clash of steel on steel, to bury the anger within him.

After everything he had done for her, she thought he was behaving like a child?

Furious at her criticism, he signalled one of the men to spar against him. He'd not allow himself to be trapped into marriage with her, regardless of what Patrick said. If it meant war, so be it.

Bevan blocked his opponent's blow with his shield, allowing his anger to erupt full force. He struck with his sword again and again, driving the soldier towards the wall as he pictured Sir Hugh's face.

Genevieve might have saved his life and Ewan's, but he had more than repaid the debt. His sword slipped, and he missed blocking a slash from his opponent.

The soldier's sword nicked his wounded shoulder. 'I am sorry, Bevan. I didn't mean—'

The intense pain made him gasp, and Bevan signalled for the fight to end. '*Tá*, you fought well. Make no excuses. I dropped my defence and deserved the cut.'

Pressing his hand to the injury, he felt blood seeping. It sobered him, and he thought again of how Genevieve had tended his wounds. He remembered the dark bruise across her cheek, and the dried blood on her scalp from the man who had once been her betrothed. He remembered her fear.

Marstowe had always treated her as a possession, never as an equal. Bevan admitted that his own wife had never been an equal—she had been far above his reach. Beautiful, nearly perfect in every way. He had felt unworthy to be her husband. He would have given Fiona anything she desired, had he been able.

The shadow of grief closed in on him again, but he blocked it away. When he reached his chamber, he stripped off the tunic and stanched the flow of blood with a cloth.

Patrick might believe that an alliance with Genevieve was the best way to claim Rionallís, but Bevan would not wed her. Or any woman, for that matter. He tossed the bloodstained cloth aside, letting the familiar sorrow envelop him.

Stop behaving like a child.

Genevieve was right. His pride had kept him from forgiving her. But, more than that, he was denying the attraction between them. She had looked so fragile, so vulnerable, he'd wanted to give her comfort. He had wanted to feel the touch of a woman once more.

The primal urges rising within him were the result of years of staying away from all women. He was not a monk, and at the moment his body ruled his thoughts.

Were it any other woman, he might have been able to wed her, make the alliance to keep Rionallís. Patrick's suggestion might not have bothered him as much, for it would be easy to stay apart from a stranger.

But he feared that if he let Genevieve get too close she might try to usurp Fiona's place. And he couldn't let that happen. Not ever.

Chapter Six

Genevieve followed Isabel into a small chamber where a hot bath had been prepared. From a chair nearby, Isabel held up a silk cream-coloured *léine* with close-fitting sleeves. 'It will be perfect with your dark hair.' She lifted a burgundy over-dress and a golden girdle.

Genevieve marvelled at the rich shade and smiled. ''Tis beautiful.'

Isabel helped her remove the torn kirtle, but did not remark upon Genevieve's bruises. 'Bevan will not be able to keep his eyes from you this evening.'

Genevieve rather doubted he wanted to see her again, but instead she responded, 'You have been very kind to me.'

She eased into the tub of water, grateful for the healing warmth. She knew Isabel wanted to ask about the bruises, but she wasn't ready to answer any questions.

At the moment she felt lost. She had wanted peace between Bevan and herself, but there was too much turmoil. When she had stood atop the battlements he had touched her. God help her, she had been unable to pull away from him. She'd found herself drawn to him, wishing he could be the one to obliterate her dark memories. Yet Bevan wanted nothing to do with her. He despised her people and blamed them for the loss of his family and home. Somehow she had to prevent the inevitable war between her father and Bevan. But how?

Isabel added fragrant oils to the water, and Genevieve luxuriated in the feel of the bath. She dipped her head below the water and washed her hair with a rose-scented soap Isabel gave her. She touched the bruises along her ribs, soaping them lightly. The colour had turned a dark purple. She imagined her face must look the same. Suddenly she wanted to see it for herself.

'Have you a mirror?'

Isabel nodded. 'I'll bring it.'

When Genevieve spied her reflection in the polished metal, she could not believe what she saw. A heavy dark bruise marred her left cheek, running along the side of her jaw to her temple.

Her hands trembled as she handed the mirror back to Isabel. Though she fought against it, a single tear ran down her cheek. 'I had no idea it was that bad.'

''Tisn't, really. It seems so, but it will heal.' Isabel gave her a drying cloth, and Genevieve stood, wrapping herself in the soft linen. 'I have some tinted salve,' Isabel offered. 'The bruise might not be so noticeable if we try to cover it.'

Genevieve saw the sympathetic look on Isabel's face, and realised that the woman genuinely wanted to help.

'I am glad I left Rionallís,' Genevieve whispered, swiping at the tears. 'I could not marry Hugh, no matter what betrothal was arranged.'

'Hugh is the one who did this to you?'

Genevieve nodded, and combed her fingers through her hair. On impulse, she decided to trust Isabel. 'Without Bevan's help

I could not have escaped him.' She touched the bruise on her cheek. 'Hugh said that if I were more obedient he would not have to punish me.'

Resting her chin on her knees, she stared at the fire. Its flames licked at the peat moss, sending airy wisps of smoke into the room. Hugh's constant criticism had made her question whether she was fit to be anyone's wife. The fortress was never clean enough, the food never to his tastes.

'I had started to believe him,' Genevieve said. 'I knew I had to leave.'

Isabel brought over the *léine* and helped Genevieve dress. The hem of the cream gown was long enough to touch her ankles. Isabel adjusted the garnet overdress on top, draping the folds over the girdle fastened about Genevieve's waist. Then she took a comb and began easing it through the tangled dark strands on Genevieve's head. The motion soothed her.

'It was right that you left him,' Isabel said.

'I wish I had never been betrothed.' Genevieve gave a half-smile. 'But I am glad I was able to save Bevan and Ewan. I could not let them die—not after Bevan tried to help me.'

'He cares for you,' Isabel said. She opened a chest and began looking through sets of jewelled earrings and necklaces. 'I've not seen him with a woman before. Not since his wife died.'

'He told me her name was Fiona.'

Isabel nodded. 'He never talks of her, but we all know how much he mourns. Sometimes I see him walking along the water's edge, where she—'

Abruptly, she broke off and stood. She picked up some golden earrings. 'These might look well with your *léine*.'

'Where she what?'

Isabel seemed torn on whether or not to say anything.

After a time, she relented. 'Where she was captured. Bevan tried to save her, but the soldiers took her before he could reach her.'

'What happened?'

'Fiona escaped her captor and tried to hide in one of the cottages. It caught on fire during the battle, and Bevan found her body afterwards. He blames himself for her death.'

Genevieve remembered how Bevan had reached out to her during his illness. 'Did he love her?'

Isabel nodded. 'Aye, he did. He would have given his life for her.'

A thread of envy wound across Genevieve's heart—envy for a woman who had been loved so much.

Isabel took out a small pot. She studied Genevieve's face, and used her finger to smear a light dab of a coloured salve over the bruise. 'In the firelight, no one will see this.'

'Thank you.' Genevieve allowed Isabel to conceal the bruise. Last, Isabel fastened a gold torque around her throat. Though Genevieve did not feel like celebrating, she knew it was important to her hostess. When both of the women had finished their preparations, they went below to the Great Chamber.

Genevieve was startled to see such an array of people. It seemed that everyone, from the lowliest serf to the wealthiest nobleman, was engaged in feasting and merriment. She thought of Bevan's comment days ago, when he had said they did not use titles here. There seemed to be no distinction between any man, and it created an atmosphere like a large, boisterous family. Peasant and lord alike were dancing, laughing, and enjoying the celebration.

Isabel put a hand on Genevieve's arm. 'Welcome to our home. May you enjoy our hospitality for as long as you have the need.'

Genevieve searched for a sign of Bevan but did not see him. All around her torches lined the walls. A laughing young man played a lilting melody on the pipes, while another struck a rhythm upon a rounded drum.

Men and women joined hands, dancing intricate steps and clasping each other's waists. Others drank cups of mead, feasting on roasted meat, pastries and cheeses. Isabel found her husband, Patrick, who presented her with a squalling infant. Genevieve watched as Isabel took her son to a corner and began to nurse. In England, such a thing was out of the ordinary. The lady of a castle would have hired a wet nurse to care for her babe. Never would she have taken the child into her own arms.

The love and contentment on the young mother's face made Genevieve envious for a child of her own. She slipped away from the crowd, her back towards the wall. The lively music faded, and a woman began to play a harp. The room grew quiet; all were listening as another man sang a ballad of the tragic love between a shepherd and a maid.

Genevieve drank in the lyrical song, closing her eyes. It had been so long since she'd heard any kind of music. The harpist's melody faded into silence, and another dancing song began. A hand touched her shoulder, and she jumped at the contact.

Hoping to see Bevan, she turned with a smile. A bearded man smiled in return. He had long reddish hair, braided at his temples. 'I've not see you here before. Would you care to dance?' He spoke in Irish, and his eyes showed open admiration. 'You're a lovely one.'

Genevieve's smile faded. 'No. That is, I don't dance.'

'All the more reason to learn. My name is Seán.' He took hold of her hands and started to pull her towards the crowd, where couples had joined hands.

'No, really. I would prefer not to.' She tried to free her hands, but the man refused to let go.

Another man, taller and also bearded, joined in and took her by the waist, laughing as he pushed her forward. 'We'll both dance with her, Seán. Then she can choose one of us. Or both.' He gave a wicked grin.

A sense of panic pervaded her, and Genevieve struggled to get away from them. 'Leave me—please.'

They paid her no heed, and soon she found herself in the midst of the dancers. Seán gripped her around the ribs, and Genevieve gasped as searing pain ripped through her bruised side. She tried to push him off, but he ignored her.

Then suddenly the hands were gone, and she had space to breathe once more. She looked up and saw Bevan. He glared at the men. 'No one touches her.'

At his furious tone, the men relented and went off to find other partners. Genevieve let Bevan escort her away, and he took her to a darkened corner.

'Did they hurt you?'

She shook her head. 'But they would not listen to me when I told them I had no wish to dance.'

Bevan glared at the crowd of people. 'They know better than to force a woman. I'll see to it they remember next time.'

'No, it is all right.' Genevieve sank back against the wall. 'They meant no harm.'

He stood beside her, not touching her, not saying a word. She gained comfort just by being near him. When the harpist began another tune, her lips curved upwards at its haunting refrain.

'You enjoy music?'

'I love it.' She closed her eyes, listening to the feel of each note. A moment later his hand brushed hers. Genevieve jolted at the sensation, but let her hand remain where it was. Her mind scolded her body for its weakness. But Bevan brought her comfort.

She should move away from him, escape the rush of heat that flooded through her. An instant later he drew her to face him. His hands framed her cheeks, tilting her to look at him.

'Your bruise is better.'

'Isabel helped me to cover it.' She was barely conscious of her words as his thumbs touched her hair. She had let it hang down with no veil, as Isabel had suggested. It felt strange to have her hair uncovered in the Irish fashion. Bevan's fingers threaded through the strands, his touch barely more than a breath of air.

'You look…well tonight.'

The intense gaze made her breath catch in her throat.

Move away, Genevieve, her heart reminded her. *He will bring you nothing but pain.*

Her traitorous body remained in place.

Bevan started to pull back, but Genevieve covered his hands with her own, keeping them against her hair. The touch of his hands made it impossible to keep a clear thought in her mind. She longed to know how it would be to have a man kiss her with tenderness, without the desire to punish.

'Bevan?' she asked, her voice hardly more than a faint whisper.

In his eyes, she saw him fighting to hold his distance. He didn't want to be near her. At his rejection, she started to pull away.

'I've gone mad,' he murmured.

Without warning, his mouth came down upon hers, warm and tender. He treated her like a cherished possession, as though she might break in his arms. The kiss was a healing balm, soothing away the past moments of pain and fear.

Her mouth parted, and the kiss turned feverish. His tongue

met with hers, and raw feelings of need pulsed within her. She clung to him for balance, aware of his desire pressing against her body. His lips travelled a path down to her throat, igniting a wild storm of yearning.

When his strong arms caught her waist, she felt trapped. A moan escaped her, but before she could struggle against his embrace Bevan stepped away. His breathing was laboured, like her own.

'I am sorry.' He moved back several paces, not looking at her. 'I should not have touched you.'

Genevieve closed her eyes, trying to gather her thoughts. Foremost, she saw the aversion on his face. It angered her.

'Because I am a Norman and therefore your enemy?'

'*Tá.* It is best not to complicate matters between us.'

Genevieve veiled her emotions, not wanting him to see how much his rejection hurt. Had the kiss been that terrible? Had her lack of experience repulsed him? Or could he not see past her Norman heritage?

'I have to take you back.' Bevan turned from her, fighting the need within him. Never had he wanted a woman as much as this. It terrified him, the way she made him forget. A few moments more and he would have taken her back to his chamber.

Two years of celibacy made the fierce need even worse. He had known it was wrong to kiss her. But when he'd seen those men pressuring her to dance, and her fear, he had overreacted. The need to keep her safe had destroyed every rational thought.

Just as the way she had looked at him had been his undoing. For the first time he had not thought of Fiona. When he'd felt her lips beneath his, an undeniable longing had ignited within him.

What bothered him most was that his own wife had never

inspired such feelings of lust. He had honoured Fiona, loved her with everything in him. Their lovemaking had been sweet, tender.

But this was far more. Though he had done nothing more than kiss Genevieve, there had been a connection between them. He didn't want to desire another woman. He had promised his wife that he would love her until the day he died. He couldn't imagine being with anyone else.

But he could not deny that he wanted Genevieve. He berated himself for his lack of discipline. The Normans were his enemy, those he had sworn to kill.

And yet he could never raise his sword against Genevieve. Her innocent presence unravelled his plan for vengeance. If he conquered Rionallís and put her family to the sword, it would make him no better than Sir Hugh Marstowe.

By Lug, he needed to put as much distance between them as possible. Else she would divert his path and weaken his purpose.

Chapter Seven

The next day, a blizzard howled outside the castle walls, blanketing the landscape in white. Genevieve saw little of Bevan, and it soon became clear he was avoiding her. She had slept little the night before, and her thoughts were elsewhere when she looked up and saw Bevan's brother Patrick.

'Good morn to you,' he said. 'I had hoped for an opportunity to speak with you.' From his formal tone, she sensed the matter held a great deal of importance.

'I hope I have not caused trouble among your tribe,' Genevieve offered.

'Some are uncomfortable,' he admitted. 'But since you are here at my invitation, they must accept it.'

He led her towards a more secluded area, away from those who might overhear their conversation. 'I have spoken to Bevan about an arrangement.'

His piercing grey eyes stared at her, as though assessing her worth. Genevieve waited for him to explain the proposition, but she sensed hesitation in his tone, as though he knew not how to broach the subject.

'This is about Rionallís?' she guessed.

'*Tá.* I know a way to bring peace among our people, and I believe you wish to do the same.'

His sincerity and calm manner put her at ease. 'What do you want me to do?'

'I want you to wed Bevan. His alliance with your family would divide Rionallís between you, and I believe your king would welcome the union.'

Though at one time Genevieve might have considered this as a solution, she knew Bevan would never agree. 'Your brother would die before wedding a Norman.'

Her prediction did not deter Patrick. 'He will obey if I command it.'

Turmoil and disappointment gathered in her heart. She knew Patrick's offering was the best solution—a way for her to protect her family from war. But in return she would have to spend her life with a man who didn't want her.

'Will you agree if I bring the matter before King Henry and our High King?'

'My opinion holds no bearing. You must have my father's approval before a betrothal can be made.'

'I sent word for him to meet us at Tara. His messenger brought a response today. He has agreed to join us there.'

A combination of numbness and relief settled over her. At last her father would come. She didn't know if he had received any of her missives, but she felt certain he would help her end the betrothal to Hugh.

But would he want her to wed Bevan? She had her doubts. In all likelihood her father and Bevan would war against one another, fighting for the rights to Rionallís. Unless she stood between them.

She wished Papa would come to Laochre and take her home again, avoiding the problem entirely.

'What is your opinion, Lady Genevieve?' Patrick asked

quietly. 'Will you wed my brother if it mends the breach between us?'

She had no choice. No more than Bevan did. It was the only way to avoid bloodshed. 'If my father agrees, I will do it.'

The blizzard slowed, thick snowflakes cloaking the ground in white. Genevieve decided to walk out of doors, to think about her conversation with Patrick.

Clad in a woolen *brat* that surrounded her shoulders, and a cloak to protect her gown, she stepped out into the freezing cold. Snowflakes whipped against her face, and she could hardly see beyond a few feet in front of her.

Beyond the outer bailey wall a blanket of snow covered the hills of Erin. As she studied the horizon, she wondered what Hugh's intentions were. Not for a moment did she believe he had given up his pursuit.

She had been at Laochre for only a few days, and yet she could not let go of her fear. She sensed she was being watched, though the idea was foolish. At night she awoke at the least sound, imagining an unseen assailant. It bothered her to know that she was behaving like a coward even now. She despised the way Hugh controlled her, even in his absence.

Though she had escaped his physical presence, his grip upon her emotional state angered her. Gritting her teeth, she took a few steps forward. Then a few more, until she stood at the entrance to the outer wall.

'It is not wise to venture forth in such a storm,' the guard said, blocking her path.

'I will only go to the bottom of the hillside,' Genevieve promised. Only far enough to face her fears. She had remained inside the fortress, hiding from the threat of Hugh's men. Though he was not here, she still felt his controlling presence.

'I'll not venture beyond where you can see me,' she promised. With that, the guard relented.

Genevieve trudged through the thick snow, the hem of her gown growing damp. There was a peacefulness here, the muffled silence of winter's beauty. She saw a single tree, its branches laced with a snowy covering. All around her the green of the hills had fallen beneath a glistening mantle of white.

No one was here to threaten her. She inhaled deeply, breathing the scent of freedom. Snow danced across her face, and she thought of the feast yestereve, when Bevan had kissed her.

Though he did not seem to hate her, was it even possible to gain his friendship? She disliked the idea of escaping one marriage only to endure another prison.

Their alliance would prevent a battle over Rionallís, but only if her father and Bevan agreed. Although Patrick claimed he could command his brother to wed her, such would only increase Bevan's animosity. He would grow to resent her presence, unless she could convince him she would be no threat to him.

The idea rooted and began to blossom. If she persuaded Bevan to wed her knowing that she held no expectations from him, it might not be so bad. They could marry and maintain their distance from one another.

The more she considered the plan, the better it seemed. She was afraid of his reaction. But perhaps if she presented it in a way that offered him complete freedom, he might understand her reasoning. The arrangement would protect her family, which was of the greatest importance. Her former dreams of wedding a husband who would love her had faded into reality. She had learned the hard way not to trust her heart.

In the distance, Genevieve heard a faint noise like the call of a bird. It was the only sound to break the stillness. She nearly turned away, but then heard it again. Frowning, Genevieve moved in the direction of the noise. She studied the landscape, searching for the source.

When she heard the cry for a third time, it dawned on her what she was hearing. She picked up her skirts and raced towards it. Ignoring the needles of snow falling against her skin, she fought her way towards the sound.

A small pond crusted with ice and snow lay just at the base of a hill. Spindly cattails danced in the wind, revealing a deep crevice in the centre of the pond with floating chunks of ice. She spied a small head bobbing beneath the surface. Her heart pounding, she prayed that she would not be too late.

When she reached the pond, she couldn't tell if the surface of the ice would support her weight. She spread herself out on her stomach, inching towards the child, who struggled to free himself from the water's death grasp.

'Hold on, love,' she called out in Irish. 'I'll be there in a moment.'

The ice splintered beneath her weight, but she kept on at a steady crawl. The boy's sobbing heightened her determination to get him out. When her fingers touched his hand, she pulled with all her strength.

The ice shattered, and Genevieve fell into the freezing water. She gasped, half-choking as she came up for air, her arms gripping the child. She would not let him go.

The water was not deep, but she struggled to free herself from the ice. Her skirts dragged her down with the weight of the wool.

The child lay still in her arms. He breathed, yet his body was cold—terribly so.

'Help!' she called out to the guards, hoping they could hear her.

Within moments, one of them came down the hillside. He ordered another guard to come and assist him, and soon Genevieve was supported by the two men as she struggled back up the incline. Her skin had never felt so freezing. The numbness in her legs made it difficult to move, but the soldiers kept her from collapsing.

Her teeth chattered as she continued up the path, holding the body of the young boy. He could not be more than three years of age. His face was a bluish colour, which frightened her. If he was to live, she would have to get him inside soon.

She reached the outer bailey, and it was not long before a group of people surrounded her, all talking at once. Genevieve cuddled the boy closer, but did not answer the flurry of questions.

At long last she reached the Great Chamber. Isabel gave orders for hot water and dry clothing. She had started to bring Genevieve above stairs when Bevan appeared.

'What were you doing?' he demanded, grabbing her arm.

Genevieve could barely speak, but she managed to answer. 'The child fell through the ice. I could not let him drown.'

'You should never have left the fortress in weather like this. Not for anything.'

'He would have died,' Genevieve insisted. 'Look. He lives yet.'

'And you could have died. I've seen men drown in less water.'

Genevieve started to argue again, but realised there was concern behind his words. 'I am all right, Bevan. But I cannot say what will happen to this child. He's hardly more than a babe.'

Bevan took the child from her, his face grave. 'Go with Isabel and dry yourself off. I will care for the boy.'

'No. I'm not leaving him.'

'I know how to care for a child.' Bevan's expression was furious. 'And you need to warm yourself. Do it now. Unless you want me to drag you up there.'

She stepped back, but only because she saw the way he cradled the child, as though the boy were his own. 'All right. But I will come and help you with him.'

Isabel led Genevieve back to her chamber, where a fire blazed upon the hearth. She helped her strip off her clothes, wrapping her in a warm blanket and drying her briskly.

'You can bathe later,' Isabel promised. 'You need to get some feeling back into the skin before that.'

Genevieve succumbed to Isabel's ministrations, accepting a fermented drink that burned a path down her throat.

Her skin burned with a searing ache, and her limbs felt heavy as she dressed in a dry *léine,* then wrapped a warm *brat* about her shoulders. She did not dwell upon her own discomfort, thinking only of the child.

'Do you know the child's parents?' Genevieve asked. 'They should be brought here.'

Isabel bowed her head. 'His father was one of the soldiers who went to Rionallís with Bevan. He has not returned. I will send word to the tenants to bring his mother to Laochre.'

Genevieve started for the door, but Isabel held her back. 'Before you go, know this. Bevan lost his daughter to a fever while he was away in battle. She was about the age of this boy when she died.'

Genevieve stilled. She had not known he was a father. No wonder he had been insistent upon tending the child himself.

'Take me to him.'

The healer had helped Bevan massage warmth back into the child's limbs, swaddling him tightly in a blanket. Bevan held the sleeping boy in his arms, closing his own eyes. The soft cheek rested against his forearm, the child's rasping breath the only sound besides his own.

Don't die, he prayed silently. The fragile band of his control strained. He had pushed away the anguish of losing his wife and child for so long he did not know how much longer he could bear it. Not once had he visited their graves at Rionallís. As long as he kept far away, he could handle the numbing pain that had haunted him for the past two years.

Now, holding this child in his arms, it was as though he held his daughter again. He stared at the flickering fire on the hearth, forcing the grief away.

The door opened, and Genevieve entered. She started to speak, then stopped. Instead, she closed the door and walked over to the bed. Without a word, she sat down beside him, drawing her hand across the child's dampened hair. Together, they held the boy.

He felt something pressed into his palm. Unfolding it, he saw the frail scrap of linen Genevieve had returned to him at Ennisleigh.

'Where did you get this?' he managed.

'From among your things,' Genevieve said. She covered his hand with her own. 'It belonged to your wife, didn't it?'

He clenched the tiny bit of fabric and nodded. 'It belonged to both of them. Fiona carried it on our wedding day. Later, she sewed it into a bonnet for our daughter's baptism.'

Genevieve saw the pain etched in the lines of his face. She wished that she could somehow ease it, but words would not be enough. Instead, she touched her palm to his cheek. The scar had become a harsh red line, but she sensed there were far worse scars Bevan carried inside.

His pain was almost a tangible thing, and her eyes clouded with tears. Long moments passed between them. Genevieve did not ask questions, but she brought his hand to her lips. 'May God ease your grief.'

His fingers tightened around hers, and together they kept vigil over the child. Hours later, Bevan lay down beside the boy, his breathing softened into sleep. Genevieve drew a strand of hair out of Bevan's face, studying him in the firelight.

Tonight she would not leave him, nor the child. She cared not what the rest of the household might think. She would stay beside this man and the child they had saved.

It was dangerous, thinking about him the way she did tonight. The walls of her heart crumbled against the knowledge of what he had suffered. And she feared what he would say when she offered to become his wife.

Bevan sat at one of the trestle tables in the Great Chamber. Outside, the sky remained dark, and much of the household was still abed.

Although the boy had lived through the night, his breathing was laboured. He coughed frequently, his small body shuddering at the effort.

Had his daughter suffered like this? Had Fiona tended their child in this way before Brianna had breathed her last? He could not forgive himself for being away in battle. War had robbed him of the last chance to hold his daughter. They had buried her before he had returned.

This morn, Bevan had awakened to find Genevieve beside him, her arms curled around the boy. He had tried to deny to himself how good it was, waking beside a woman once more.

After a while, he saw Patrick approach. 'Walk with me a moment, Bevan,' his brother said.

Bevan accompanied Patrick outside. The weather was crisp and frigid in the dawn. The moon lay hidden behind a mist of clouds, but a thin haze shone through. Snow crunched beneath their boots as they walked along the inner bailey.

'I have sent word to the High King, Rory Ó Connor,' Patrick said. 'He has summoned you to Tara.'

Bevan tensed. 'For what purpose?'

'The Norman King is there. Ó Connor informs me that he and King Henry will pass judgement on the matter of Rionallís.'

Bevan glowered at his brother. It should have been a simple matter of prior ownership, but Patrick was allowing politics to dictate the future. He knew what the *Brehon* judges would say.

'You still want me to marry her,' he said flatly.

'*Tá.* It is the simplest solution, and both kings will be satisfied.'

'I cannot.' The words came out too quickly. But he meant them.

At first it had been his vow never to betray Fiona's memory. Now it was because of Genevieve. Were it any other woman, he could keep his distance. But not with her. She tempted him, alluring in her innocence.

He imagined a blue-eyed babe, with dark hair and Genevieve's smile. The crushing reminder of his own daughter's death stiffened his resolve. He could not marry again and face the prospect of losing another wife, possibly another child.

'You may not have a choice,' Patrick said. 'I have received an invitation to meet with King Henry, along with the other kings.'

'Will you go?'

'I've not decided. Isabel thinks I should. As a Norman herself, she believes it would be a strong gesture towards peace.' Patrick turned back to the donjon, nodding to a kinsman as they passed. 'The Norman King may demand your marriage to Genevieve.' He added, 'And I may demand it of you.'

Surprise and resentment filled him at the words. 'You've no right.'

'I am your king.' His brother's voice assumed an air of authority. 'And you are risking the lives of my people. I have been lenient in allowing her to stay, knowing the abuses she suffered. But if it comes to war—'

Bevan recognised the unspoken promise. But he would not allow anyone to force him into marriage. Not even his brother.

'I will travel to meet with the High King,' Bevan said. 'And when the matter is settled Genevieve will return home to her family.' He turned his back on Patrick, focusing his mind on the journey preparations.

Genevieve sponged cool water on the boy's forehead. Despite their efforts the entire day, no one had been able to find his mother. She had tried to get him to drink some broth, but to no avail. His forehead felt hot to the touch, and he still laboured to breathe.

The healer had tried different poultices, but nothing seemed to relieve the boy's breathing. Genevieve could only hold him in her arms, praying that somehow he would survive. Since they had been unable to find his mother, she felt all the more protective.

Bevan returned to the chamber, his face shadowed with worry. 'He hasn't improved?'

Genevieve shook her head. 'I fear we may have to send for the priest. I do not think he has enough strength left in him to survive another night.'

Bevan reached out and took the boy into his arms. With a nod, he dismissed the healer. The child whimpered, but Bevan lifted him upright. 'Bring me a basin.'

Genevieve complied, and Bevan instructed her to pour some hot water inside. Supporting the limp body with one arm, he placed a cloth around the child's head, allowing him to inhale the steam.

'Will that help, do you think?'

'It can do no harm. One winter it helped my daughter, when she had trouble breathing.' His face grew tender at the memory. 'Fiona and I never left Brianna's side for a moment. I don't think either of us slept for three days.'

When the steam had cooled, Genevieve refilled the basin with fresh hot water. 'And Brianna was better afterwards?'

'One morn she woke up and informed us that she wanted honey cakes to break her fast. I think we would have given her anything she wanted, so thankful we were. She demanded that I take her out riding that day.'

'And did you?'

'No. Though I considered it.' He ruffled the boy's hair, smoothing a stray cowlick. 'Isabel told me they haven't found his mother. I ordered some men to search the pond.'

Genevieve winced at the thought of them finding a body. She couldn't conceive of how such a young boy would be alone, or why. He had been dressed warmly, as though for a journey. From the manner of his clothing he was not of the noble class, and yet not a slave either.

'His father was one of my men,' Bevan said. 'I can only assume he was captured with the others, at Rionallís.'

Genevieve shivered. No doubt the boy's father was dead by now. Hugh would not allow a single enemy to live, nor any man to threaten him.

'Are you going after them?'

'My brother Connor has already left with a group of soldiers. I asked to go, but it seems I must go to Tara instead.'

He didn't look at her, and Genevieve recognised his resentment. Were it not for her, he would be back at Rionallís.

'What if Hugh attacks your brother?'

'He can take care of himself. Connor's fighting skills are strong. He'll not be taken captive.'

She reached out and touched the child's shoulder. Her eyes met Bevan's. 'I know you want to be with them.'

'I know my duty.'

But beneath his tone she heard the underlying meaning. He believed his duty was to his men, not being forced to wed a woman he didn't want.

She drew back from him and took the basin, forcing herself to concentrate on the child's needs. She emptied the cooled water and refilled the container with hot water. They kept up the pattern, not knowing whether their efforts were in vain. After a few hours, Genevieve reached out for the boy. 'I'll keep trying the hot steam. If you like, you may retire.'

Bevan shook his head. 'No. I've a need to be here.'

Though his words were purely for the child's sake, she became aware of Bevan, of the contrast between strong warrior and tender father. His fighting spirit fascinated her, just as it frightened her. He could easily be as dominant as Hugh, taking whatever he wanted. And yet he had never asked more of her than she had given.

His kiss had been gentle, though it had drawn out such yearnings within her. She sensed that he guarded his feelings, locking them away inside. If he were ever to release them, she wondered what sort of man would lie beneath the surface.

Genevieve rose and brought the basin back to the table where Bevan sat. 'When are you leaving for Tara?' she asked.

'In three days. The High King intends to settle the property dispute of Rionallís there.'

Now was the time to tell him of her conversation with Patrick. She had to convince Bevan to accept the compromise. Yet the rigid cast to his face gave her pause. She was afraid of what he might say to his brother's proposition.

'Patrick believes we should wed.'

'I'll not wed you to regain what rightfully belongs to me,' Bevan said.

The painful finality of his words cut her down. She sensed the fury behind them, the frustration of being forced into an arrangement he didn't want.

But somehow she set aside her hurt feelings and gathered a strength she hadn't known she had. 'You are trying to push me away because I am the enemy,' she whispered. 'And yet I am the only woman you could marry. I would not expect a true marriage from you.'

Moving closer, she laid her hand upon his shoulder. His muscles were hard, his skin warm beneath her fingers. 'I would not expect you to…share my bed.'

His pulse quickened beneath her palm.

'You could come and go as you pleased, just as you do now.' His breathing tightened, and she could see the effect she was having upon him. 'Rionallís would be yours without raising a finger. Without losing a single man in battle.'

He caught her wrist in his. 'You know not what you are doing, Genevieve.'

The nearness of him, the warm male scent, had her blood racing. His mouth was only a breath away from a kiss. She shivered, afraid of this warrior who could not forgive her for being a Norman.

'Will you consider it?'

He said nothing, but his thumb moved upon her wrist in an unmistakable caress. His firm lips softened, his green eyes drinking in the sight of her. He desired her, though he denied it.

She pulled away, and a tendril of hope was suspended in the space between them. 'Think upon it, Bevan. You would have your freedom and Rionallís, too.'

Chapter Eight

The soldier entered the darkened fortress, its torches casting shadows upon the walls. He moved towards the men he had fought alongside in battle. Friends, rivals—they did not deserve what he was being forced to do.

The *Gaillabh* wanted him to betray the MacEgans. If he did not, they would hurt his wife, Kiara. The soldier swallowed back his helpless rage, knowing he had little choice but to follow their commands.

'What happened?' A guard blocked his path, recognition dawning over his face. 'We thought you were dead. The Normans—'

'I escaped,' he said. 'The others are still held captive.'

'Are they alive?' his friend asked.

He nodded. 'For now.'

'Good. Bevan has sent a rescue party. Connor went with them days ago.'

'And why did Bevan not go after them himself?'

'Our king forbade it.' His friend walked alongside him into the inner bailey. 'But they should arrive back soon. If they're still alive.'

The soldier did not mention his wife, though he feared for Kiara's safety. Had Sir Hugh kept her chained with the others? Or had he moved her elsewhere? He'd seen the look of interest upon the Norman's face, and he prayed to God that she remained untouched.

'And what of you? Did they harm you?'

The soldier shook his head. They had not harmed him, only because he was of use to them. His gut twisted at the thought of his wife falling victim to the Normans.

Dark fear and anger burgeoned within him. All of this was for a woman—Genevieve de Renalt. Were it not for her, none of it might have happened.

Sir Hugh wanted the woman, had spoken of nothing but Genevieve. And if he returned her safely to Rionallís, Sir Hugh would be appeased. The soldier felt certain that the Norman would let his wife go free in exchange.

'Has Bevan returned?' the soldier asked. 'I must speak with him.'

'He is in his chambers.'

'And the Lady Genevieve?' Anticipation caused a thin film of sweat to break out over his skin. He had to find her—find some way of bringing her back to Rionallís. Only then could he exchange her for Kiara.

'She is still here.' His friend added, 'Some of us will accompany Bevan to Tara in a few days' time. Will you come?'

'I know not what my orders are yet.' He clapped his friend on the back, and was about to make his excuses when the man stopped him.

'We found your son a few days ago.'

'My son?' Kiara had sworn she'd left young Declan with a trusted friend. He had not thought any harm would befall him. 'What has happened?'

'Do not fear. We brought him here. Your wife—'

The soldier's expression tightened. 'She is held captive by Sir Hugh's men. She came to try and free us.'

'The MacEgans will not rest until all are freed.' His friend tried to set him at ease.

But the soldier could not voice his agreement. Bevan had abandoned them for days, without any attempt to retake Rionallís. The men had suffered in captivity while his commander had done nothing.

If the MacEgans had attacked immediately, Kiara would be safe. The soldier laid the full blame upon Bevan.

'Where is my son?' he asked.

'Above stairs.'

He excused himself, but other friends greeted him before he could venture forth. With each good wish, each welcome, his guilt grew stronger. He had no wish to betray them to the enemy.

Cursing his weakness, he slipped into the shadows. As the minutes stretched, his breath grew steadier. After he had ensured his son's safety, he would find Lady Genevieve and bring her back to Sir Hugh.

His heartbeat hastened at the fear of failure. Stealthily, he opened the door, not knowing what he would find inside the chamber. The only sound came from the crackling of the fire at the hearth. He saw Bevan sleeping in a chair, and at the sight of his commander the soldier stopped short.

If Bevan awakened, there would be questions.

The soldier's gaze travelled over to the bed. There he saw Lady Genevieve, along with something else that made his heart stop.

His son, resting in her arms.

The soldier closed the door, his plan no longer possible. It was as if God had asked him to choose between his wife and his son.

And the soldier had no answer for it.

* * *

A low cry woke Genevieve from her sleep. The young child stirred in her arms, murmuring for his mother.

'We will find her, love,' Genevieve whispered, pressing a kiss to the boy's forehead.

She had hardly slept that night, in between holding his head over the steam and trying more poultices recommended by the healer. Just before dawn he had slipped into a more restful sleep, and his breathing seemed easier. Genevieve now believed that he would live, though it would be a while before his full strength returned.

In his sleep he cuddled close to her, and Genevieve felt a pang of tenderness for him. His baby-fine hair was soft, like featherdown. He placed his thumb in his mouth, sucking for comfort.

Genevieve eased the boy to a sitting position. She saw Bevan slumped in a chair, his head resting on the table. In spite of the awkward circumstances between them he had stayed all night, refusing to leave the child's side.

He had said nothing more about her proposition, and heat rose in her cheeks at the memory of his refusal. She had thought he might consider the arrangement, only to be rebuffed.

Genevieve held the child in her arms, tiptoeing towards the door. Bevan did not awaken, and she brought the boy below stairs. He had barely eaten in two days, and likely was hungry.

She had slept past Mass, and most of the family was already engaged in their morning duties. Genevieve spoke with one of the servants, asking for a bowl of broth.

The boy stirred in her arms. He opened his eyes, which were a greenish-brown hue, and regarded her solemnly.

'What is your name?' Genevieve asked.

He said nothing, but tangled his fingers into her hair, pulling it against his mouth. When the broth arrived, Genevieve helped him to eat. Relief filled her when he ate with a good appetite.

She had just finished feeding him when a man strode into the Great Chamber. His fair hair hung to his shoulders, and he walked with an airy confidence. When he saw her, he smiled.

It was one of those smiles that could make a woman's bones melt. She nodded, and pretended to be fascinated with the boy. The man approached her and sat beside her on the bench.

'You must be Genevieve.'

Her cheeks flushed. What had got into her? Stealing a glance up at him, she saw his smile broaden.

'I am Connor MacEgan.' He reached out and ruffled the boy's hair. 'He's a good lad, isn't he? Patrick told me you rescued him from the pond.'

'Aye. They are still looking for his parents.'

'That is true.' A shadow crossed Connor's face, and Genevieve wondered if he knew something. Switching topics, he added, 'You are fair of face, I must tell you. A pleasure it is to see you this morn.'

'Do you always greet women thus?' Genevieve blurted out, then covered her mouth. The man had done nothing more than compliment her, but his handsome looks made her uncomfortable. Too often a handsome face hid a treacherous heart. She had learned that from Hugh.

'*Tá.*' Bevan's voice interrupted from across the room. 'He has his eye on many women, Connor does.' He strode towards them, his face glistening with drops of water. The dark bristle of his unshaved beard shadowed his cheeks, though it did not cover the matching scars. His feral looks made Genevieve's skin grow warmer as she thought of their conversation the night before.

Though he had stayed with her to look after the boy, he had avoided her, behaving as if he could not bear to be near her. Genevieve did not understand what she had done wrong. And yet during a few stolen moments she had caught him watching her, his expression inscrutable.

She held the child tighter, pretending to give the boy her full attention.

Connor leaned closer. 'And has my brother his eye on you? If so, I could battle him for you.'

'Leave her be.' Bevan leaned against the trestle table, glaring at Connor. 'Did you find the men?'

Connor's expression turned serious. 'We brought back three of them. Two died in captivity. One went missing.'

'You were not detected by Hugh's men?'

'Your people helped us. And Sir Hugh was not inside the *rath.*' Connor glanced at Genevieve. 'He's looking for her.'

Invisible threads of apprehension wrapped around her throat, making it difficult to breathe. She'd known Hugh would not give up.

'He knows where she is,' Bevan said.

'*Tá.* But he is also aware of our strength. He hasn't the men to attack Laochre. I saw them returning to their encampment later that evening.'

Genevieve's shoulders drooped with relief. She wouldn't put it past Hugh to slip through their defences. His battle skills were deadly, honed from years of experience.

With a glance towards the child, Connor added, 'It is the boy's father who has gone missing. But I've learned he escaped on his own.'

'Is he here?' Without waiting for a reply, Bevan ordered, 'Send him to me. He'll want to see his son.'

Connor's gaze shifted to one of unease. 'He was here. Except he's disappeared again. Something is wrong. The men told me Sir Hugh holds his wife captive. He wanted him to turn traitor against us.'

Genevieve held the child tightly, stroking his hair. She pressed a kiss upon his temple, praying for the safety of his mother. For if Hugh had the woman in his possession, he would show no mercy.

'There was no woman there when we freed the men,' Connor added. 'I know not what has happened to her.'

Genevieve's vision swam with unshed tears as she held the boy close. Though she wanted to believe everything was all right, in her heart she knew the truth. If the Irishwoman held no use for Hugh, he would kill her.

'Then we must find him,' Bevan emphasised. 'And his wife.'

'I'll see to it.' Connor shot his brother a roguish look. 'While you are visiting the High King, that is.'

He reached inside his tunic and withdrew a sprig of holly, its berries red and glistening from melted snow. 'For you.' He offered it to Genevieve, raising her hand to his lips.

At his kiss, Genevieve tried to pull her hand away. Connor's excessive attentions reminded her too much of the way Hugh had once courted her.

'I'll be leaving for Tara on the morrow,' Bevan said, behaving as though nothing had happened. 'Patrick has agreed to lend soldiers from Ennisleigh to accompany me.' With a nod to his brother, he added, 'Look after her, won't you?'

Connor placed the sprig of holly into her hand, his smile becoming more heated. 'Oh, I believe I will be taking very good care of her.'

Bevan's words made Genevieve feel as though she'd just been handed over to another man. And she found she did not like the notion.

'I can care for myself, thank you both.' Rising to her feet,

Genevieve balanced the boy on her hip. As she left the Chamber and continued through the first set of doors, the boy struggled in her arms.

'Da!' he cried out, arching his back.

Genevieve stopped and turned around. She thought she saw a flicker of motion, but back in the Great Chamber, Connor and Bevan remained deep in conversation. The boy whined, trying to pull away. Genevieve hushed him, bouncing him against her shoulder. She saw no one. But her spine prickled and she grew suspicious.

In time, his fussing gave way to quiet crying. At last he tucked his head beneath her chin and pulled her hair close for comfort. Her heart gave a tug, and she wished for a moment that the boy were her own son.

She climbed the stairs, and his relaxing body succumbed to sleep. A softness filled her while she held him close. Her thoughts of children abruptly shifted to the marriage bed.

She knew the necessity of submitting to her future husband in order to bear a child. And yet a cold darkness flooded her at the thought of yielding beneath a man. With Bevan it might not be so bad. He, at least, knew the beatings she had endured, and would not raise his fists to her.

But then, she had offered herself with the promise of granting him his freedom. She had sworn not to make demands of him. Bevan would not want to share her bed even if she somehow overcame her fear. He had made it clear that he still regarded her as the Norman enemy. Even if he stayed with her at Rionallís as her husband, she doubted if he would ever change his mind.

In the next few days her father would decide her future while she waited at Laochre. She hated this lack of control over her future. There had to be some way to guide the hand of fate. She mulled over the possibilities.

Above stairs, she found Isabel, instructing her ladies on tasks to be done for the evening. Baskets of greenery were being spread around the room, and Isabel herself held an armful of pine branches.

'Oh, Genevieve.' Isabel turned and smiled gratefully. 'I could use your help, if you're willing.' She took the boy from Genevieve's arms and handed him to the healer, an older woman Genevieve recognised. 'Siorcha will look after him for now.'

She didn't like the idea of relinquishing the boy, but Isabel seemed to understand her discomfort. 'Siorcha has grandchildren his age, you needn't worry. And his parents will be found soon.'

Genevieve kept silent, for she doubted if the boy's mother lived. And there was no way of knowing where his father was. Though she sent up another unspoken prayer for both of them, she ached for the child's loss.

Isabel placed another basket of greenery into Genevieve's arms. 'Tonight we celebrate Alban Arthuan. 'Tis similar to our Christmas celebration, but the Irish have their own unique customs. You will enjoy it,' she promised.

Genevieve followed the women below stairs, but she did not believe she would find much to celebrate. With Bevan soon to be gone, she felt alone and uncertain. And Connor's attentions, though friendly, threatened her sense of security. His forward manner bothered her, and she preferred not to see him this evening—particularly if Bevan was not there to shield her from unwanted affection.

As she helped the women hang garlands of greenery, Genevieve reprimanded herself for her cowardice. She needed to rely on her own strengths and face her fears.

She was tired of waiting for others to make the decisions affecting her life. She wanted to take control of matters, to prevent war between her family and the MacEgan family she had come to care for.

Bevan's aversion to marriage cast a shadow upon her plans, but she believed he wanted to avoid bloodshed as much as herself.

Perhaps she should journey to Tara with them, to seek the aid of King Henry.

The Alban Arthuan celebration marking the beginning of the winter solstice was both enchanting and comforting. The warm flicker of candles, the roaring fire on the hearth, and the garlands of greenery reminded Genevieve of home.

Connor was charming her with humourous stories, coaxing a laugh out of her even as he brought her delicious morsels of food.

'It is good to see you smile,' he said.

'I have not had reason to smile for some time now,' she admitted. 'I like your family.'

'They are good people, yes.' He took a sip of mead and added, 'We protect those in need.'

His remark reminded her of the young boy, lost without his own family. 'Will you be searching for the child's parents?'

'At dawn,' he said. 'But for tonight I intend to celebrate the solstice.'

Genevieve caught several women's jealous glares as Connor remained by her side. But her mind had wandered, and she watched in a detached manner. She wondered if Bevan had gathered his soldiers from Ennisleigh. Was he returning to Laochre for the celebration? Or would he avoid her on this last night, pretending she did not exist?

Stop thinking of him. She berated herself for her errant thoughts.

'Your attentions are elsewhere, I can see,' Connor said, holding her palm lightly. 'Shall I leave you alone?'

Genevieve shook away her reverie. 'No. I am sorry. It's just that I cannot seem to concentrate tonight.'

'Dance with me.' He took both of her hands in his. The warmth of his palms and the intensity of his gaze both captivated and frightened her.

'I would rather not.' But the music had grown sweet once more, and she savoured the notes that echoed inside the chamber. The delicate harpstrings tugged at her emotions, and she drank in the sound of each note.

'Then listen.' His hand cupped the back of her neck in a light caress. Genevieve started to move away, but reminded herself that Connor had done nothing untoward.

After they had listened to several songs, he managed to cajole her into a dance. Genevieve could not follow the rapid steps, but in time she gave up and simply let Connor whirl her around in his arms.

All the while she danced with him, she thought of Bevan. He did not seem the sort of man who would dance or make merry. She wondered what he had been like before he had lost his wife and child. She had seen him smile only once, and never had he laughed.

The wine she had drunk, coupled with her dizziness, made her lose her balance. Connor steadied her, embracing her in strong arms.

Her smile faded as she recognised his intent to kiss her. 'Please don't.'

His thumb trailed down her lips to her throat. 'You care for him, don't you?'

Her heartbeat thrummed in her chest as she tried to find the right words. 'Bevan is my friend.'

'Your feelings run deeper. Were it not for him, I would

have stolen far more than kisses this evening.' His arrogant smugness suddenly struck her as funny.

'You believe that, do you? Just because you are handsome, it does not mean I am longing to kiss you.'

He broke into a laugh. 'So you do find me pleasing? I'll have to tell him that.' He cupped her face between his hands. 'I think we should make him jealous.'

'Bevan is not here,' Genevieve said. 'He went to Ennisleigh for soldiers.'

Connor caressed the line of her jaw. 'He has returned, and has been watching you for some time now. Come now. One kiss.'

'Do women never refuse you?'

'Never.' He puckered up his lips. 'Aren't you curious as to what he'll do?'

'I don't believe you. I think you are only trying to get me to kiss you. He's not there.'

Connor expelled a hearty laugh. 'That would be a good jest, lady. But in truth he *is* watching.'

Genevieve turned in the direction Connor pointed, just as his lips brushed against her cheek. He had not been lying. Bevan was standing against the wall, a cup of mead in his hand. She could not read the expression on his face, but he remained motionless, watching her as Connor had claimed.

'Wait,' Connor warned. 'He will come after you. My brother never could resist a challenge.'

But his prediction did not come true. Instead, Genevieve saw Bevan turn away and leave. Her insides turned frigid as he walked from her. He didn't care. He was leaving her in Connor's arms, knowing that Connor would not let any harm come to her. She was an obligation, nothing more.

A warm hand cupped her cheek. 'If he is too brainless to see the beauty in front of him, I am not.' Connor's lips descended upon hers, and Genevieve fought to keep herself from struggling.

The gentle kiss should have made her feel wanted, but all it did was make her feel trapped. A suffocating thickness rose in her throat. Like Connor, Hugh had once been light-hearted, and had taken his time wooing her. But the bold strength she had admired had become the arms of a prison.

She trembled, and a frightened moan escaped her. Connor steadied her shoulders. 'Are you all right?'

'No.' She pushed back from him, needing to get away. He let her go, but she knew he watched her. Genevieve fled to a corner staircase, sinking down upon the steps. She rested her head against the side of the wall, unable to calm her rapid breathing.

Her fears were foolish. Connor had not intended to harm her, only to steal a kiss. But the familiar anxiety had risen up and conquered her once more. Tears stung her eyes, but she held them back.

The ghost of Hugh's abuse tormented her. And as long as he held such power over her she would never escape him. Though her eyes remained dry, inside she wept for the future she could not have.

It took every ounce of his control not to go to her. Connor's stolen kiss and Genevieve's subsequent flight infuriated Bevan. His brother had exchanged with him a silent question, and Bevan had answered it with a glare, telling him to leave Genevieve alone.

He remained in a hidden alcove where he could keep watch over her. From the shadows of the corner he saw her seated on the steps, her head leaning against the wall. A lock of her hair had come loose, a dark silken tress that slid across her cheek. Her arms were locked around her waist, but she did not weep.

He hadn't expected Connor to kiss her, and he chastised himself for leaving her alone. She had been terrified of his brother. Any man would have that effect after the abuses she'd suffered.

And yet she had not run from *him*. He remembered the delicate feel of her in his arms, like a summer's rose. When he'd kissed her she had driven all thoughts of Fiona from his mind.

She had offered to sacrifice herself in marriage to prevent fighting over Rionallís. She had sworn not to make demands of him, to let him live his life as he chose.

He believed she would do it, too. But honour demanded that he refuse. He'd watched her cradling the boy to her breast, singing a soft ballad when she thought he didn't hear her. It was not fair to deny her the chance to become a mother.

Bevan took a step towards her, knowing that he should not. If he closed the path between them, there would be no turning back. But he wanted to comfort her, to drive away the past that haunted her.

Why did she get under his skin in such a way? Why did she make him feel again? His throat tightened with anticipation as he moved closer. He suddenly felt like Ewan, an adolescent boy who knew nothing of how to speak to a woman. What should he say?

Genevieve lifted her chin to look at him. The emptiness in her eyes made him wish more than ever that he had never sent her towards Connor. Though his brother would cut off his arm before harming a woman, he did not understand what Genevieve had suffered.

'I leave on the morrow for Tara,' he told her. 'The King will decide the matter of Rionallís.'

As if she didn't know that already. He wanted to bite his tongue and take back the ridiculous words.

Genevieve revealed a guarded smile. 'I should wish you well, but I am afraid I cannot.'

He did not know how to respond, but she continued, 'I have been thinking about Rionallís, and I believe it would be best if I accompany you to Tara. I can speak with my father and intercede if necessary.'

'No. You will remain here, where our soldiers can guard you.' He knew he would have to face Genevieve's father, but he'd not let her fight his battles for him.

'I will not be a prisoner here,' she argued.

Bevan took her hands firmly in his. 'Heed me on this, Genevieve. Believe me when I say you will not go anywhere.'

'You cannot keep me.'

'Can't I?' He gripped her wrists. 'Hugh's men are waiting for their chance to take you. I won't allow you to endanger yourself,' he said. 'And that is final.'

'You have no claim over me, Bevan. I can and I shall do as I wish.' Her eyes blazed in rebellion, and he wanted to shake some sense into her.

'Do not defy me on this, Genevieve.' He moved forward until her back was pressed against the corridor wall.

She winced, and he relaxed his grip, taking a deep breath. 'I am sorry. I did not mean to hurt you.' With his thumbs, he massaged at the sore spots on her wrists.

His thumb drew lazy patterns across her skin, touching its softness.

'Why does it matter to you what I do?' she whispered.

He held her gaze. He could not answer her question, for he did not know the reason himself.

She stepped back, pulling her hands away. 'Bevan, I need to do this. I made the mistake of asking my father for a betrothal to Hugh. I should be the one to petition the King for its severance.'

'That is your father's task,' he argued. 'And he should never have allowed Hugh to harm you.'

'Things are different in England,' she said. 'A woman must be subservient to a man's wishes.'

'It should not be thus. A woman holds equal value to a man in Éireann.' He did not understand why the English would treat their women so poorly. 'You do not deserve to suffer at Marstowe's hands.'

'No. But sooner or later I will wed. And I shall have no choice in that arrangement. I can only trust that my father will choose someone better than Hugh.'

The idea of her marrying another man discomfited Bevan. He didn't want any man to touch Genevieve. 'You could enter an abbey.'

'I am not suited to being a bride of Christ,' she admitted. Though she did not say it, he saw the wistfulness in her eyes. A woman such as Genevieve ought to bear children.

Her words confirmed his decision not to wed her. He could not be a father again. The thought of holding another child of his own was like a sword to his gut.

If Genevieve belonged to him, he was afraid he would not be able to resist touching her. Even now he wanted to pull her into his arms and kiss her. She looked so vulnerable, and he feared what might happen were he to act upon his body's wishes.

Clearing his throat, he changed the subject. 'How is the boy?'

'Better. Siorcha spoiled him today, feeding him sweet-meats. He's been crying for his mother, though.'

Her face dimmed, and Bevan said, 'All children want their mothers. Brianna sometimes would not let me hold her, wanting only Fiona.'

'It hurts,' she admitted. 'I am afraid of what Hugh has done to the boy's mother.'

'You should not grow attached to him. He belongs with his father.'

'I know.' A tear escaped her, though she summoned up a half-hearted smile. 'Sometimes you cannot help the feelings inside you.'

He brushed away the tear, grazing the side of her cheek. She'd covered the bruise again, but the colour had started to smear. Even still, she was beautiful to him.

Bevan tried to suppress the intense need rising within him. He longed to forget Fiona and the bitter taste of loss.

'You're right.' His voice caught in his throat as he drew nearer. 'Sometimes you can't help what you feel for someone.' His palm rested against the wall, his other arm drawing around her waist. He waited, letting her pull away if she would.

She didn't move. Slowly, he moved the dark strand of hair, tucking it behind her ear. The world seemed to hold still in that instant when her sapphire eyes met his. His skin grew warm as he moved his fingers up her spine.

She leaned back against the wall, letting it support her as he slid a soft kiss against her neck. He could feel her yielding to him, her warm breath against his cheek.

His mind ordered him to stop. The voice of reason demanded that he release her. She was not his, would never become his. This was wrong.

Her hands tentatively touched his chest, her palms light against his pectoral muscles before she lifted her arms around his neck. Tentative and unsure, she looked terrified and yet determined.

Lug, but he could not remember the last time a woman had held him. There was goodness here, a rush of fire. His body grew impatient, and at last he surrendered to the need. He captured her lips, tasting the sweet warmth of her mouth.

She trembled in his arms but did not turn him away. A ragged breath escaped her. 'We should not do this,' she whispered. 'I can't—'

His hands trailed down her back to cup her hips, pulling her closer. 'I know.' But even as he spoke the words he knew he could not stop wanting her.

He kissed her again, moving his hips against her in a sensual dance. The music from the celebration was ending, and he took her hand, leading her down the corridor. He stopped before his chamber, waiting. Her lips were a deep red, moist from the kiss. More than anything he wanted to take her inside and join with her. But honour demanded that he stop this madness before it consumed them both.

With great reluctance, he released her. 'Leave me, Genevieve. You don't want this.'

She took a step back, then another. For a moment she looked as though she were about to run. But she stopped, uncertainty lining her face.

'Do you care for me, Bevan?' she asked. 'Am I still nothing but a Norman to you?'

He saw her eyes filling with tears and the weakness of his body betrayed him. He cupped her face in his hands, letting her see the full force of desire in his gaze.

'Just a kiss,' he swore. He would not take more than that.

He traced the outline of her jaw, skimming his fingers across the bruise. With his lips, he kissed the injury. Her eyes remained transfixed upon him as he kept his touch light, gentle.

Her lips parted, and she closed her eyes. He bent to taste her, no more than the barest brush of his lips across hers. She trembled, arching her head back. He pulled her hips closer until they moved against his, cradling his length. This time she embraced him tighter, until he could feel the softness of her breasts against his chest.

His hands moved beneath the fabric of her gown, inside the voluminous sleeves, until he felt the softness of her shift. His thumbs were poised at the curve of her breasts, waiting to see if she would allow him to go further. She froze, terrified, but he saw the awakening desire in her eyes.

The intense need to touch her overcame any hesitancy he might have had. Slowly, gently, he moved his thumbs across the sensitive nipples. Genevieve's breath shattered, and he moved her up against the wall, stroking her breasts until she moaned with pleasure.

Her mouth met his in a heated frenzy. She was the rain that brought him to life, quenching the thirst within him. All the years of wanting, of hurting, seemed to melt away as she kissed him back, meeting his tongue with her own. He silenced the guilt of old memories, telling himself he was only human.

Their breaths mingled while he fought to control his urges for more. Then he tasted the salt of her tears. At that moment he despised himself. He had hurt her without meaning to.

'Go,' he commanded her. 'Now.'

When she did not move, he opened the door. Another tear slid down her cheek, but she obeyed. When she was gone, he drove his fist against the heavy oaken door. He had no willpower where Genevieve was concerned.

In the corridor, Genevieve leaned her forehead against the wall. She had no one to blame for her humiliation but herself. Her body pulsed with a fiery storm of feelings. She had never known it could be this way, and a part of her had wanted him to continue.

With him, she had felt cherished. She could not help the falling tears. And then he'd pushed her away. Why had she thought he might want her? Her cheeks suffused with colour. Now that she knew what it was like to be desired by a warrior such as Bevan, her body yearned for more. Her mind spinning with thoughts of him, she stumbled back to her chamber. On the morn he would travel to Tara, to battle for the rights to her land.

But more than that she feared the siege he had already begun upon her heart.

Chapter Nine

The soldier departed Laochre a few hours before dawn. Sir Hugh's commander had ordered him to report his findings within a single day, to avoid suspicion. The Norman encampment lay a few miles beyond the fortress. As he neared the enemy, his heart grew heavy. He'd caught a glimpse of his son, and the sight of Declan had torn him apart. He'd wanted to go to his child, but he could not reveal himself to Bevan or to Lady Genevieve. Instead, he had sent a message to his wife's sister, asking her to come for his son.

Already he sensed his cause was doomed to failure. His friends had seen him, and would wonder why he had not taken Declan home. They would want to know how he had escaped—an answer he could not give them. He had avoided them, pretending his duties required his presence elsewhere. But their suspicions were rising.

When he arrived at the camp, the Normans escorted him to their captain.

'What information do you have for me?' Robert Staunton asked.

'There is a section of the outer wall where the wood is

decaying. I can arrange for it to be left unguarded,' he offered. 'Even now they have only a few men positioned there. Many are accompanying Bevan MacEgan to Tara.' He tried to keep his gaze steady, careful not to let Staunton suspect his lies.

He gave the captain half-truths about the MacEgans—information designed to lead the Normans into a trap.

'What of Lady Genevieve?'

'I will bring her to Rionallís myself,' he said. 'And I want my wife in return.'

'Good.' Staunton mounted his horse and turned to leave. He smiled. 'I pray your words are the truth. For your woman's sake.' Then he tossed a small bag to the soldier. 'A token for your assistance.'

The bag was far too light to contain pieces of silver. The soldier waited until Staunton had returned to his tent before opening it.

Inside he found long tresses of hair belonging to his wife Kiara. Her lovely hair, sheared by the enemy.

His hands shook. The bleakness of failure sharpened his fury at those who had taken Kiara. And with it emerged a sudden anger at Bevan MacEgan. Bevan had abandoned his own men for a Norman woman. Kiara had tried to save them after the MacEgans had deserted them in their time of need.

Were it not for Bevan's ill-fated attack his wife would be safe at home, spinning thread. His time was drawing short if he intended to save Kiara's life.

After Bevan left for Tara he would seize his opportunity. The only way to save his wife was to deliver the Lady Genevieve into the enemy's hands.

Genevieve tickled the young boy's stomach, laughing at his deep giggles. His temperament had shifted to one of delightful play, and he had spent the morning toddling around.

Last night she had tried to ready her belongings, to go with the men to Tara, but Bevan had refused to let her join them. Were it not for the threat of Sir Hugh's men, Genevieve would have travelled without Bevan's permission. She resented having to stay at Laochre when she preferred to speak to her father in person.

A soft knock interrupted her. When she called out for the person to enter, she saw a petite young woman with light brown hair and a plump figure. At the sight of the boy, the woman's face lit up with joy, and she held out her arms.

'Sheela!' he cried out, and raced into her arms, clinging tightly, while the woman murmured softly in Irish, caressing his hair.

A sinking feeling spiralled in Genevieve's stomach. 'Are you his mother?'

The woman shook her head. 'His aunt. My name is Sheela. And you are Lady Genevieve, I understand?'

Genevieve nodded. Sheela had used her title as a courtesy, though it was unnecessary here in Erin.

'My sister went after her husband and left Declan with one of the tenants,' Sheela said. 'He wandered off that morn, and though they searched for him they could not find him.' She drew Declan into her arms, stroking his hair. 'When I received a message that he was here, I came at once.' The boy squirmed, wanting to be let free.

Releasing her nephew, she said, 'I must thank you for saving him. Isabel told me of how you rescued him from the pond.'

'I am only glad I found him in time,' Genevieve replied.

Declan picked up a wooden toy sword and began striking it against the floor, singing a nonsense song to himself. Genevieve managed a smile, but as she watched the young boy she felt a pang of regret. Sheela would take Declan away, and Genevieve would not see him again.

During the past few days, while she'd nursed him to health, she had grown accustomed to waking beside him, his warm body cuddled next to hers. For a time Genevieve had allowed herself to dream that the boy belonged to her.

'You look a great deal like Fiona MacEgan,' Sheela remarked. 'I saw her at a distance last summer, when my husband and I visited family in Leinster.'

Genevieve picked up her needle, trying to act uninterested though her curiosity was piqued. 'I have been told I look like her,' she said. 'But you must have seen someone else. Fiona MacEgan died two years ago.'

Sheela frowned. 'I was certain it was she.' Then after a moment she shrugged. 'But it could be that you are right. I did not see her except from far away.'

When they were about to leave, Genevieve asked if she could hold Declan once more. Taking him into her arms, she smoothed his hair, pressing a kiss to his temple. 'I am glad you are well, little one.' Declan squirmed to get back to his aunt, and Genevieve let him go, feeling a tug of regret.

One day, she promised herself. One day she would have a child of her own.

'And you believe he lies?' Sir Hugh asked his commander.

Robert Staunton gave a nod. 'I do. His loyalty to MacEgan is stronger than we predicted. He will not betray him.'

'Then kill the woman.' Marstowe's eyes glittered with impatience. 'Send her body to the traitor. And prepare our men for attack.'

Staunton concealed his distaste. 'My lord, would you not rather wait for the Earl? With his men to join ours we would be better prepared.'

'No. I'll not let it appear that our men are incapable of protecting my betrothed.'

It was a suicidal mission, and Staunton knew it. 'I hear that MacEgan intends to journey to Tara.'

'You said the man was lying.'

'That may be true. But King Henry is holding court at Tara. You could bring the matter to his attention. I am certain the Irish could not withstand an attack by the King's army.'

Marstowe's expression changed and grew calculating. 'You are right. The King would never allow an Irish barbarian to threaten one of his subjects. And the Earl would, of course, want me to bring it before our sovereign lord.' He stared, lost in thought. 'I was supposed to take Genevieve to Tara for the King to witness our union.'

He smiled. 'This will work to our advantage. Have our belongings packed. We will go to Tara and ensure that King Henry knows exactly how my bride has been threatened.'

In his mind's eye he was certain Henry would take his side. And as for Genevieve, he would cleanse all thoughts of the Irishman from her mind until the only man she desired was himself.

The faint sounds of music came from inside a chamber. Bevan frowned, following the tones into the solarium. The haunting song was one he'd never heard before, and delicate strings filled the room with sorrow. When he stood at the doorway, he saw Genevieve seated at the harp.

Lightly her hands moved over the strings, as though she didn't want anyone to hear her playing. Her eyes remained closed as she lost herself in the music. He hadn't known that she knew how to play.

He cleared his throat and she jolted, her hands moving back from the strings as though they were on fire.

'I am sorry. I didn't—I shouldn't have—'

'You needn't apologise. You play very well. Did your mother teach you?'

'No. When I was fostered in Wales I learned. One of my foster-sisters was from Ireland. She brought her harp from home and taught me.'

Colour heightened in her face, and he saw then that she had been crying. She rose and faced him. 'What is it you want?' Her eyes were red and swollen, and he wondered what had made her weep.

'I am leaving now.' He searched for the right words, wondering if she was angry with him for the way he had touched her the night before. He should apologise for it, for his actions had gone further than he'd intended. 'I wanted to see that you are well before I go.'

'I am fine.' She cleared her throat and regarded him with a cool expression. 'Though I do not understand why you have forbidden me to see my father.'

'He will come for you after we have settled the matter of my lands.'

'I understand that those lands were yours,' she said. 'But my father is not the enemy. You were not there to defend Rionallís. My father protected your people when Strongbow attacked last spring, else your enemies would have destroyed the fortress.' Her posture straightened. 'He saved their lives.'

At the mention of Strongbow, Bevan felt his temper flare. Strongbow's forces had landed at Hook Head, destroying *raths* and murdering hundreds of Irishmen only two years ago. It was during that battle he'd lost both Fiona and his eldest brother, Liam. Patrick had barely managed to defend Laochre.

And then, last spring, the invaders had attacked Rionallís.

'Your people do not belong here,' he said, 'and I'll not surrender to your father what is mine. Nor will I be forced into a marriage not of my choosing.'

Genevieve's eyes flashed with anger. 'And do you think *I* choose to wed a man who does not want me? I know how much you despise my people, but I'll not let blood be spilled for the sake of my pride.'

Gritting his teeth, he finished, 'I am leaving. After I return we need not see one another again.'

She paled, and he noticed her trembling hands. A hollow feeling invaded his skin, but the words of apology would not come forth. Genevieve was right. He had not been there for his people. His grief had consumed him and he'd left his kinsmen to the mercy of the Normans.

Genevieve held her composure and inclined her head. 'As you say.'

Without another word, she turned and strode away from him.

Her anger increased with each step, until she realised she had gone outside without her mantle. The bitter winds whipped her hair into her eyes, and she shivered.

'Here,' a voice called out. She caught the *brat* just as Ewan threw it.

'You are wrong about my brother,' he said.

'Were you listening?'

He gave a sheepish grin and nodded. 'Of course.'

Genevieve sighed and wrapped the blue woollen *brat* about her, shielding her head. She supposed it was foolish to chastise the boy. 'What am I wrong about?'

'Bevan does want you. And if you weren't a Norman I know he would take you as his bride.'

The beliefs of a boy hardly older than four and ten did little to reassure her. Genevieve continued her walk towards the inner bailey, Ewan following at her heels. 'Well, it is fortunate for him that I *am* Norman. And he is so thick-witted he cannot see past it.'

'He came to say goodbye to you,' Ewan pointed out. 'Come to the gate with me. We can watch as the soldiers ride past.'

'I have no wish to see him again.'

'If we climb up to the gatehouse we can throw snow upon him as he passes,' Ewan suggested.

In spite of her anger, Genevieve laughed. 'No.'

They stood in the courtyard, and as she watched the men riding past her good humour faded.

Bevan caught sight of her and drew his horse to a stop. Flakes of snow drifted across his dark mane of hair. He stared, his gaze fastened upon her. Her heart beat rapidly as he leaned down to her.

'Tá brón orm.'

His gloved hand touched hers, pressing against her palm. The intensity of his gaze almost undid her.

Genevieve blinked back tears and nodded in response. 'I am sorry, too.' She swallowed hard, and in a wistful moment she imagined his lips upon hers. Her body remembered full well his touch, the way his hands had moved over her bare skin.

His apology was genuine, and it eased the resentment she held within her. He joined his men, and Genevieve ignored the curious stares of the people around her. Though some would never call his scarred face handsome, it had become dear to her.

She was afraid the King's decision would alter their lives irrevocably. For when Bevan returned he would become either her enemy or her husband.

The High King Rory Ó Connor's fortress of Tara loomed over the vast lands of Éireann. His wooden structure dominated the landscape, with several mottes surrounded by palisades. Each of the five ancient roads converged at this place.

As their horses drew near, Bevan heard cries for mercy from the dugout mound used for hostages. Though a fair High King, Rory Ó Connor was not fond of the Normans. Bevan wondered how Rory would respond to the issue of his land. The Norman King Henry was visiting him, accepting allegiance from the Irish kings and chieftains.

On the far side, he spied the large Lia Fáil stone. At the sight of the grey standing stone he wondered if the stories were true. It was said that the stone would cry out when the true High King was present. Bevan rode past the Lia Fáil, hiding his disappointment when the legendary stone remained silent. Instead, he focused on his task. If all went well he could put the matter of Rionallís to rest once and for all.

Yet he resented the fact that Patrick had involved the Norman King. The dispute could easily have been resolved in the *Brehon* courts. A foreign king had no right to interfere with land that belonged to him.

The men busied themselves with eating and drinking, enjoying the attentions of serving wenches. Bevan awaited his opportunity to speak with the High King, the food tasting dry in his mouth.

Rory Ó Connor was speaking with Ailfred, the chief poet. As his advisor, Ailfred enjoyed a position of honour, but the man cared little for ceremony. He wore frayed robes, and his grey beard hung well below his chest.

Seated beside the High King was King Henry, laughing and jesting with his men. He appeared confident and relaxed, but there was no mistaking the shrewd politics of the Norman King. Bevan knew that Henry wanted nothing more than to add Éireann to his kingdom. Rory Ó Connor was also aware of it, from his strained expression.

In time, Bevan was summoned to speak before them. Ó Connor sat upon the dais, his hand cradled over a goblet of mead. He handed Bevan another goblet, inviting him to sit beside him.

'I know why you are here,' the High King began without prelude. 'And I have agreed to grant Henry the authority to pass judgement upon this matter, since it concerns his subjects.'

Bevan drank the mead, keeping his face impassive. He didn't know why the High King had bowed to the foreigner, but no doubt it was a political agreement. He didn't like it at all.

The smile on Henry's face was guarded, as if the man were judging him.

'We understand that you once dwelled upon the lands called Rionallís,' Henry began. 'What we do not understand is why you left it unguarded and free for the taking.'

Bevan met the King's gaze evenly. 'Those reasons are my own. But Strongbow did not earn the right to take the land from us and grant it to the *Gaillabh*.'

'And so you thought to take it back?' Henry remarked. 'Your men attacked the lands belonging to Thomas de Renalt, the Earl of Longford, but did not succeed in retaking them. And then you tried to murder their daughter's betrothed, Sir Hugh Marstowe.'

Bevan's grip tightened upon the goblet. 'I defended myself against his sword, *tá*.'

'You wounded him and took his bride. But, thanks be, he has recovered from his injuries and is here now, to claim the rights to Rionallís and to his betrothed.'

Bevan turned and saw the face of his enemy as Marstowe entered the chamber. Clothed in fine silk and gold, Marstowe sent him a triumphant smile.

Bevan's hand went automatically to his sword, but it was not there, as the King would not allow weapons in his presence. His fists curled, fury rising. Knowing that Hugh had struck Genevieve, hurt her, made him long to sheathe his blade in the knight's heart.

'Kidnapping is a punishable crime,' Henry said.

'I am not subject to your laws,' Bevan responded.

The Norman King's face darkened with anger. Rory Ó Connor intervened. 'But you are subject to the laws of your king and to the laws of our land.' With a nod towards Henry, Ó Connor continued. 'We will find a solution to satisfy both parties.'

It was then that the chief poet Ailfred spoke up. 'The penalty for abduction must be made. You may pay the *cumals* to Sir Hugh Marstowe, her betrothed.'

'She came willingly,' Bevan argued. 'And she suffered beatings from Sir Hugh. He must pay restitution for his crimes against her.'

'If she came of her own free will, then you must pay to her family her body price and her honour price,' Ailfred said.

Bevan sensed where the conversation was heading. 'I want my property returned to me,' Bevan said, barely keeping his temper in check. 'The Lady Genevieve has asked to return to her parents. She awaits them at my brother's fortress.'

Ó Connor directed his gaze to Henry, and the King's expression tightened. 'It seems that our Irish warrior refuses to compromise,' Henry remarked. 'Since he is unwilling to pay the penalties, we should simply remove the Lady Genevieve from his custody. And we would not advise returning Rionallís to him, since he has already shown himself incapable of defending it.'

Bevan took a sip of the wine, his hand gripping the goblet so hard the metal bent. Hugh sent Bevan a slow, knowing smile. Bevan returned it with a hardened gaze.

The fermented beverage did naught to appease his anger.

A knot coiled in his stomach at the thought of Marstowe possessing his home. Worse was the prospect of Genevieve falling beneath Marstowe's fists. If he did nothing to prevent it, he would be responsible for any harm that befell her.

The invisible noose of duty tightened about his throat. He had no choice but to offer for her.

'What if Lady Genevieve wed me instead?' Bevan asked softly.

'If she were to become your bride, then Rionallís would be returned to you,' Ailfred admitted. 'This could be a fitting solution. Though you would still owe a fine to her family, and to Marstowe.'

'Her father would never permit such an alliance,' the Norman King argued.

If it meant recapturing Rionallís and keeping Genevieve out of Marstowe's grasp, Bevan would do it, despite his misgivings.

'Bring Lady Genevieve to Tara,' Bevan suggested. 'And let her choose between Marstowe and myself. Whomsoever she chooses shall have Rionallís.'

The High King turned to King Henry. 'Would this be a suitable compromise?'

Henry shook his head. 'The Earl of Longford has the right to choose a husband for his daughter. But we have no objection to either suitor, so long as the Earl grants his consent.' With a nod towards Bevan, he added, 'If her father agrees, she may choose her husband. But MacEgan must pay restitution for his actions. His fines must be heavy for attacking the fortress and kidnapping the Earl's daughter.'

Sir Hugh looked displeased, but to Bevan's surprise he voiced no objection. 'She may choose.'

Bevan was immediately suspicious. Surely Marstowe knew Genevieve would never choose him? His quick agreement made Bevan grow cautious.

Everything about the man made Bevan tense. His richly-embroidered clothes, the golden hair, and the way he sent a mocking smile towards the women of Henry's court—it made Bevan all the more determined to keep Genevieve away from him.

'MacEgan,' Sir Hugh said, by way of greeting, 'I shall look forward to emptying your coffers.'

Bevan's eyes burned with fury as he met Marstowe's gaze. 'And I look forward to the day my sword will end your life.'

Hugh folded his arms across his chest. Beneath his breath, he murmured, 'Do you really believe I will allow you to take her from me?'

Bevan stepped forward, using his height to look down upon Hugh.

Anger flashed across the knight's face, but Hugh centred his attention upon the King, bowing. 'I propose another alternative, Your Majesty. I would challenge this Irishman to face my sword.'

'And I would accept that challenge,' Bevan replied, watching the man as though he were a deadly serpent.

'Stand down, Sir Hugh,' King Henry said. 'The matter is yet to be settled.' The King sent a nod towards a group of soldiers, and two stepped forward to prevent the fight. Bevan did not struggle against the guards, but he kept his attention fixed upon Marstowe.

'We have already passed judgement, Sir Hugh,' the King said. 'You will respect it, as a loyal subject of the crown.'

The warning was clear. To defy the King meant treason. With great reluctance, Marstowe stepped back. Bevan never took his gaze off his enemy.

Ó Connor turned to Henry. 'Inform the Earl of Longford to join us.'

'He is here now?' Bevan questioned.

'*Tá,*' the High King replied. 'He has come at your brother Patrick's bequest.'

King Henry signalled a servant, who exited the chamber. Within moments the man returned with Lord Thomas de Renalt, the Earl of Longford.

The Earl was a sturdy man, with greying hair and a beard. Although he stood a full head shorter than Bevan, there was no denying the man's strength, nor the corded muscles in his forearms.

Bevan took a measure of satisfaction as the colour drained from Marstowe's face. Hugh bowed to Genevieve's father while Bevan remained standing.

'Your Majesty,' Longford greeted the King. He bowed before his gaze fell upon Sir Hugh. Bevan sensed a bridled fury towards the knight.

'An agreement has been made,' King Henry informed the Earl. 'We have granted your daughter the right to decide between Sir Hugh Marstowe and Bevan MacEgan for a husband. The disputed property rights to Rionallís will go to the man she chooses.' The King smiled, his expression mocking. 'With your permission, of course.'

Longford chose his words carefully. 'I am honoured by Your Majesty's interest.'

He stood before Bevan and Sir Hugh, his expression impenetrable. 'I understand my daughter was taken from Rionallís?'

Bevan perceived that somehow his question was a test. '*Tá,* I helped her escape.' He met the Earl's accusation with his own silent message of contempt. 'After I found her bruised and beaten. She awaits you at my brother's fortress, Laochre.'

Bevan sent a look towards Marstowe and caught the flash of anger in the man's eyes.

'And do you think my daughter would consent to wedding

a man such as yourself?' The Earl's tone made it clear that he would not offer his own support to a match between them.

'Given the alternative, I have no doubt she would.' Bevan made no effort to hide his insult to Marstowe. He remembered all too well Genevieve's slender body suffering beneath Marstowe's fists.

'I disagree,' Sir Hugh said. 'I understand you lost your first wife because you could not keep her guarded. The same might happen to Genevieve,' he remarked. 'She does seem to run off whenever the mood strikes her.'

High King or not, Bevan wanted to kill the man with his bare hands. Before he could reach Marstowe, soldiers held him back.

'Enough of this arguing,' Longford said, his voice deadly. 'No decision will be made until I have seen my daughter.'

The soldiers restrained Bevan until the Earl had passed. At last, with a nod from Rory Ó Connor, they let him go.

The High King exchanged glances with the Norman King. 'Bevan, you must understand that by agreeing to let the lady choose, you forfeit all land rights to her. Should she wed Sir Hugh, you will have no further claim upon Rionallís.'

Bevan did not concern himself with the warning. His only thought was to reach Genevieve before Marstowe did.

Chapter Ten

Thomas de Renalt, the Earl of Longford, observed the Irish warrior. Bevan MacEgan was intent upon returning to Genevieve, and he rode like a man possessed. There was urgency in his every move, and all of his energies were directed towards reaching Genevieve.

Not the behaviour of a man only interested in land.

MacEgan was a puzzle, Longford thought to himself. This new alliance offered an intriguing possibility. He had never liked the betrothal between Genevieve and Sir Hugh, but because the King had initiated the arrangement, it had been difficult to break. Now he had the means, and he intended to see it severed before nightfall.

Longford knew he was soft-hearted when it came to Genevieve. As his only daughter, she held a unique place in his heart. She asked for little and it pleased him to grant her desires. When she had begged to wed Sir Hugh, his instincts had warned him against the match. He would have refused, despite her pleas, had it not been for King Henry's desire to reward the young knight with an ambitious marriage.

Though the Irishman had accused Sir Hugh of harming

Genevieve, he already knew the truth. Genevieve's own words had proclaimed the knight's guilt, and the Earl would not allow Marstowe near his daughter again.

Yet he did not know whether he could trust MacEgan.

It was already the second day of their journey south, and the late afternoon sun had begun to descend. The two men rode hard, sweat glistening upon the flanks of their destriers. The wind slashed at their faces, bitterly cold, but neither MacEgan nor Sir Hugh showed any interest in breaking camp. The Earl remained behind them, and at one interval he caught a fragment of their conversation.

'Genevieve belongs to me. Your foolish idea of letting her choose means nothing. Her father will never allow her to wed an Irish barbarian over a Norman,' Sir Hugh said.

'You fear he will learn the truth,' MacEgan predicted. 'And which of us is the true barbarian.'

At that, Longford urged his horse forward to ride between the men. 'When do we arrive at Laochre?'

'By nightfall,' Bevan predicted.

'And how can you be sure she is well and unharmed?'

When the Irishman did not respond, Longford pressed further. 'If what they say is true, you could not keep your own wife safe.'

'If what Genevieve says is true, you could not answer her pleas for help when she begged for it,' MacEgan retorted. 'Or do all Normans find it necessary to beat their women into submission?' His posture grew rigid. 'We value our women here.'

MacEgan's rejoinder confirmed what Longford had already suspected. Though he recognised the Irishman's intense prejudice against Normans, he felt certain MacEgan would never raise a hand against his daughter in rage.

Which was more than he could say for Sir Hugh.

'Sir Hugh, I would speak to you alone,' Longford said,

moving his horse to the side. The knight followed, his expression wary. Longford waited until the others had passed far ahead of them. 'What say you to MacEgan's accusations?'

'I would hope that a man of your stature would not stoop to believe the lies of an Irishman,' Sir Hugh said calmly. 'We both know he will stop at nothing to control the land that was once his. We owe it to Genevieve to protect her from this man.'

The Earl made no comment, but he could see Sir Hugh's face beginning to perspire. 'I spoke with some of the soldiers I sent to escort Genevieve. Can you guess what they told me about your treatment of her?'

Marstowe blanched. 'I would guard Genevieve with my life, my lord. She is a highborn lady with a strong spirit.'

'So strong you found it necessary to tame her? You are not her husband yet, Hugh.'

'A betrothal is nearly the same as a marriage.'

'But I am still her father. And my authority supercedes yours before she is wed.' He paused, watching Sir Hugh fumble for another excuse. Before the knight could argue again, Longford drew his horse to a halt. 'I asked to speak with you in private so as not to draw shame upon you before the others. You will not wed Genevieve. While we continue on to Laochre, you will return to England. I will have your belongings sent to you, along with all gifts and coins you brought to Genevieve. Do not show your face before me again.'

Longford reached into a pouch and withdrew a crumpled parchment. Holding it out to Sir Hugh, he read the priest's handwriting that dictated one of Genevieve's petitions for help. 'This alone is not why I want you away from Genevieve. I have heard tales of your cruelty from my own men. They spoke of the soldier who tried to protect her, whom you killed for it. I'll not wed my daughter to a murderer.'

Sir Hugh's face turned scarlet with barely controlled rage and embarrassment. Longford kept his voice even. 'I would rather Genevieve wed an Irish barbarian who would give his life to protect her than a man who values her dowry over-much.'

He turned his horse away, not waiting to see Sir Hugh's reaction. But it was enough to know that Genevieve would be safe once more.

'My Lady Genevieve, I am sent to tell you of your parents' arrival.'

Genevieve had been mending a basket of clothing when the soldier interrupted. She rose and set aside her needle.

'They are below stairs?'

'No, my lady. They await you beyond the gates of Laochre.'

Genevieve frowned. 'Why do they not come inside?'

The soldier looked embarrassed. 'King Patrick did not bid them welcome. He calls the Normans his enemy still.'

Something about the soldier's words rang false. Although Bevan had threatened to deny her family entrance, she had not expected it of Patrick. The king reserved passing judgement until he had all the truths he required. He had granted Genevieve sanctuary. To forbid her parents the right to enter seemed unlikely.

She studied the soldier. His face appeared familiar somehow, though she knew not where she had seen him. A strange premonition warned her to be wary.

'Am I to bring my belongings?' she asked.

The soldier shook his head. 'Patrick has agreed to send them to Rionallís later.'

Genevieve lifted a woollen *brat* from inside a chest, hiding a small dagger in the folds as she wrapped the length of

GET FREE BOOKS and FREE GIFTS WHEN YOU PLAY THE...

7 Lucky

SLOT MACHINE GAME!

Just scratch off the silver box with a coin. Then check below to see the gifts you get!

YES! I have scratched off the silver box. Please send me the 2 free Harlequin® Historical books and 2 free gifts for which I qualify. I understand I am under no obligation to purchase any books, as explained on the back of this card.

349 HDL ELWX   **246 HDL EL4M**

FIRST NAME   LAST NAME

ADDRESS

APT.#   CITY

STATE/PROV.   ZIP/POSTAL CODE

7	7	7	**Worth TWO FREE BOOKS plus 2 BONUS Mystery Gifts!**
			Worth TWO FREE BOOKS!
			Worth ONE FREE BOOK!
			TRY AGAIN!

www.eHarlequin.com

(H-H-05/07)

DETACH AND MAIL CARD TODAY!

© 2000 HARLEQUIN ENTERPRISES LTD.
® and TM are trademarks owned and used by the trademark owner and/or its licensee.

The Harlequin Reader Service® — Here's how it works:

Accepting your 2 free books and 2 free mystery gifts places you under no obligation to buy anything. You may keep the books and gifts and return the shipping statement marked "cancel". If you do not cancel, about a month later we'll send you 6 additional books and bill you just $4.69 each in the U.S. or $5.24 each in Canada, plus 25¢ shipping & handling per book and applicable taxes if any.* That's the complete price and — compared to cover prices of $5.50 each in the U.S. and $6.50 each in Canada — it's quite a bargain! You may cancel at any time, but if you choose to continue, every month we'll send you 6 more books, which you may either purchase at the discount price or return to us and cancel your subscription.

HARLEQUIN READER SERVICE
3010 WALDEN AVE
PO BOX 1867
BUFFALO NY 14240-9952

BUSINESS REPLY MAIL
FIRST-CLASS MAIL   PERMIT NO. 717   BUFFALO, NY

POSTAGE WILL BE PAID BY ADDRESSEE

NO POSTAGE
NECESSARY
IF MAILED
IN THE
UNITED STATES

If offer card is missing write to: Harlequin Reader Service, 3010 Walden Ave., P.O. Box 1867, Buffalo NY 14240-1867 cloth around her shoulders. She did not trust the soldier's words, but there was a slight chance he spoke the truth. It was best to be prepared for anything.

After she had donned her mantle, the soldier led her out of doors to the inner bailey. It was there that Genevieve halted. There was no escort of soldiers to take her outside the gates. Now she was certain of his lies.

'I will go no further with you,' she said. 'Not until I have spoken with the King of Laochre.'

The soldier gripped her wrist tightly, and Genevieve tried to break free. She fought against his grasp, using her fists, her elbows. Anything. But before she realised what had happened, he had located the dagger she'd hidden and manoeuvered it until it rested against her skin.

'Why are you doing this?' she asked, her voice hoarse. 'I thought you were loyal to the MacEgans.'

The soldier's countenance was weary. 'Sir Hugh holds my wife prisoner. If I do not bring you to him, he will kill her.'

Genevieve's expression faltered. 'How do you know Sir Hugh has not killed her already? Then your betrayal would be for naught.'

She saw him glance towards a small pouch at his belt. His face sullen, he replied, 'I don't. But I intend to find out.'

In a flash of recognition Genevieve knew where she had seen his face: in the softness of a child's countenance.

'You are Declan's father,' she whispered. When he did not deny it, she recalled the day Declan had called out to him. 'He saw you that day.'

At the mention of his son, the soldier eased his grasp. 'He is safe now.'

'I saved his life,' Genevieve insisted. 'Does that not mean anything to you?'

Pain flickered across his eyes, but he said only, 'Were it not for you, my wife and child would be safely at home.' He spat, cursing the Normans beneath his breath in Irish. 'This is your fault.'

A desperate man took desperate measures, and she realised he would not listen to reason. When he forced her towards the main gate, Genevieve screamed.

The soldier moved the dagger until it rested against her throat. Genevieve tried to step back and use the technique Bevan had taught her to escape. Instead, the soldier caught her off balance and dragged her forward.

'Let us pass,' he told the guards. 'Or I slit her throat.' The guards moved to block him, and to prove his point he pressed the blade until blood welled up from Genevieve's skin. The burning sensation filled her with terror. She believed he would act upon his threat if need be.

The guards lowered their weapons and let him pass. The soldier took only a few steps past the gate before Genevieve heard a dull thud. The soldier's arms loosened their hold, and she moved away. An arrow lay embedded in his throat.

In the distance, she heard hoofbeats approaching. Within seconds she saw Bevan and a large army of men. Relief streamed through her at the sight of him. He still held the bow, though when he dismounted he set it aside.

Her breath caught when he crushed her into an embrace, drawing her so close she could smell the pine scent of him. His beard was rough against her cheeks, his hands cupping her face.

'Are you all right?' he whispered huskily. His fingers wiped away the smear of blood on her neck.

She managed a nod, though she could hardly stand. He enfolded her within his cloak, massaging warmth into her shoulders. It felt so good to be in his arms, and she laid her cheek against his chest while he rubbed her spine.

'I tried to get away from him,' she whispered.

'I know.' He drew back and motioned towards the parapets. 'But he would not have made it any further.' Genevieve looked up and saw the archers waiting. Though she understood his meaning, she was grateful it was Bevan who had saved her. She had missed him more than she'd thought possible.

'Your father is here. He sent Sir Hugh back to England. He will not trouble you again.'

She could hardly believe that Hugh was gone. It was as though the chains of her fear had shattered and fallen away.

Bevan's intense green eyes burned into her. He released her, and the distant warrior's demeanour returned. Suddenly she did not want to know the King's decision.

'I am cold,' she whispered.

Bevan removed his cloak and pulled it across her shoulders. She felt the heat from his body, but it did nothing to warm the fear that froze her from within.

'Your father approaches,' Bevan said gruffly.

At the sight of her father, Genevieve ran to him. Thomas de Renalt caught her in his arms, hugging her with a fierce intensity. 'Are you harmed? Tell me, daughter.' Frowning at the bruise on her cheek, he turned his anger upon Bevan.

'Who did this?'

Genevieve held her father back. 'It is not as bad as it looks. It was my punishment from Sir Hugh for helping Bevan to escape.'

Thomas took her hand in his, squeezing it. With a knowing gaze towards his daughter, he asked, 'Do you wish to wed Bevan MacEgan?'

Her father's question took Genevieve by surprise. She watched Bevan's face for a sign of encouragement. When he gave none, the spark of anticipation disappeared, and she felt torn at the question.

'Why do you ask me this?' She knew better than to think her personal wishes mattered where political alliances were concerned.

'A new betrothal agreement was created. I have not yet given my consent.'

Genevieve sensed her father's silent question. He wanted to know if she held reservations about a marriage to Bevan. Unlike most fathers, he had always listened to her opinion before making a decision about her future. Even with Hugh. What a fool she had been, she thought darkly.

'Did you agree to this arrangement?' she asked Bevan, afraid to hear his answer.

'The King will grant Rionallís to me,' he replied. When she looked into Bevan's eyes, she understood that he wanted his property, and could only be granted that right if he wed her.

'I can arrange a marriage for you when we return to England,' her father suggested. 'There are many men who have offered for you, and several would make a sound alliance.'

She considered her father's suggestion, but with one look towards the unyielding determination upon Bevan's face she knew that men's lives were more important than her desires. If she did not wed Bevan, it meant war. She could not live with herself if she went back to England and wrought the deaths of her father's men.

She cleared away the turmoil of emotions and lifted her chin. 'I will wed him.'

'Are you certain?' her father asked.

'Aye, Papa.' She hoped that one day she would overcome Bevan's antipathy. 'I have made my choice.'

She did not look at Bevan, afraid of the resentment she might see. Though he had saved her from the soldier, had embraced her as a lover would, he would blame her for this marriage.

Thomas sighed. 'Then I suppose you will be wanting your mother to help with the celebration. I will bring her here, for your sake.'

She embraced her father, and Thomas tucked her head against his chest. In that moment the gesture reminded her of when she had been a little girl, sitting upon his broad lap. A single tear spilled onto her cheek.

'Well, let us not stand out in the cold,' her father said. 'We will finish the arrangements.'

As they entered the fortress, Genevieve risked a glance at Bevan. There was no sign of contentment or joy, only an impassive expression she could not read. She tried to bolster her courage. Somehow she would find a way to please him and earn his respect, if not his heart.

Chapter Eleven

Days later, Bevan MacEgan and the Earl returned to Tara to finish the new betrothal agreement. The Norman King conceded that no *cumals* would be given as retribution to Sir Hugh, upon the Earl of Longford's request.

While they were gone Genevieve returned to Rionallís, stripping away anything that reminded her of Hugh. It was then that they found the body of a female prisoner—the wife of the soldier who had tried to kidnap Genevieve. Her hair had been shorn, and Genevieve pressed her fist to her mouth, imagining the woman's fear. Tears streamed down her face, for this might have been herself one day. She made arrangements for the woman to be buried, and a wave of sorrow enfolded her. Declan had lost both parents. Though he had his aunt to care for him, it was not the same.

She regretted both deaths. When Bevan had seen the soldier threatening her, he had not hesitated to kill the man. Her hand moved to her throat in memory. He had killed one of his own men on her behalf. The thought sobered her.

She knew not why he had done such a thing. In truth, Bevan remained a mystery to her. What had made him change his mind about the marriage? And what sort of husband would he be, once her father returned to England?

It was easier to start anew at Rionallís without Hugh's presence. Yet it took two days before she gathered the courage to enter her former bedchamber.

Genevieve entered the room with an armful of fresh rushes, hoping to occupy herself with the activity. The maids worked alongside her, and she stacked peat in the hearth to provide a long-burning fire. The heavy loam scent enveloped the room in time, offering comfort.

She stared at the bed. Nausea twisted at her stomach at the memories it evoked. Hugh holding her down, striking her until she lay still beneath him. Her vision swam, and Genevieve clenched her fingers, fighting the surge of hurtful anger. Hugh had wanted to control her, to make her feel desire for him. He had bragged about his skills, ridiculing her fears and insisting he could make her want him. It was the only reason he had not breached her, though he had come close.

'Are you well?' a young maid asked her.

'Take the bed out of here. I don't want to see it again,' Genevieve said. 'Burn it, if you like.'

The girl nodded. 'I will see it done.'

'Leave me,' Genevieve ordered. The maids complied, and she stripped the bed of its coverings. One by one she fed them into the fire, watching them erupt in flames before fading into ashes.

In another few days she had to face her own marriage bed. Though she knew Bevan did not want her, he had to consummate the marriage to make it binding. Her nerves were so tight she closed her eyes to will the fear away. Once, she reminded herself. It need be only once. And she did not believe Bevan would harm her.

She needed a distraction. Rising to her feet, she left the chamber. Isabel had sent Ewan to keep her company, along with a dozen escorts. Genevieve found him at last in the weaponry room. He held his arm out, as if clutching an imaginary sword. His gaze remained intent upon the ground, his feet moving in intricate patterns while he muttered to himself.

'Forgive me,' Genevieve interrupted, 'but what on earth are you doing?'

Ewan's gaze darted towards her. 'Close the door, and I'll show you.'

He picked up a sword from the wall and moved to attack an unseen adversary. His feet moved in the same patterns, while his sword arm slashed and parried imaginary blows.

Genevieve leaned against the wall, watching. 'Does it work?'

Ewan shrugged. 'I practise every night. Some day I shall use my skills on the battlefield.'

'It seems terribly complicated.'

'It is. It takes years of practise.' Ewan repeated the footwork sequence, his concentration focused on his feet.

'Shouldn't you look at your opponent?'

'What?' He lowered his sword. 'Oh. Well, as soon as I've mastered this new pattern I shall.'

Genevieve let him continue and remarked, 'I used to watch my brothers practise swordplay when I was younger. They would never let me try.'

Ewan sent her a doubtful look. 'The swords are heavy.'

'Aye, they are. But I never saw my brothers watching their feet. They swore that, no matter what, I must always keep my eyes upon my attacker.'

'Bevan says that. I've never seen anyone move faster than him. He's undefeated in battle.' Ewan gave a self-deprecating laugh. 'I've never won a battle.'

'Neither have I.' Genevieve smiled at him. 'But I'd imagine that would come in time.'

His eyes glittered. 'I want to be the greatest warrior in all Éireann. I want to be a legend.'

'I think you will be one day,' Genevieve encouraged. 'But if it were me, I might look more at my opponent than my feet.'

Ewan pondered her words. 'Whenever I fight, my feet tangle up. I thought if I practised my footwork it wouldn't happen.'

He adjusted his stance and practised some more. 'You're very different from Fiona, you know.'

'How do you mean?'

Ewan slashed at the air and stumbled before regaining his footing. 'She never laughed. Bevan was always trying to make her smile. She didn't smile often.'

'Don't you think she was happy here?'

He shook his head. 'She would take long walks alone when Bevan wasn't around. Sometimes she wouldn't return for hours.' He lowered his sword and paused for a moment. 'One night when Bevan was away she didn't return until the next morn. That was a few weeks before she died.'

'Surely someone went after her?' Genevieve suggested. 'Your brother would never have allowed her to be harmed.'

'They didn't know she was gone. I only knew because I followed her.'

Genevieve itched to ask where Fiona had gone, but from the masked expression on Ewan's face she doubted if he would tell her.

'I am glad you are to marry Bevan,' Ewan said.

Genevieve was taken aback by his comment. 'Why do you say this?'

'The way you look at him. You like him more than Fiona ever did.' He scowled, and Genevieve wondered again what had made him dislike his sister-in-law so much.

'He doesn't want to marry me,' she said. 'He cannot see past my Norman blood.'

'Oh, 'tisn't that.' Ewan jabbed the air and stumbled when his footwork caught him off balance. 'Bevan takes his vows to heart. When Fiona died he swore he'd never wed again. Thinks he's being faithful to her, he does.'

She knew Bevan had cared for his first wife, but now she wondered how deep his feelings ran. Was she comparing her to Fiona?

Genevieve picked up one of the heavy swords from the wall. The unfamiliar weight caused her to tighten her muscles, but she held it. 'So what would soften your brother towards me?'

Ewan's mouth twitched, and he shrugged. 'You could try pastries or tarts. Especially those with dried cherries or apples. I thought I saw some.'

Genevieve suspected he spoke more of his own adolescent wishes than his brother's. She gave him a warm smile. 'Mayhap you are right.'

She raised her sword and touched his. 'You might visit England one day. You could train with some of my father's knights, should you wish it.'

He shook his head. 'My place is here. And now so is yours.'

Genevieve did not answer. Each day was a battle to drown out the terrible memories. She was grateful for Ewan's presence. His enthusiasm helped keep her mind off of Hugh.

She held the sword out towards Ewan. 'Will you teach me what you know?'

He gave a self-deprecating smile. '*Tá*. But that won't take very long.'

Bevan rode among his men, his muscles paining him at the old injury on his shoulder. One night the wound had reopened, but thankfully the bleeding had stopped within minutes of rebinding it. He knew many men who had died from wounds as bad as his. He was grateful that Genevieve had tended it so well.

At the thought of her, Bevan stiffened. He had been ordered to wed her immediately upon returning to Rionallís. And it seemed necessary for the haste, should Sir Hugh threaten the marriage in some way. Protecting her was foremost in his mind.

Genevieve's parents travelled at the back of the entourage, keeping far away from his kinsmen. Bevan had spoken little to them, for the Earl's wife, Lady Helen, regarded him as the devil incarnate. Longford was more affable, and Bevan detected a note of respect from the man since he had rescued Genevieve.

Connor rode up to greet him, a few miles beyond the gates of Rionallís. 'You look as though you are going to meet your executioner,' he remarked. 'But I suppose you *are* getting married.'

The teasing annoyed him, but Bevan would not rise to the bait.

'I would be happy to take your place with such a one as Genevieve.' Connor gave a sly grin and drew his horse up alongside Bevan's. 'Her lips taste like the sweetness of honey.'

His fist shot out towards his brother's jaw, but Connor blocked the blow, laughing. 'Fear not, brother. You'll wed her when we arrive.'

Bevan glared at Connor, jealousy consuming his rational thoughts. *Tá,* he had all but pushed her into Connor's arms, but now he didn't want any man near her.

It reminded him of how friendly Fiona had been towards strangers. She had always been kind whenever visitors had come to Rionallís. But when it had been just the two of them she'd seemed to remove herself to some faraway place.

Though he had been able to bring her body to a state of ecstasy, her mind he had never been able to touch.

It seemed that more and more he was remembering his wife's faults. Why should that matter? She was dead, and they had enjoyed many happy years together.

He thought of his last embrace with Genevieve. Soon he would have a husband's right to bed her. She would belong to him.

That, he decided, was what bothered him. He had been forced into this match, and he didn't want to dishonour the memory of his first wife with another woman. If he let himself soften towards Genevieve he would betray the vow he'd made upon Fiona's death.

Could he touch Genevieve, satisfy his longings, and yet keep himself apart from her? He didn't know. He desired Genevieve, but she had endured such pain. He did not want her thoughts to linger upon Hugh.

More than that, he felt guilty for the lust he felt. Every time he saw Genevieve he wanted to caress her softness, to bring her body to a flushed state of fulfilment.

He dared not risk letting a woman close to him again. Especially not Genevieve, who occupied his mind at every moment, despite his attempts to shut her out. What kind of man could he call himself were he to abandon his vow?

Straightening his posture, he increased the horse's gait until Rionallís emerged over the horizon. The snow-encrusted fields would ripen with a golden harvest come the summer. He would add another section to the fortress—one of stone. And as the years passed he would eventually replace all the wood with stone until nothing could destroy it. He envisaged prosperity among the people, close friendships with the tenants upon the land.

He hadn't realised he'd missed it. It had been easier to stay with his brother and neglect that part of his life, his former home. Bittersweet memories flooded him as he rode towards the gates. He remembered Fiona waiting for him, standing atop the steps.

He ached to think she would never be there again, waiting. But Genevieve would await him. And each time he rode back from battle she would be there, as a part of his life.

He slowed his pace as they drew nearer to the familiar walls. It was as though he could somehow preserve the old memories by not entering the fortress. A few sparse flakes of snow skimmed over the wind, settling upon his gloves before fading into nothingness.

With a silent farewell to all that had been, he rode through the gates towards a new future.

Genevieve raised a sword to block Ewan's blow. Her grip had grown stronger, but she winced at the arm-numbing contact. Over the past few days she had spent her afternoons with Ewan, letting him teach her the art of swordplay. She knew almost nothing about it, but she enjoyed the exercise. It also gave Ewan a sense of pride to show off his skills, particularly when he was far better than herself.

He had also revealed more about Bevan. From the way he spoke of his elder brother, she knew he both worshipped Bevan and was jealous of him. It seemed that he wanted to be exactly like his brother in every way.

'Except I would never marry,' he said now, sheathing his weapon when their sparring match had finished.

'Why is that?'

'I've no need to marry. I have little of my own, save a few head of cattle.'

As the youngest son, his inheritance would be the smallest of the brothers, Genevieve realised. Here it seemed that cattle and sheep, rather than coins, measured a man's wealth.

'Wouldn't Patrick grant you a portion of land?' she asked. 'Or could you not buy your own?'

'They want me to become a priest,' he said. 'But I've no wish for that lifestyle.' His expression grew thoughtful. 'I'll fight as a mercenary, like Bevan, and save my earnings. Then it might be that I could afford some land of my own.'

'And you wouldn't want sons to inherit the land?' Genevieve prompted. 'Surely you would want a wife for that?'

His face reddened, and he withdrew his sword once more, practising lunges. 'They laugh at me, the girls do. They know I cannot fight.'

The embarrassment on his face made her want to box the ears of such foolish girls. 'Then you must find a woman who knows your true worth inside.'

Ewan said nothing, but went back to his practising. Genevieve knew he wanted to be alone, and so she withdrew from the weaponry room.

In the Great Chamber below, she tried to occupy herself with her needle. Her fingers moved across the linen, the row of even stitches belying the nervousness she felt. She wished she had her psaltery, to lose herself in music.

Ewan was right. Bevan would return soon, and their marriage would take place.

Her needle moved across the linen as she visualized his face in her mind. Unbidden came thoughts of his kiss, and the way he had touched her.

Did he have any feelings for her at all? If he did, she sensed he fought them. According to Ewan, Bevan's loyalty to his first wife transcended anything he might feel for Genevieve.

And therein lay another problem: Ewan's dislike of Fiona and the strange details Genevieve had learned bothered her. All her instincts warned her that Fiona had held secrets—ones that Bevan knew nothing about. The one that bothered her most was Ewan's claim that Fiona had left the fortress more than once, not returning until morning.

There was no plausible reason for it save one: infidelity. Genevieve knew Bevan had loved his wife completely. But would he still grieve for her if he knew the truth?

In her heart, she realised that she could never be the one to reveal such secrets. What good would it accomplish? It would only turn Bevan against her. Silence was the best course of action. She wanted to win his heart, but not at the cost of destroying his memories.

Loud voices interrupted her thoughts. Genevieve turned and saw her mother entering the Great Chamber. A smile of joy broke across Genevieve's face. 'Mother!' Rising to her feet, she ran to embrace Helen.

Tall and slender, Lady Helen de Renalt wore her dark hair concealed beneath a veil. Genevieve knew her mother used plant dyes to prevent the silver strands along her temples. Fine age lines edged the corners of her eyes and mouth— lines that curved upwards at the sight of her daughter.

Her mother hugged her tightly. 'Tell me what has happened.'

Genevieve explained, but could not keep the bitterness from her voice when she spoke of the beatings.

'Only one missive arrived—a short time ago,' Helen admitted. 'Had it not been for his illness, I am certain your father would have come for you sooner.' Her face was filled with regret. 'And it was our fault for sending Sir Peter of Harborough and his wife. They are friends of ours, but I suppose Hugh deceived them.'

'Sir Peter believed Hugh's lies that I deserved punishment. He did nothing to stop him.'

'I am sorry, daughter.' Helen touched her face tenderly. ''Tis a good thing Hugh and Peter are already gone, for I would likely flay them both alive. Your father will have words with Sir Peter, of that you can be sure.'

Never one to dwell on unpleasant matters, Helen changed the subject. 'I want to know about this Bevan MacEgan. Do you truly wish to wed him?' Her mother spoke of the matter as though Genevieve had volunteered to throw herself from the top of a tower.

Hedging, she said, 'He is a good man, and a fine warrior, but his heart will always be with his first wife.'

Helen sighed. 'I did not ask about his heart, Genevieve. This is a marriage, not a love ballad.'

'I know.'

'I am not certain you do. I know the King wanted you to wed Sir Hugh, but he was not your only suitor. We could have wed you to any number of men. Had you been thinking with your head, you might not have ended up where you did.' Helen added, 'And I am not certain marriage to this Irishman is a good idea at all.'

'Bevan is a strong protector, Mother,' she argued.

'But can you endure living here in Erin with him?' Helen glanced around, as though she would rather be dead than dwell here.

Genevieve hid her smile. She had grown to love Erin and its green hills. She found it no hardship to live in a wild land filled with untamed beauty. 'I can.'

Helen continued voicing her opinions on marriage, but Genevieve had stopped listening. Her gaze moved towards the entrance to the Great Chamber.

A small group of soldiers entered the room, followed by Bevan. He stood, awaiting her.

'Mother, pray excuse me for a moment.'

Helen turned and frowned. 'I am not certain about this man, Genevieve. He is little more than a barbarian.'

'Go, Mother. Please,' Genevieve said. 'I would speak with him alone.'

Helen began to shake her head, but Bevan stepped forward. With a dark glare to Helen, he commanded, 'Leave us.'

Her mother stiffened. 'I shall stand over by the fire. If you have need of me I will—'

'Mother—' Genevieve warned. 'Go to my chamber above. I will speak with you there later.'

With a shake of her head, Helen left. Genevieve lifted her gaze to Bevan. 'I am sorry about this. I never meant to—'

He stepped forward, so close to her that Genevieve could feel his breath upon her face. His nearness disconcerted her, but she struggled to hold her ground. Her warrior's green eyes glinted with a firm resolve. Reaching up, she touched the fresh scar on his cheek. 'Your wound is healing well.'

He covered her fingertips with his own. His voice was a deep baritone as he leaned in. 'The marriage will take place today.'

She knew how much he didn't want to wed her. It hurt more deeply than she had imagined.

'Why did you change your mind?' she asked.

He did not respond, but said firmly, 'I am holding you to your promise. After the wedding, we lead separate lives.'

Her heart bruised at his words, though she had expected them. 'I know.'

'Can you accept this?' he asked. 'All I can offer you is your freedom to do as you please.'

'I have no choice, have I, Bevan?' Her voice sounded tired, but she managed to nod. 'I will wed you and avoid a battle between our people.' Her anger grew until her teeth hurt with the effort to clench them.

Bevan released her hands. 'Go and prepare yourself. I will see you when the priest arrives.'

Genevieve's eyes burned as he departed. He wanted nothing to do with her—something she had to acknowledge.

Her nerves strained at the thought of sharing his bed even a single time. Though it was necessary, in order to bind the marriage, she hated the thought of being naught more than a duty. She did not know if she had the courage to yield to him in such an intimate way.

Isabel MacEgan interrupted her. Patrick's wife, the Queen of Laochre, had journeyed for the wedding, and she offered a joyful smile to Genevieve. 'Genevieve, will you come with me? I would help you dress for the wedding.'

Though her feet felt leaden, Genevieve followed Isabel to another chamber. Upon the bed, Isabel had laid out a *léine* of saffron silk with an emerald overdress. A bathing tub filled with water awaited her.

Helen de Renalt selected jewels for Genevieve to wear, muttering her disapproval of the marriage beneath her breath. Genevieve sank into the tub of warmed water, allowing Isabel to wash her hair with scented soap.

Her mother helped her comb her hair, drying it before the fire. Afterwards she wound Genevieve's hair into elaborate plaits, pinned atop her head.

'You look beautiful,' Isabel proclaimed, adding a cream-coloured veil trimmed with pearls.

'He is unworthy of her,' Helen said. 'I like it not.'

Genevieve sent a sharp look towards her mother. 'I'll not hear words against the man who is to be my husband.' Helen shrugged and placed a golden necklace encrusted with jewels around her daughter's throat. Deep emeralds accentuated the colour of the gown.

Isabel hugged Genevieve. 'All will be well. You'll see.' Touching Genevieve's cheek, she added, 'The bruise is gone.'

Genevieve lifted her fingers to the spot. Though her

wounds had healed, her spirit remained fragile. She gathered her courage and mustered a smile. 'Let us go.'

The ceremony began at twilight, after Genevieve and Bevan had bathed the feet of their guests in welcome. The young ladies had fought over the silver coin left in the basin, for it was said that she who won it would be the next to marry.

When the vows had been spoken, Bevan took her hand and the priest blessed their union. The warmth of his touch emanated through her skin, but his eyes stared forward, focused upon the priest and not her. She saw sadness in his gaze, and it hurt deeply.

Was he remembering his first wedding to Fiona, the woman he loved? Genevieve tortured herself, wondering what he was thinking.

Bevan's lips brushed against hers in a kiss of peace, so swiftly she might not have known they were there. Afterwards, the wedding guests cheered.

Tankards of mead were passed around, and the feasting began. Genevieve and Bevan were ushered to a table where the most sumptuous meats and pastries were piled.

Her parents watched them, and Genevieve tried to put on a face of happiness for their sakes. It was like seeing herself through a pool of water, silent beneath the surface, drowning amid a sea of guests. Her husband smiled when others smiled at him, answered questions, and pretended to be having a good time.

Genevieve knew better. He wore a mask of joviality, even kissing her when others teased them. His act suddenly upset her.

Was she unworthy of a husband's affections? Was she not deserving of a good marriage with a man who genuinely wanted her?

She had thought it would not be so bad, wedded to a man who would never harm her. She believed that in time they could be content with one another. But as she watched him, it hurt to know that Bevan did not view their union as a reason to celebrate.

She set down her goblet, narrowing her thoughts to that which troubled her most. Though she was not his chosen bride, not the woman he wanted, somehow she must find a way past the enmity in his heart. He desired her; that much she knew from their stolen kisses.

An icy chill grasped her spine, and she took another sip of wine to fortify herself. He would expect her to surrender her virginity, but the thought of baring herself before him was daunting.

With each passing minute her anxiety heightened. At home, the bedding ceremony embarrassed many brides. Genevieve remembered laughing women who would strip the bride of her shift, tucking her into bed naked to await her husband's embrace. She glanced around, but only friendly smiles greeted her.

When she could wait no longer, she rose from the table. If there was not a bedding custom here, then she preferred to prepare herself. She might be able to calm the terrified beating of her heart.

'Where are you going?' Bevan asked.

'To our chamber.' She offered him a weak smile. 'I am weary.'

The lie flowed from her mouth. She didn't know if she would sleep at all tonight. For that matter, she knew not if he would consummate their marriage. She had offered him the choice of not sharing her bed.

She walked away, not waiting for him to reply. She moved above stairs, turning once to look back. He met her gaze from below, and for a moment she stood transfixed by him. His tunic was an unusual shade of blue, a colour that made his strong features arresting. His hands cupped a goblet, but he did not drink.

The crowds of people seemed to disappear, and he looked upon her as though seeing her for the first time. There was a hint of reassurance upon his face.

Genevieve took a deep breath and forced herself to take another step. When at last she closed the door to their bedchamber, she sat upon a wooden stool to await him. She noticed that the servants had indeed disposed of the massive bed. In its place was a smaller bed, with new coverings. She had completely redecorated the chamber, removing all traces of its former design. Even the tapestries were gone. It was bare now, but she would make new ones.

Her fingers tapped nervously against the silk of her gown. Minutes passed, and still Bevan did not come. Genevieve removed her gown, laying aside the finery and the jewelled necklace. She slipped beneath the bedcovers, the linen soft against her bare skin.

With her eyes closed, she tried to curb her fears. He was not Hugh. Never would he strike her or humiliate her.

After an hour of waiting, she realised he did not intend to claim his bride, either.

Had she made a mistake? Was she not supposed to await him within her chamber? Her cheeks coloured as she donned a shift. Their customs were different here. Mayhap she should have gone to his room instead?

Though the idea of invading his private room made her insides go numb, she steadied herself. It need only be this one time. It was expected of her, and she'd not shirk her duty.

Closing her eyes, her last thought was that a bride should not have to go and claim her husband upon their wedding night.

Chapter Twelve

Bevan had not missed the question in Genevieve's eyes. He endured the ribald jests of his men before realizing that he could not stay below stairs for much longer without embarrassing his new wife. He took his leave from the guests, and Patrick prevented several drunken men from accompanying him.

Bevan entered his chamber alone, bolting the door behind him. Thankfully, it was not a chamber he had shared with Fiona when they had lived here. He had left that one to Genevieve. His brothers had used this room upon occasion, and it held no memories for him.

But the fortress held many memories. This time, coming home had been far different. He had recognised former servants, neighbouring tenants, and old friends at the feast. They'd seemed wary of the wedding but happy to see him once more. Bevan realised that they had been here when Genevieve had come with Hugh. He wondered if there was any animosity between them, since she was Norman. It did not seem so, but he could not be certain.

Bevan saw the wooden tub by the fire. It had been brought up before the ceremony, but he had not taken the time to bathe then. Now, the cold water offered a distraction from Genevieve. He did not doubt that she would invite him into her bed, were he to visit her. Still, he sensed fear within her. Whatever she might say, he did not think she had forgotten Hugh's beatings.

He was not even certain if she was a virgin. From the magnitude of her intimidation, he suspected other nightmares might haunt her.

Bevan stripped and sat down, sluicing water over his face and chest. As he'd hoped, the frigid bath quelled any desire he'd felt. He rose from the tub and took a drying cloth. After towelling off the water, he wrapped the cloth around his hips and sat beside the fire.

It was then that he noticed a shadow away from the bed. He reached for his dagger, but saw Genevieve step from behind one of the bed curtains. Her dark hair spilled over the thin shift she wore. She walked towards him in silence.

'Genevieve—' he began.

He could see the fear and uncertainty in her eyes. He remained motionless, not wanting to frighten her with the lust growing within him.

'I did not know if I should come,' she whispered. 'Your customs are not the same, and I thought—' She broke off, her shoulders hunched forward.

He said nothing at first, and in time she straightened. Through the thin outline of her shift her womanly curves beckoned to him. At the sight of her slender frame, he understood the courage it had taken for her to come to him. Though he should force her to go, he knew that if he uttered the words it would devastate her.

Bevan craved the feel of her in his arms, wishing that he could be the bridegroom she deserved. He took her hands in his, exerting a gentle pressure until she stood before him. He brought his palm to her cheek, his thumb coaxing her lips to open. When she allowed him to kiss her, he was lost.

She tasted of the warm summer sun, of honeyed mead and the promise of loving. In spite of his intent not to touch her, his arms slid around her waist. The feel of her soft skin made him harden, and he sat upon a stool, drawing her down to straddle his lap.

At the intimacy of their position, she tried to pull away. Her cheeks flamed, but he held her fast, until she surrendered. Though he did not intend to claim her as his bride, he wanted to ease her fears. Gently he drew his palms up her back, stroking her. Through the thin shift he saw her breasts tighten.

The drying cloth fell away until he felt her damp womanhood pressing against his shaft. He grew rigid, inhaling sharply as she tried to stand up. The motion caused her to ride against his length, and he eased her back down again.

His mouth possessed hers, the kiss intoxicating him with heat and lust. The voice of reason cried out for him to stop, but he could not find the strength to deny her.

Genevieve broke away from the kiss first, trying to catch her breath. This time he released her. She looked ready to flee from the chamber.

'Forgive me,' she breathed. 'I thought I could let you—'

'Not this eventide, Genevieve,' he breathed in a husky whisper.

Her face paled, shadowed with dismay. 'I am sorry for displeasing you.' She turned from him, but he stopped her.

'Genevieve, I cannot be a husband to you. Not in the way you want.' His body burned, but he willed himself under control. Leaning down, he picked up the fallen drying cloth and wrapped it around his hips.

'If you would grant me time, I will do what I must,' she insisted.

He led her over to the bed and turned down the covers. 'Sleep, now.'

Genevieve wanted to curse with frustration. She had managed to break through his wall of indifference for the briefest moment, only to be shut out again. It had taken all of her courage to seek him out, while she struggled to block out the terrible memories of her past.

The taunting voice of Hugh rose up in her mind. *You are a poor excuse for a woman. You should be grateful that I grant you my attentions at all.*

And here, too, she had failed. In the darkness, she huddled in the bed alone. What would it take for Bevan to see her as a wife and not a burden?

She lifted her gaze to watch him. In the firelight, his skin was molten bronze. Scarred from battle, his thigh muscles flexed as he put on his trews. His chest was bare, the sculpted torso covered with a fine mat of dark hair.

'Bevan?' she whispered.

'Tá?'

'Don't leave me. Not tonight,' she pleaded.

He met her ashamed gaze. 'I would not humiliate you in such a way, *a chroí*. Those below will think that this marriage is consummated, do not fear.'

'What about the sheets?' she asked, eyeing the clean linen. Her face turned crimson. 'The blood—' She broke off, too embarrassed to continue. At home, the sheets of a new bride were proudly displayed to show her loss of virginity.

A hint of amusement lined his face. 'It is not a custom of ours. My men will believe me when I tell them you are no longer a maiden.'

But her parents would expect to see the sheets, she realised. Custom or not, they would ask.

'May I borrow your knife?' she asked.

'Why?'

'To satisfy my father. He will expect to see my blood spilled.'

Bevan rose and unsheathed his knife. Never taking his eyes from her, he slashed a shallow cut in his hand, letting drops of his blood spill upon the sheets. 'It need not be your blood.'

Genevieve winced, but he behaved as though the gesture were of little consequence. Afterwards, he made his bed before the fire, lying on the hard wooden floor.

Genevieve thought of asking him to sleep beside her, for the sake of comfort. But she could not bring herself to speak the words. Her body aching with frustration and embarrassment, she buried her face in the mattress. Within Bevan's bedchamber dwelled the ghosts of his past. She had tricked herself into thinking she wanted a separate life away from him.

When he'd kissed her tonight, she had dreamed of a time when she could relinquish all fears and welcome him into her arms.

In the flickering of the firelight, she saw him stretch out to sleep. His back held silvery scars from former battles. His was a body that had witnessed death and vanquished its foes. But beneath the surface lay other scars. A father who had lost his only daughter. A husband who hadn't been able to protect his wife from the enemy. And a man forced to wed a woman he didn't want.

'Bevan?' she whispered, unable to stop the question tormenting her. 'Why did you wed me?'

He had been so adamant before he'd left for Tara that he could not wed her. He would have done anything to avoid it.

For a time he didn't answer, and she wondered if he'd heard her. Then at last he said, 'To keep you away from

Hugh. You would have been forced to marry him. No woman deserves such a life.'

Her eyes swam with tears at his admission. 'But my father ended the betrothal,' she whispered. 'Hugh couldn't have harmed me any more.'

Bevan turned to face her. 'I offered myself in Hugh's place. Hugh is one of the King's favourites, do not forget. But an Irish alliance is better for King Henry than an English one.'

'I suppose you are right.'

'And I don't trust Hugh. I don't believe he will give you up so easily. If anything happened to your father, he would come for you. And for Rionallís.' He softened his voice, as if to allay her fears. 'You're safe from him now.'

When he turned away from her she clenched her fists into the sheets. It would have been easier to dismiss his change of heart had she cared nothing for him. She could have closed off her heart to the stoic warrior who held her at a distance.

But not to the man who had wed her to keep her safe. And not to the man who had kissed her, awakening her body to a man's touch.

She prayed that one day he could release the memories that haunted him. Until that day there was no hope for their marriage to become anything more than an arrangement.

When Bevan awoke, Genevieve was gone. He rose from the floor, wincing at his sore shoulder, aching from the long night. He hadn't slept at all, thinking of her. Though he had considered joining her upon the bed, he did not trust himself not to touch her. She had a way of disarming his willpower and shattering it into dust.

He donned his tunic, and as he entered the Great Chamber delicious smells of pastry and warm fruit tantalised him. Ewan sat at a long table, stuffing his mouth with food.

At the sight of his brother, Bevan asked, 'Where is Genevieve?'

'I have not seen her this morn. But you should break your fast,' Ewan suggested. 'Try the apple cakes.' He used his forearm to swipe a dribble of honey away from his mouth.

The table was piled high with bowls of steaming oat pottage and cakes dripping with honey and dried apples. Bevan reached out to sample one of the pastries. The sweet crust practically melted on his tongue, and he reached for another.

'Did she make these?'

'No, but she ordered them for us. I've not had such food before in all my life,' Ewan commented. 'I may never leave.'

'Soon,' Bevan said firmly, 'you must return to Laochre.' His brother's response was to shovel in another mouthful of pottage.

Though he knew there was no reason for concern, he wondered about Genevieve's motives. He had never bothered much with food in the morning, and the sudden change gave him cause to worry about what other changes she intended to make.

After he'd finished, he went outside to find her. The frosty winter air cut through his cloak, but while traversing the grounds he saw her in the inner bailey. He stood back, watching as she helped the laundress with a steaming cauldron. Genevieve used a long pole to stir the laundry. The heat from the boiling water dampened the strands of hair at her temples, and her cheeks shone from exertion. A linen veil kept her hair back from her face.

The way she fitted in with his people, engaging in their everyday tasks, made him realise that she could belong here. She knew their language, and there was none of the cool demeanour of a Norman noblewoman. Already they did not view her as an outsider—a fact that troubled him.

She saw him and raised a hand in greeting. Bevan nodded in acknowledgement, but returned to the fortress without speaking to her. He entered the Great Chamber and went above stairs, to the old chamber he'd once shared with his wife.

He had never considered that she might make changes to Rionallís. The original bed was gone, and in its place stood a smaller one. The wooden frame was new, along with the coverings.

The tapestries were gone, too—the ones Fiona had woven with her own hands, working long hours, sometimes into the night. He remembered coming up behind her to steal a kiss while her fingers worked on the loom.

His memories had been stripped away, leaving behind only poor substitutes. The walls were bare, the room devoid of any decoration. Hurt and resentment rose up within him. Had they sold the tapestries? What had happened to the bed where he used to fall asleep with Fiona's warmth pressed against him? Their child had been conceived in that bed, and now it was gone.

Moments later the door opened, and Genevieve stood at the entrance. She offered a smile of greeting. 'Good morn to you.'

'Where is the bed?' he asked. 'And the tapestries?'

Her smile faded. When she did not answer, he gripped her by the shoulders. 'Where are they?'

'I know not where the tapestries are,' she said. His fingers tightened upon her, his fury so great he knew his grip would bruise her delicate skin.

'I ordered the bed destroyed,' she said. 'I told them to burn it.'

Burned. He couldn't understand why she would do such a thing. He should never have given this chamber to her. It would have been better to lock it up, giving him at least one place where he could hold fast to his memories.

Now they were gone, seared into ashes. All because of her orders. Bevan closed his eyes and released her. He feared what he might do, and so he stepped away.

'Why?' he demanded.

She shook her head, tears welling in her eyes. 'Because I couldn't face it again. I could never lie there with you without remembering the way Hugh used to beat me.'

'I never intended to lie with you,' he said coldly.

Her face blanched, and she swiped at the tears. For a moment it was as if he were standing outside his body, as another person. He knew his words cut her deeply, but he could not stop them.

'Leave me,' he said, his voice weary. 'And make no more changes here. This is my home, and I want it the way it was.'

When she did not move, he shouted, 'Go!'

She fled, and he buried his face in his hands. He regretted marrying her, letting her make changes. Rionallís was not, and never would be, the same.

Genevieve sat beside her parents at the midday meal, the food tasting like dust in her mouth. Bevan's rebuke had hurt, and she could not anticipate what else might provoke his temper.

She endured another hour of the meal, forcing herself to drink a goblet of elderberry wine. Her mother retired up to her chamber, and Thomas de Renalt reached out to touch Genevieve's hand.

'So glum are you? Is aught the matter? Did he harm you?'

An embarrassed look crossed her father's face at the mention of her wedding night. The servants had shown him the sheets, and she knew the bloodstains had satisfied him. Even so, guilt suffused her at the deception.

She shook her head. 'He did not harm me, Papa.'

'The Irishman will make a good husband for you, I am certain,' her father stated. 'His fighting skills are legendary among his people.'

'He was forced to wed me,' she said. 'What kind of a beginning to marriage is that?'

'Some of the best marriages have inauspicious beginnings,' he commented. 'And they turn out rather well in spite of them. Give it time, Genevieve. You shall remain here, and King Henry will have loyal Normans near to him whenever he has the need.'

A bitterness rose up within her. 'Aye, I will remain here. Wed to a man who despises me.'

'Now, now. You are a grown woman, Genevieve. Not a child. Sulking does not become you.'

She knew he was right, and he successfully coaxed a smile. 'Will you stay for a time?'

He shook his head. 'I'm afraid not. Henry has ordered our return to England within a sennight. But I will send a servant to you—one who will summon your mother and me if MacEgan lays a finger upon you.'

'Bevan would never do that,' Genevieve said. 'He nearly killed Hugh for harming me.'

The Earl gave a nod of approval, laying a hand upon her shoulder. 'I am sorry for what happened. Had I known of it sooner I would have come for you. You must know this.'

Genevieve bowed her head, hiding the tears that threatened. He squeezed her hand. 'You are a beautiful woman, Genevieve, with a loving heart. Go to your husband. Show him who you are.'

'It will be all right,' she said wearily.

Her father smiled. 'You will conquer this warrior's heart, my Genevieve. Of that I have no doubt.'

Genevieve embraced him, and he tapped her chin with his finger. 'We depart on the morrow for England. Should you need us, you have only to send word.'

With her father's strong arms around her, she took comfort. 'Thank you, Papa.'

'Now, off with you.' Her father gave a wave of dismissal. 'I intend to sample this fine poteen before your mother finds out.' He took a sip of the strong liquor, coughing while raising a toast to her.

'I'll send a barrel home with you,' Genevieve promised.

'You are my most beloved daughter,' he sighed, downing another sip.

Bevan did not sleep in their chamber that night, and Genevieve slept poorly. She tossed upon the straw mattress while imagining him in his own chamber, thankful to be away from her.

The following morn she said farewell to her parents, and her mother promised to visit again in the spring. Lord Thomas had teased about grandchildren, and Genevieve had struggled to maintain her smile. There would be no children in her future. Not with Bevan.

After they had gone, she busied herself with tasks around the fortress. Her arms strained as she struggled to lift a heavy sack of grain. She had long since dried her tears, and vowed she would not pity herself. She had married Bevan knowing he did not want a wife. The hard labour kept her mind from the sorrow coiling around her heart.

'Put that down, Lady Genevieve!' A barrel-shaped woman with speckled raven hair swatted at Genevieve with a rag. 'We've men for lifting heavy things.'

'I can manage,' Genevieve said. She dragged the sack of grain into a corner, her arms burning with the effort.

''Tis not your place to do such work,' the woman argued. 'Ye could injure a babe, if ye've one started.'

'There will be no babe,' she said dully.

She thought of young Declan, his baby softness nestled against her cheek, and the raw ache threatened to consume her. Why had she ever thought she could gain Bevan's affections? He had been honest with her from the first moment. She would never win his heart, and it was useless to try.

'Oh, there'll be a babe, sure enough. Those MacEgan men…' The woman gave an appreciative sigh. 'There's not a woman I know of who can resist them. It's lucky ye are, being wed to Bevan. He's a good master, and a fair man. Much better than that Norman ye were betrothed to.' The woman spat on the ground in memory.

Genevieve braved a smile. 'Aye, you are right. What is your name?'

'I am Mairi.'

Genevieve clasped Mairi's hands in greeting. 'I am glad to meet you.'

Mairi led Genevieve by the hand. 'The women and I wondered about ye. We saw what Marstowe did, and I hope his soul burns for it. But there was naught any of us could do.' She crossed herself. 'He'd only have killed another innocent.'

'Another?'

'*Tá.* He had poor Maureen killed when she told him where Bevan had taken you. The bastard.' Mairi led Genevieve outside, handing her a *brat*. She accepted the long length of wool, wrapping it around her shoulders. 'Ye must cover up, for 'tis quite cold.'

'Where are we going?'

'To visit the tenants. They're eager to meet ye, as I was. We never had the chance when ye were betrothed to that demon.' With a nudge, Mairi added, 'They want to know what sort of woman would wed our Bevan.'

'A foolish one,' Genevieve said. 'I am a MacEgan now, but his name is all I have.'

'Feeling sorry for ourselves, are we?' Mairi said, pulling Genevieve into the inner bailey. The icy air sliced against her face, and she pulled her *brat* tighter around her shoulders. 'If ye want a good marriage, heed my advice. Be a strong woman and know your own mind. When ye have your own happiness, a happy marriage ye'll make. There's no quicker way to lose a man than to chase after him. Make him come after ye. That's what I say.'

'Are you married?' Genevieve asked.

Mairi laughed. 'Five times, counting this last one. I've buried four of them, God rest their souls. But those that died, died happy. A good romp in the bedchamber keeps a man faithful.'

Genevieve blushed at the bawdy reference. When they reached the stables, Mairi told the groom to bring out a horse for Genevieve. 'What about you?' Genevieve asked.

'I've no need for a horse. I'll walk. But, as the lady of Rionallís, you should ride.'

Genevieve shook her head, dismissing the groom. 'I'll walk alongside you.' She thought she detected a glimmer of approval in Mairi's eyes.

As they journeyed towards the tenant farms, Mairi pointed out the names of the people, adding gossip whenever she could.

Genevieve saw an expanse of farmland, neatly divided into smaller plots with thatched cottages. Herds of cattle and pigs huddled around grain that had been set out for them in wooden troughs amidst the snow. One tenant broke a layer of ice over the water in another trough. He smiled and waved at Mairi as they passed.

Genevieve wanted to meet them and grow better acquainted. An idea occurred to her, and she stopped walking. 'We've not decorated Rionallís,' she said. 'Alban Arthuan is past, but we've not had any feasting or celebrations here for Christmas. With all that's happened, I did not think of it.'

Mairi brightened. 'You are right, my lady. I'll bring some girls up to help. A celebration is exactly what ye need to take your mind off of the troubles ye have.'

'Call me Genevieve,' she said. A part of her warmed at the idea of decorating the Great Chamber for the Christmas celebration. 'Is there anyone here who could play music this eve?'

She remembered the harp she had played at Laochre, and longing rose up at the memory. Bevan had not seemed to mind, but she grew nervous at the thought of playing before the Irish people. Perhaps they would not like her songs.

No, it was best to let others play. She would enjoy their songs and learn them when she could.

'Every man here thinks himself a musician,' Mairi said, rolling her eyes. 'But I'll see if Eoin can bring his pipes. Do not ask him to sing, though.'

Genevieve hugged her *brat* around herself, brimming with excitement. She would *not* let Bevan's anger diminish the celebration. But there was one way to ease his ill spirits.

'Do you know where the women put the tapestries that used to hang in my chamber?' Genevieve asked. Mairi nodded. 'Bring them. We'll hang them in the Great Chamber.'

She could do that much for Bevan, by way of apology. But she refused to have any trace of Fiona or Hugh in their chamber. She would begin weaving tapestries of her own, adorning the chamber with wall hangings that had no memories save the new ones she would make.

Mairi was right. It was time to stop feeling sorry for herself.

Chapter Thirteen

Genevieve supervised the decorating of the Great Chamber, while outside another winter storm raged. She had not seen Bevan since that morn, and she suspected he was avoiding her.

She had arranged for Fiona's tapestries to be hung on the back wall of the Chamber. She spread garlands of holly and greenery around the room, placing candles in the windows to light the path of the Holy Child. The cook had agreed to roast a suckling pig and to prepare salmon, lamb, and salted eels for the feast. Her father had replenished the stores of food depleted by Hugh and his men as part of her wedding gifts. Bevan had given twenty horses, several barrels of poteen, and gifts of silver as her bride price. The silver would satisfy her mother, Genevieve knew.

A maid had brought forth elderberry wine, mead, and poteen from the cellar, to quench the thirst of the guests. For dessert, Genevieve had the cook prepare cakes dripping with honey and finely chopped hazelnuts.

Mairi had introduced her to some of the tenants' wives, and Genevieve befriended them as they worked alongside one another, adding festive touches to the Great Chamber. They spoke not of her betrothal to Hugh, and for that she was grateful.

Hugh had never allowed her to leave Rionallís, claiming that as a noblewoman she had no place among the freemen. She had tried to protest that as the lady of the castle it was her duty. The argument had earned her another beating, and so she had held her tongue while the steward performed her duties.

Now, she recognised that it had been yet another way to hold her prisoner. Hugh had trusted none of the Irish, and Genevieve knew his reputation was that of a cold-hearted *Gaillabh*—a Norman outsider.

Behind her, she heard Ewan chattering to Bevan, boasting of his new skills in swordplay. Genevieve busied herself adjusting a garland, wondering what her husband would say when he saw their decorations. His gaze travelled the length of the room, surveying her handiwork.

When he saw the tapestries, she noticed a change coming over him, a subtle relaxation of his features. His eyes met hers, and Genevieve sensed forgiveness in the nod of greeting.

'The tenants are going to celebrate Christmas with us this eve,' she said. 'Will you come?' She hoped that he would not deny her the chance to welcome the people.

He seemed agreeable. '*Tá*, I will come.'

'Good.'

The discomfort stretched on, and finally Genevieve excused herself to finish the decorating. Bevan did not stay to watch, and she felt relieved without his eyes watching every move.

At last, Genevieve dismissed the ladies to prepare for the feast. Ewan hung around, casting glances at an auburn-haired girl with deep brown eyes. The girl ignored him, and Genevieve pitied Ewan's lovesick expression. He consoled himself by snatching a honey cake from a platter.

'Those are for the celebration tonight,' Genevieve reminded him. Ewan started to put it back, but she shook her head. 'Just the one.'

He nodded his thanks and devoured it, licking his fingertips. A servant interrupted Genevieve moments later, giving her a small folded parchment sealed with wax.

She thanked him and broke the seal. Inside no words were written, but a frayed blue ribbon fell out. She recognised the token immediately. It was a ribbon Hugh had given her once, from when he had courted her affections.

It was a reminder. A chilling one. He had not gone to England, as ordered.

'Did you see who sent this?' she asked the servant.

The servant shook his head. 'One of the tenant's children gave it to me. It was given to him by a messenger he did not recognise.'

A shadow crossed over her chair, and Genevieve saw Ewan standing before her. 'What is it?' he asked.

'It is from Hugh,' she answered, showing him the ribbon.

Ewan straightened and rested his hand upon his sword, as if poised for a fight. 'Has he threatened you?'

'No.' Genevieve did not know what Hugh intended by the ribbon, but she would not allow him to frighten her. She rose to her feet and moved towards the hearth. Tossing the ribbon into the flames, she watched as it curled and caught flame. 'We will let the matter rest.'

'Bevan should know of this.'

'No.' Genevieve knew the ribbon was meant to cause her fear. She had no desire for Bevan to track down Sir Hugh and risk further injury. Her marriage had ended any threat Hugh might have posed.

'You are certain you do not wish for me to find out why he sent it?' Ewan asked.

'It's part of the past now.' As the ribbon darkened into ashes, she resolved not to think of it again. She would host the Christmas celebration, and in time Hugh would understand that she was not going to allow her past to rule the future.

When the roasted pig's bones lay exposed, the tender meat devoured until only fragments remained, all gathered around to hear the stories of Trahern MacEgan. He had spent the past few months travelling across Éireann, and had only just returned home. Bevan had invited him to share in their Christmas celebration.

Solid as an oak, Trahern had a curling black beard and long locks that fell across his shoulders. His chest was so large, no woman there could span it with her arms, and he had encouraged all to try. Genevieve had been embarrassed, but had joined in on the fun when urged by Ewan.

'How many brothers do you have?' she asked Bevan when he joined in the merriment. 'I thought I'd met all of you.'

'There are five of us living,' he said. 'Our eldest brother, Liam, died in battle years ago. Patrick is now the eldest, then me, then Trahern, Connor, and Ewan.' He settled back into a chair while Trahern began his stories.

'Six sons,' she mused, dropping her voice lower so as not to interrupt the tale. 'Most fathers would be pleased at that. No daughters?'

Bevan shook his head. 'My mother kept hoping, but God saw fit to give her us.' He passed her a full cup of mead, taking a swallow from his own goblet. 'What about you? Have you brothers or sisters?'

She nodded. 'Two brothers. James is the eldest, then Michael.' She took a deep sip of mead. 'It's a good thing Michael was in Scotland and didn't know what Hugh did to me. He has a vicious temper.'

'Then likely he and I would understand each other,' Bevan said. 'I've a vicious temper when it comes to Hugh as well.' His eyes had turned dark, watching her as though he were trying to memorise her features. Her skin grew warm, and she turned her attention to her goblet.

'Did you have other suitors besides Hugh?' Bevan asked. He accepted a pitcher from a passing servant. Then he covered her fingers with his while he refilled her cup. The contact of his palm sent a light thrill within her.

'I did.' Genevieve hid her disappointment when he withdrew his hand. 'A few were rather handsome.'

His mouth narrowed. 'I am rather handsome.'

A startled laugh burst forth before she could suppress it. 'Of course you are.'

Bevan glanced away, and she realised she'd embarrassed him. A faint colour appeared in his cheeks. 'I was not being serious.'

'I was.' She reached out to touch the fresh scar. Unable to stop herself, she caressed his cheek.

He stared at her, as if he wanted to kiss her. She held her breath, but he did not move. Instead his attention shifted back to his brother Trahern.

'I've heard this one before. He's got a knack for making any tale funny.'

Genevieve did not respond, feeling once again that she'd been pushed away. She'd drunk the mead too quickly, and her head spun with the effects.

'What happened to your parents?' Genevieve asked, though she already suspected they were gone.

'They died a few years back. Before I wed Fiona. They would never have approved of our match,' he added.

His confession surprised her. She would have thought any parents would have been glad to claim the saintly Fiona as a daughter. She mentally rebuked herself for being spiteful. But a secret part of her felt satisfaction that at least someone had not worshipped Fiona.

'Why wouldn't they have approved?'

'Da hated the Ó Callahans—every last one of them.' When Trahern's tale ended, the room erupted in laughter and applause. Bevan raised his goblet in a toast, and his brother began another story. 'He called them cattle thieves and worse. But we all knew the truth.'

'What do you mean?'

'They were enemies because of my mother. The Ó Callahan king wanted to wed her, and so did Da.'

'But your mother chose to wed your father?'

'No, she did not.' Bevan refilled Genevieve's goblet with more mead, though she had already drunk enough to make her dizzy. 'She wanted Ó Callahan, but her father forced her to marry Da.' Bevan sipped his own drink.

'Did she learn to love your father?'

'She tried to divorce him, but he'd not allow it. He had to woo her for a time, it is said.' Bevan's face twitched, as if hiding a smile. 'Every sennight she went to the courts demanding a divorce, and each time Da convinced her to give their marriage another try.'

Genevieve could not imagine a woman trying to divorce her husband. Such a thing was rare in England, unless there was a close degree of kinship between a husband and wife. 'They would allow a woman to divorce her husband?'

Bevan nodded. 'There are seven reasons why she may do so and still keep her *coibche*—her dowry. But our mother could not convince the courts without losing everything, and so she stayed. She did love him in the end,' he remarked.

'How do you know?'

'When he died from a poisoned battle wound, she lay down beside him and held his hand. That was how we found him, with her hand in his. She died a few months later.'

'Love is a rare thing in a marriage,' Genevieve said. 'Sometimes I envy the peasants, because they may wed whomever they want.'

'All can marry of their choosing here,' Bevan said. 'So long as their parents approve of the match.'

Genevieve suddenly wished that Bevan had never met Fiona. Then he would have been free to love her. They were jealous thoughts, but then again, they were in her head. She could think whatever she wanted.

'How did you meet your wife?' Genevieve asked. Her stomach was twisting from the mead. Food would settle her queasiness, so she ate a piece of crusty bread.

'She was walking alone in the woods when she came across a boar. It charged her, and I killed it. She had climbed up a tree to escape and couldn't get down again.' Bevan took another sip from his goblet. 'She never cared for heights.'

Trahern accepted a large tankard of ale from a maid and started another tale in his deep, booming voice. 'There once was a lass from Kilkenny, who took pity upon a man left for dead by the roadside…'

As the tale went on, Genevieve grew absorbed in the magical legend, of a woman who fell in love with a changeling. The voices blended together into a hazy buzzing.

Ewan approached and sat beside her. 'Don't fall asleep,' he urged. Genevieve blinked, and saw that the story had ended. Bevan had gone to join his kinsmen. All the men of Rionallís had risen, forming a line with swords.

'What is going on?'

'The games are about to begin. The men will compete to

show off their fighting skills. There are prizes for the winners.'

'What kinds of prizes?' She yawned and let Ewan lead her closer, to a bench where the women sat watching. A burly soldier had stripped off his tunic, revealing a heavily muscled chest. The other men removed their outer garments as well, to the shrill cheering of the women.

'It depends. Sometimes an animal, like a cow or a pig. Sometimes money. Sometimes a kiss from their choice of maiden.'

He'd better not kiss his choice of maiden, Genevieve thought when she saw Bevan among the fighters. The jealousy had returned, though she tried to keep more ladylike thoughts in her head.

Trahern raised his arms, and the crowd cheered. With a mighty swing, he rammed his fist into the first soldier's gut. The man gasped, stumbled, but held his ground.

'What is he doing?' Genevieve asked, horrified.

'A test of strength. A man has to be able to handle pain in battle,' Ewan explained. 'Trahern is the strongest here.'

Trahern continued down the line, felling some of the men with his punches, cracking the ribs of a few others, Genevieve was certain. When he reached Bevan, a hush fell over the crowd.

'Bevan is wounded,' she whispered, remembering his shoulder. 'He wouldn't harm his own brother, would he?'

'Especially his brother,' Ewan commented.

But even as Trahern's fist shot towards Bevan, her husband caught the man's wrist. Neatly twisting it, he moved in such a way that Trahern lost his balance and hit the floor. Bevan rested his boot upon his brother's throat.

'You've still not learned to best me in all your travels, I see.'

Trahern gave a hearty laugh. Grasping Bevan's wrist, he hauled himself to his feet. With a wicked roll to his hips, he leered, 'I can best you in one area, brother. At least, that's what the women tell me.'

Genevieve joined in the laughter, but her concentration was focused on Bevan. The mead had gone to her head, and she thought what a fine warrior she had married. Without the tunic, his corded muscles gleamed in the firelight.

Mine, she thought.

Her body grew warmer as she imagined what it would be like if he cast off his vow and made her his wife in truth.

Mairi slid onto the bench beside Genevieve. 'The next contest is one of the sword. Bevan is the best of all, but he'll not compete in this one.'

'Why not?' Genevieve's gaze followed her husband as he donned his tunic.

'The prize for this sword competition is a kiss. The winner may choose a lady, and she must grant him that boon.'

'Can anyone enter?' Genevieve asked, as she watched Bevan sit closer to the competitors.

'*Tá.* There, you see—the first match is begun.'

Two soldiers faced off with their swords, parrying blows and lunging. The heavy clang of metal echoed in the stone chamber as the fighters were surrounded by a throng of cheering spectators. A few of the women had moved closer, primping and awaiting the winner to make his choice.

At long last one of the swordsmen drew blood, and the loser bowed in defeat. The winner took the hand of one of the maidens and drew her into a lusty kiss.

Seeing the hearty embrace of the two lovers made something stir inside of Genevieve. Though it might be wrong, she could not banish the thoughts from her mind. As swordsman after swordsman joined in the competition, the idea grew stronger in her head. She wanted to destroy the memory of Hugh forever and face her fears.

The crowd had grown quiet once more as the last fighter stepped into the circle, his sword drawn.

'Will no one fight me?' he demanded.

The swordsman was Ewan. Surrounded by the other soldiers, his thin body appeared gangly and weak. Genevieve remembered the long hours he'd trained, and how he'd been practising his footwork.

They expected him to lose, she realised. His reputation as a poor fighter made them reluctant to humiliate him.

But she believed he had promise as a fighter, young though he was. She moved closer to the crowd and took a sword away from one of the bystanders. The hilt warmed within her grasp, and she steadied her wrist from its heavy weight.

The bystander started to protest, but Genevieve silenced him with a hand. She held out her sword, smiling at Ewan. 'I will fight you.'

Chapter Fourteen

Loud guffaws and jeers met her challenge. Genevieve straightened her posture and glared at the onlookers. Bevan shook his head, intending to stop the swordfight. Before he could reach her, she tilted the sword towards him. 'Step away, husband. This is my challenge, not yours.'

'I'll not allow you to—'

Genevieve brandished the sword, poking it towards his chest. 'You may fight me after I fight him.'

The crowd roared at that, and Trahern grabbed his brother across the ribs, holding him back. 'I want to see her fight.' He grinned, giving a nod of encouragement to Genevieve.

'Can you best a woman, boy?' one jeered.

Their laughter infuriated Ewan, and he started to lower his sword out of humiliation.

'Do not listen to them,' Genevieve said. 'Show them how you've been practising.'

He looked doubtful, but Genevieve repeated, 'Show them.'

When he didn't move, she decided she would have to initiate the fight by swinging her sword at him. He waited until the last moment before blocking the blade.

'Is that all you can do?' she taunted. She was rewarded with a glower from Ewan.

He circled her, and struck with an arm-numbing blow. She barely defended herself from his first strike.

His sword moved in the patterns they had practised together over the past few days, and Genevieve saw he was trying to go easy on her. He didn't want to fight her, but he didn't want to make it appear that he was incapable of fighting a woman.

She was going to have to make him look good. And the only way to do that was to fight better herself. She swung her sword at him with all her strength, and by instinct he met her blow with a parry. The effects of the mead caused her to stumble, but she caught her balance in time to dodge his next thrust.

The crowd had grown silent as the swordfight continued. Ewan's feet moved in the intricate patterns, twisting this way and that. She saw an opening to strike at him, because his eyes were on his footwork again. She let the opportunity go by, not wanting to make him look like a failure. When she saw his gaze flicker back, she struck again, only to be dealt a jarring blow that made her teeth rattle.

He had relaxed finally, focusing his attention on the mock battle. His sword moved more rapidly, and Genevieve's arm ached with the effort of defending herself. She knew she wouldn't last much longer. Ewan seemed to sense this, for he met her glance. A shared bargain was made between them, and with the next lunge they both raised their swords and ended the competition.

'I would not draw the blood of my brother's wife,' Ewan declared with a cocky grin.

Trahern gave a hearty laugh and clasped their arms, raising them in victory. 'I say they both deserve the winner's prize. Ewan, go and choose your lass.'

Ewan's face turned scarlet, but he took the hand of the young girl with auburn braids. She giggled as he kissed her, blushing at the same time.

'And you, Genevieve—whom shall you kiss?' Trahern puckered up his lips. The crowd laughed. Genevieve patted Trahern's cheek, but shook her head, stepping past the bystanders. Her concentration focused on Bevan.

'He is my choice,' she said, taking her husband's hand. The people roared their approval as Genevieve leaned towards Bevan's scarred face.

Tension lined his face, but she knew he would not shame her by refusing the kiss. He would feign interest, even kiss her back. But it would not be real.

His mask of indifference had returned. She should just kiss him and finish it. But, oh, it hurt to think that he did not want her. The pretence had ruined it all.

She brushed a soft kiss across his lips, and fled before he could react. Behind her, she heard Eoin playing the pipes. The crowd had begun their dancing. No one would pursue her. She escaped up the stairs to a narrow passageway that led to their chamber.

Bevan felt the way he had the first time he'd hunted with his father. He remembered the fear in the eyes of the doe before he'd shot her down with an arrow.

Genevieve had looked at him that way just now, fearful, and yet hoping for a second chance. He hadn't given it. He had planned to give her the kiss she wanted, making it look as if all were well between them—a hearty kiss between husband and wife. But she had left him standing alone, after granting a kiss that a child might give to a parent. He found himself going after her, not really knowing why.

He saw her standing at the door to her chamber, her face

pressed against the wall, her shoulders trembling. He had made her cry.

Regret pulled at him, and he knew there was only one way to mend the torn feelings.

'Genevieve,' he whispered softly. 'Come here.'

She turned, and he saw the despair in her eyes. Bevan closed the distance between them, cupping her face in his hands. He couldn't say why, but he felt the need to kiss her truly.

He tasted the salt of her tears, but soon the warmth of her mouth distracted him. She drew in her breath and he deepened the kiss, coaxing her mouth to open. Her arms wrapped around his neck, her thumbs softly stroking his nape.

The kiss was gentle, a humble offering of healing. Tongues mingled, and this time he didn't fight the rush of desire coursing through him. His hands moved down to her hips as he lost himself in her.

'Bevan, you don't have to—'

'Shh.' He covered her mouth with his again, ignoring the voices of protest in his mind. He knew this was wrong, knew he should never have started it. But in the name of Lug, he wanted her. He wanted to feel her softness in his arms.

He opened the door to their bedchamber and bolted it behind them. Then he took her back into his arms, pressing her against the wall. His hands fumbled with the laces of her gown, and he felt her warm skin. He cupped her breasts, stroking the tips while he plundered her mouth.

Desire roared through him with the force of a tempest. Her knees buckled and he caught her, lifting her against him. His mind was blessedly empty of everything but her.

He balanced her weight against the wall, his heart thundering while he sought her bare skin. Linen tore and laces fell away as his mouth covered her nipple.

It was then that he noticed she had stopped responding to him. Tears streamed down her face and she clutched his arms. She hadn't fought him, but the terrible fear in her eyes made him aware of what he'd done. He'd torn her clothing in an effort to be close to her, not thinking of her former suffering.

Genevieve was not ready to share his bed, no matter what she might say. The realization was like a bucket of cold water upon his lust.

'I am sorry.' He released her, and she slid in a boneless heap to the floor, her arms wrapped around her knees. 'I didn't mean to frighten you. I just—'

He raked his hand through his hair, not knowing what to say. 'I would never hurt you, Genevieve. I swear it.'

She said nothing, nor would she look at him.

'I'll leave, if that's what you want,' he said.

'No.' She kept her head down, but whispered, 'Don't leave.'

He sat beside her, shoulder to shoulder. 'You made me forget myself.'

'I thought I was over him. I thought it would be different with you.'

Her words struck him like a fist. He didn't like being compared to Hugh, not in any way. He wanted to argue that he *was* different.

But hadn't he just shown her otherwise? He'd lost his control, forcing her to kiss him. 'I won't bother you again,' he promised. 'It should never have happened.'

'I know we must consummate our marriage once,' she whispered. 'After that you need not come to me. I won't ask it of you.'

'It isn't your fault, Genevieve. I pushed you too far, and you were not ready.'

Slowly, she sat up. Though her tears remained, he saw a

fierce determination. 'I can be,' she insisted. 'Teach me not to fear. I promise I won't push you away. Just…have patience with me.'

'You don't know what you are asking me.' He didn't have that kind of restraint. And it was becoming harder to silence the voices that reminded him he was betraying Fiona. He didn't want to think of his first wife any more. He was tired of the guilt weighing upon him.

Her palm reached up to his scar. 'I trust you,' she whispered.

He didn't want this kind of responsibility. His body craved her, *tá,* but he wasn't the right man.

He started to refuse again, but the words tangled in his mouth. She laid her cheek against his, and his arms folded around her. He couldn't speak, but merely held her. He wondered if he had enough honour to turn her away.

Genevieve tried to mask her emotions. She hadn't known the fear would return like that. Not with Bevan. But she'd never experienced the onslaught of feelings that had rushed through her, a sensation as though she were burning. When he had pressed her against the wall her nightmares had returned. Hugh had once held her against a wall, beating her until she lost consciousness.

No. She would not think of him any longer. She would keep her vow to reclaim her freedom. If she could just force herself to lie still, to submit to Bevan, she felt certain he would drive away her ghosts.

His thumb grazed a path across the neckline of her gown, sliding down to her waist. Slowly, Bevan drew her to face him.

His hands moved to her veil, and he waited for her to pull away. When she did not, he unfastened it, letting her hair fall across her shoulders. The silken mass hung below her waist in dark waves.

He threaded his hands in her hair and noted the tension that returned to her body. She was still afraid, though she fought it.

Though he wanted to bed her, wanted to take the pleasure he'd denied himself for over two years, it was her fear that made him pause. He knew he could teach her not to be afraid of a man's touch. As long as he did not consummate the marriage he could keep a tenuous hold on his vow of faithfulness to Fiona.

Genevieve's hands rested upon his chest. Tentatively she explored his bare skin beneath the tunic, tracing the outline of his muscles. He closed his eyes, enjoying the feel of her fingertips.

So long. It had been so very long since he'd let anyone touch him. The goodness of her was like a balm to his spirit.

'Are you certain about this?' she asked. Her fear was audible from the tremble in her voice. 'If you do not want me—'

He placed a finger over her lips, letting his hand rest on her waist. He wanted her so badly his body was ready to ignite at her touch. She had come to him, wanting him to drive out her demons. And he would this night. He could bring her to fulfilment, chasing away her fears without forsaking his vow to Fiona.

He placed her arms around his neck and leaned in. Her lips met his, opening when he prodded her with his tongue. When at last she surrendered, he slid his tongue inside the warmth of her mouth, the fire of his need growing stronger.

The vow of fidelity was so strained he was ready to snap. This was his new wife. Before God, he was meant to make her his. And she was eager to learn everything he could teach her.

Bed her, his lust urged him.

He closed his eyes, wondering why he was keeping a vow

to a woman who was dead. Just as Hugh still ruled Genevieve with the legacy of fear, Fiona still ruled his heart.

Genevieve broke away, her hands trembling. He saw fear in her eyes, but there was also trust. She let him see every feeling, every part of her.

'What do you—?' She stumbled over the words, then took a deep breath. 'What do you want me to do?'

'Nothing.' A tightness rose in his throat at her confession. He couldn't name the feelings he had for her, but she had managed to push away the darkness in his life. 'It's too soon for you, *a chroí.*'

He was lying. It was too soon for *him.* His heart hovered on the edge of a precipice, knowing it was time to let Fiona go. But even as he touched Genevieve, even as he warmed to the idea of loving her, he wasn't ready to cast away his loyalty to Fiona.

But he could pleasure Genevieve, bring her to fulfilment and drive away her nightmares.

'Shall I leave?' she asked.

He shook his head. His hands framed her face, his thumbs stroking her cheek. He brought his palms down to her shoulders, his gaze searching.

Genevieve wondered what he was thinking, why he hadn't responded to her words. Then his mouth descended on hers again, in a hot storm of need and desire. She shivered, clinging to him as her skin grew warm. His muscles flexed beneath her palms, and she moved her hands over his skin. His kiss invoked aching feelings of need, and liquid heat rushed between her thighs.

The fear rose up in the pit of her stomach, though he did nothing more than kiss her. She fought against the rising tide of desire filling up inside of her, afraid to let go.

Bevan released her, but kept her hands in his. Confusion

clouded her mind. He brought her palm to his lips, flicking his tongue across the centre. She shivered at the strange feelings that flared again.

'You are beautiful, Genevieve.' He took a strand of her hair and brought it to his lips. 'No matter what he ever said to you, believe it.'

His hand cupped her cheek, his thumb grazing the soft skin beneath her chin. He dipped and kissed the softness, sending a violent shiver through her. Her skin warmed with anticipation.

He spoke in Irish, murmuring words of endearment, words that touched her heart. As he spoke, his lips trailed down her collarbone to the swell above her breasts.

'For this night I'll show you how a husband would seek to please his wife.'

He took her to his bed, laying her down upon it. She trembled, fighting to push the bad memories away. Bevan's mouth covered her nipple, dampening the linen of her shift. A rush of heat flooded her as his tongue circled the hardened tip. Her breath erupted in a gasp as he suckled one breast while stroking the other with his hand. His hand moved down until he reached the juncture of her hips, and his thumb found the centre of her pleasure.

She could hardly breathe as his mouth continued its sweet torment across her breast. And she sensed there was more.

'I need you,' she whispered, unable to stop the words. In response, his mouth covered hers, kissing her deeply. She was afraid he would stop, afraid he would be thinking of his first wife and push her away. But she couldn't let him arouse such sensations within her without telling him how she felt.

She pulled him towards her, running her hands over his warm skin, down to his hips. He stood and removed his trews, naked before her. His manhood was thick and hard. Genevieve sat up on the bed, staring at him.

'Do you want to touch me?' he whispered.

Genevieve shied away, but he brought her hand to grasp the length of his shaft. She had never touched any man in such a way. Hugh had delighted in overpowering her with his strength, holding her down until she wept with shame. Though he had not taken her maidenhead, had never raped her, she had known there would come a time when he would.

Had it not been for his arrogance, his insistence that he could make her want him, it might have come. But it had not.

There was no shame with Bevan, only a new awakening. And with the awakening came the realisation that she was falling in love with him. It hurt too much, knowing that he would never love her in return.

She hoped that one day he might look upon her as more than a wife and companion. And she consoled herself with the knowledge that he did desire her.

She took Bevan in her hands, and his eyes closed as he leaned back, letting her explore him. He remained motionless while she stroked his length. She found that he grew harder when she used a rhythm, his breath growing ragged.

Then he took hold of her hand and brought it to his lips. Bevan reclined on the bed beside her, tracing a single finger along the linen of her shift. 'I made a vow, and that vow I'll keep. But not if you keep touching me the way you do.'

She knew not which vow he spoke of, but it gave her a small sense of victory that she had the power to make him forget himself.

He nestled her backside against him, cradling her in his arms. With one hand he stroked her breasts, and with the other he caressed a path down her stomach to the wetness between her thighs. He slipped a single finger inside her, using his thumb to rub against her while the other hand tormented her breasts.

The violent feelings of longing rushed back, and Genevieve arched her body at the sensations of pleasure. She strained as the heat intensified. Bevan rubbed harder against her nipple, and then he slipped a second finger inside her.

She cried out as he continued to move his fingers in and out. He lowered his mouth to her shoulder, nipping lightly as his thumb increased the pressure on her hardened centre of pleasure.

All at once a stream of white-hot release shattered her, suffusing her with the most incredible feelings of fulfilment. He held her as the tremors pulsed through her, tilting her chin to recapture her lips.

He had made it beautiful for her, asking nothing in return. But she wanted to give back to him, to show him how much she cared for him.

She could feel the rigidity of his erection against her spine as he cradled her in his arms.

She moved away and sat up, straddling his hips. With her hands, she cupped his arousal. Bevan flinched as if in pain, groaning, but she sensed he felt desire at her touch. Encouraged, she stroked upward, and his manhood rubbed against her palms.

Bevan captured her wrists. 'Don't.'

'Let me,' she whispered. 'Let me give you what you gave to me.' She removed her shift, letting him see her bare breasts. Leaning down to kiss him, she grazed the hardened tips across his chest.

The feel of his hot length against her wetness only made her want to feel him inside her.

'Please, Bevan,' she whispered.

The pained expression on his face made her want to give to him every feeling, every sensation he had given to her.

Very gently, he lifted his hips and moved her to the side. He raised her arms and adjusted her shift over her body once more. The unyielding look in his eyes told her he would not change his mind.

He kissed her again and drew her against him. 'Sleep, Genevieve.'

Her body burned with unfulfilled desire, as she knew his did. She could not understand why he had turned her away. He was not indifferent towards her. She could only pray that somehow she could break through the shield around his heart.

The small garden lay covered in snow, its barren shrubs laced with a frosting of ice. In the quiet before dawn, Bevan walked towards the gnarled walnut tree and the twin mounds beneath it.

He knelt before the graves. A rosebush had been planted between them to offer flowers in the spring. The canes stood bare and thorny, devoid of life. He laid his palm across the snow covering his daughter's grave first.

He was grateful that at least he had known the sweetness of his child's embrace and the song of her laughter. Even though her time had been short, he had that memory to hold fast.

His fingers dug into the snow, his shoulders drooping as he let the sorrow come forth. He mourned his loss alone, letting the grief sweep over him like the tide of the sea. Then, at last, he knelt beside Fiona's resting place.

His grief for her was not less, but it had softened. Memories washed over him of Fiona's quiet industriousness, of the way she had made Rionallís into a true home. Her fingers had never been still, always embroidering or weaving or spinning.

He admitted the truth to himself. She had not been happy here. He had tried to give her everything—his love, her every desire. But it had not been enough. Her smiles had been rare, and usually reserved for their child, never himself.

It hurt even now to acknowledge that she had not loved him the way he had loved her.

He might have been able to deceive himself into thinking she had, were it not for his new wife. Genevieve had given herself to him, heart and mind. When he had looked into her eyes he had seen the intensity of her feelings, the complete trust. And he had hurt her because he could not give the same in return.

His breath formed clouds in the frozen air as he touched the earth covering his wife's grave. He knew the pain Genevieve felt, and he wished he could mend her torn feelings. He wasn't even sure he knew how to love again.

But it was time to let go of the past. The vow he'd made, never to let another woman into his heart, was no longer one he wanted to keep. He had wed Genevieve believing that he could keep himself apart from her. Such was not possible.

'Forgive me,' he whispered to the grave of his wife. Silence curled about him and the wind moved over his face. Were she alive, he believed she would release him from the vow.

He kept his vigil over the graves, praying for their souls. He prayed that he would find the strength to let them rest and to begin anew.

Behind him, he heard the soft crunching of footsteps. Turning, he saw Ewan.

'Lionel Ó Riordan has sent for you. The Normans are attacking his lands once again.'

It was the fight he had anticipated. Bevan had given his word to his friend and ally, promising to help when he was needed. 'Tell the men to arm themselves. We ride without delay.'

'I am coming with you.'

'No. You are not ready for this kind of battle. Ó Riordan's men have faced the enemy before, but if he has asked for our garrison, then they are losing the fight.'

'I'll never be ready for any battle,' Ewan argued. 'Not in your eyes. How can I ever gain experience if I must always stay at home?'

Bevan gripped his brother's arm. 'Do you remember the night Liam died? Do you? Well, I do. I watched the Norman bastard bury his sword into our brother's flesh. I'll not lose another brother. Not when I can prevent it.'

He saw the rising adolescent rebellion in Ewan's eyes and realised the boy might do something dangerous if he did not soften his words. 'Besides, I need you to guard Rionallís and Genevieve.'

'They are well protected,' Ewan said, his eyes hot with resentment.

'I am trusting them to you, Ewan. I know that if anything were to happen I can depend on you to come and fetch us back again.' He gave his brother's shoulder a squeeze. 'Can I rely on you?'

Ewan's face was stony, but he nodded his assent. Bevan knew his brother must feel like a nursemaid.

'Good. Now, give the orders for the men to prepare themselves. And send Genevieve to me,' he said. She would not like it were he to ride off without saying farewell.

His brother left to make the arrangements and Bevan remained a moment longer in the garden. For his wife and child he sent up a silent prayer, that their souls would find everlasting peace in the arms of God.

Genevieve met him in the inner bailey. Her cheeks were reddened from the wind, her eyes bright. Bevan took her hands, warming them in his.

'I missed you this morn,' she said.

He drew her into an embrace, breathing in her scent. 'And I you.' He meant it. More and more she occupied his thoughts, and he was glad to have her with him.

They walked alongside one another, and though she did not speak of the forthcoming battle he knew she saw the men, armed and ready to depart. He regretted having to leave, especially since he had at last made his peace with Fiona. But the time away from her would give him the chance to ponder his next move. He intended to court his wife, making theirs a true marriage.

'I am sorry for last night,' Genevieve said, speaking rapidly. 'I should not have asked you to come to my bed. The mead—'

He kissed her, silencing the needless words. 'I did not sleep last eve,' he said, caressing her cheek. 'And when I return, if you are willing, you'll not sleep the night either.'

Her blush told him she knew exactly what he meant. With a smile, he left her standing in the bailey, his thoughts fired with the promise of making her his wife.

Chapter Fifteen

Genevieve wondered what had brought about Bevan's change of attitude, but instead of it filling her with joy, she felt only wariness. Self-doubts plagued her, with little voices reminding her that she had never been able to please Hugh. How long would Bevan's desire for her last? Would he, too, become dissatisfied with her?

She tried to drown out the voices by working. Over the next few days she occupied herself with any task that would busy her fingers.

Ewan had remained behind to look after Rionallís, on Bevan's orders. Genevieve wondered how long her husband would be gone, and Ewan reassured her that it would likely be a matter of days. In the meantime, he took it upon himself to learn more about the ribbon Hugh had sent, despite her protests. He insisted that it could not be pushed aside.

Genevieve suspected that he was more interested in having a reason to spy on others than to uncover the mystery. But it kept him occupied, so she ignored it.

With the help of the servants, she swept the hearth and recovered the floors with fresh rushes. When she found herself scrubbing the walls, searching for cobwebs, she decided she had done enough.

Bevan had forbidden her to touch the chamber he had shared with his first wife, save for cleaning. The new bed reminded her of his promise to consummate their marriage, and she wondered if he would keep it. Would he love her upon it? Or would the ghost of his wife haunt him still? She did not fear his touch any more, but she worried about pleasing him.

Her gaze travelled to a chest against the wall. She knew its contents well, from even before Bevan had forbidden her to open it. Inside were a woman's gowns, a length of rose-coloured linen, and an infant's bonnet. Only months ago Genevieve had tried on a gown, though it had been too short for her. She had wondered about what their lives must have been like.

Now she knew, and understood the sorrow that went with that knowledge. Love lay in that chest, tucked away with packets of herbs to preserve it. His memories were there.

She opened the chest again, lifting the gowns aside, holding the bonnet in her palm. So tiny. The grief he must feel she could not imagine.

Had he truly let go of them? Or had she merely incited his lust? She wanted him to love her in the way he had Fiona.

Why open this Pandora's Box? Why let herself dream again when he held the power to break her heart? Genevieve closed her eyes. Though it might make her a fool, a fool she would be.

All at once, Ewan burst in. He sounded out of breath from running. 'A small party of Normans. To the north. I've ordered the men to be on guard.'

Genevieve rose to her feet. 'And their intent?'

Ewan shook his head. 'I do not know. But I'll find out.'

He departed the chamber with all haste, and Genevieve stifled the rush of nervousness. She straightened her attire, ensuring that her hair was properly covered. Below stairs, she gave orders for refreshments and a footbath for the guests. She would treat them as such until she knew the reason for their visit.

Some time later, Ewan returned. A scowl rested upon his face. 'Sir Hugh Marstowe is with them. Shall I give the order to attack?' His eyes gleamed with excitement.

Genevieve's heart seized. She steeled herself, trying to remember that she was well protected, even without Bevan.

'How many of them are there?'

'Only ten. A short battle it would be,' Ewan urged.

She knew she should deny Hugh entrance and have the guards send them away. It was the right thing to do.

And yet she thought again of the frail ribbon he had sent. What did Hugh mean by it? What did he want? She had already wed Bevan, and their children would inherit Rionallís. If there were any, Genevieve thought with a sigh.

She recalled her husband's promise and her body warmed at the memory. Before she gave herself up to Bevan's embrace there was one memory left to excise: the terrible night when Hugh had tried to force himself upon her—and nearly succeeded.

He had held her down, crushing her with his weight. 'You cannot deny me,' he had said. 'I am to be your husband.'

His fists had bruised her, tearing away her clothing until she lay exposed to him. She had fought him, but his strength had overpowered her.

'If you do this, I shall hate you forever,' she had whispered.

And for some reason he had stopped. His wrath had not diminished, nor his lust, but her words had stayed his hand. He had tried to woo her once more, insisting he could give her pleasure. She had sobbed until finally he'd left her alone.

The devastating fear had been with her ever since. She would never be free of it until she faced him.

Here was a chance to reclaim her pride, to look upon the face of her enemy and let him see that she would not be beaten. Her hands trembled as she straightened her *léine*.

'Allow them to enter. I will speak with him.'

Ewan looked incredulous, but Genevieve added one further order. 'And I want twenty guards in the room with me. Along with yourself.' She offered him a faint smile. 'You will protect me, will you not, brother?'

Pride burst over his face, and he nodded. 'I will.'

As the moments passed, she paced. With each step her heart hammered faster, until she felt the fear starting to overtake her.

'Genevieve.' She turned, and Hugh gave her a thin smile. His face was clean-shaven, his fair hair cropped short. He wore only light armour, his conical helm tucked beneath his arm. 'I see you received my message.'

'What do you want?' she asked. To her surprise, her voice sounded calm.

'I wanted to apologise for my past actions,' he said. 'I know I lost my temper on occasion. You bore the brunt of it, and for that I am sorry.' He looked embarrassed, particularly with all of her guards looking on. 'Could we not speak in private?' he asked. 'There is more I wish to say to you.'

'What you have to say must be said here,' she replied. 'You lost my trust long ago.'

He bowed his head in assent. 'Aye.' He let her see the regret in his face. It appeared genuine, something she had not expected. His expression held a fleeting glimpse of the young man she had once loved, the man who had treated her with kindness.

'I came to offer my good wishes upon your marriage. And to ask forgiveness for my earlier actions.'

Genevieve did not believe him. 'What other reason brings you to Rionallís?' She spoke directly, not wanting to prolong his visit.

His forced smile tightened. 'Are you happy with the Irishman?'

Genevieve said nothing as Hugh sat upon a bench and unlaced his boots. As hostess, she was expected to bathe his feet. But she could not abide the thought of kneeling before him. Instead, she signalled for a servant to attend him.

She folded her arms across her chest. 'I am. And I would not defy our King's command.'

He took a drink of the mead offered by a maidservant, and donned his footwear once more. 'Do you remember when I first gave you that ribbon? At the fair?' He smiled as though reminiscing. 'You gave me a kiss for it.'

'That is in the past, Hugh. Why do you speak of it?'

He moved in closer and tried to take her hands in his. Genevieve stepped back, repelled by his touch. 'Once, you loved me,' he said. 'Once, you desired me, and we belonged to each other.'

No, you thought I belonged to you, she wanted to say. Instead, she clenched her teeth and met his gaze. 'Tell me what it is you want, Hugh.'

'What if I could have your union annulled?' he offered silkily. 'We could be together once more. Give me a chance, Genevieve.' He motioned to a servant, who brought forth a small wooden chest. 'I have brought this gift for you. I ask only that you consider it.' Lifting the lid, Hugh presented her with a golden torque set with sapphires.

Genevieve could barely conceal her anger. Did he think he could eradicate the past with a golden gift?

'I do not want an annulment, Hugh.' And, to be certain he would not mistake her meaning, she added, 'And I would not wed you if you were the last man on earth.'

His face turned scarlet with rage. 'You have not lost your haughtiness, have you? You would do well to learn how to submit to a man's authority. I'll wager your Irishman does not know how to tame you.'

'Get out,' Genevieve gritted. 'I will not be insulted in my own home.'

'It may not be yours for very long,' Hugh insinuated. 'Not with your husband away in battle. He could be killed. And then what?'

Genevieve swallowed hard, but held her ground. 'I asked you to leave. My men will see you out.'

'Think upon my words, Lady Genevieve. It only takes a single arrow to end a man's life. Your husband fights against the Norman army of Richard de Clare's men. My sword may meet his yet.'

With those words, Hugh departed. Genevieve waited until he had gone before sinking onto a bench. She covered her face with her hands, rubbing her temples. Hugh was right. If anything happened to Bevan, she would not be safe.

Genevieve did not sleep that night, nor the next. Each time she closed her eyes she saw the face of Hugh, taunting her. Then his fists would come down upon her until she woke, sweating with terror.

Mairi noticed her sleeplessness, and offered to brew an herbal remedy. At Genevieve's refusal, she clucked like a maternal hen, fussing over her until she at last agreed to drink the tea. She tasted chamomile and mint, and lied that it did make her feel better.

'Ye need to get away from your sadness, Genevieve,' Mairi chided. 'Séan the brewer has invited you to his home this evening. Ye'll be coming, won't ye?'

Genevieve did not feel like visiting, but she thought it

would be rude to refuse. Her relationship with the tenants was slowly improving. They were a proud folk, some less forgiving than others. She decided to go, in the hopes that she could win over the hearts of those who resented her Norman heritage.

Mairi led her to the small tract of land, its field covered with snow. She hustled Genevieve out of the cold wintry air and into the beehive-shaped cottage, where a peat fire burned brightly. 'Ah, here we are. This is Séan. If ye are wanting gossip, he's the man to find. Knows everything, does our Séan.'

A portly man with ruddy cheeks smiled and handed Genevieve a mug of ale. 'It's welcome you are, Genevieve.'

Inside the small cottage, several women and men had gathered to share food, drink and entertainment. Genevieve drank, and found the brew to be quite good, though strong.

'I imagine you're wanting to know about Fiona MacEgan, is that right?' Séan asked, lighting his pipe.

The web of jealousy snared her, but Genevieve pushed away the emotion. 'I would rather know more about Bevan,' she said, correcting his assumption.

Her jealousy must have given her away, because Séan laughed. 'Well, you'll have to be knowing about our Fiona before you can understand Bevan.' He launched into a tale about the Ó Callahan feud, much of which she had already learned from Bevan. But throughout the tale it was clear that the people had adored Fiona.

'The prettiest Ó Callahan of all, she was,' Mairi remarked.

'What happened to her?' Genevieve asked. 'I know little about the night she died.'

Séan refilled everyone's mug. Sitting back on a bench, he lit his pipe. 'That I can tell you. And it might be that you'll understand why Bevan grieves so when you hear the tale.'

Séan exhaled a puff of smoke. 'Two years ago, Bevan had

taken Fiona for a visit to Laochre. Only a month had passed
since they'd lost their daughter, Brianna, from a fever. Both
were grieving. At Laochre, they were attacked, and Bevan
told Fiona to stay in the donjon. He prides himself upon his
skills in battle, you know. Bevan slew more than thirty men
on the day Strongbow attacked.'

The room grew hushed, and Séan continued. 'Our tribe
fought against the Norman invaders—' he glanced at Genevieve, not wanting to offend '—and though Fiona was not the
sort to disobey, she did this day. It must have been a madness
brought forth from the battle, or a fear for Bevan's life. She
left the fortress in search of him.'

'Bevan saw her running from a group of Norman soldiers,
and he heard her cries for help as they pursued her. He fought
with all his strength to prevent them from carrying her off,
but a soldier struck him across the head. No one could reach
her in time.'

'What happened then?' Genevieve asked.

Séan cleared his throat and set the pipe aside. His features
turned sorrowful. 'Her body was found later. Burned. She
must have escaped into one of the cottages that was set on fire
by the Normans. Had she not left the fortress she might be
alive still.'

The mood in the cottage had shifted to one of sadness, and
Genevieve sensed the evening drawing to a close. She
thanked Séan for his hospitality and he sent her home with
the promise of a barrel of his finest ale for a bridal gift.

When she reached the gates of Rionallís, activity in the
bailey drew her attention. A large group of men, weary from
battle, were giving their horses to the stable boys. Genevieve
searched the crowd of men until she located Bevan.

His armour was caked with mud, and bloodstains covered
his face and clothing. A rough beard covered his cheeks and

chin, and his green eyes seared her with intensity. Genevieve ran to him, and he dismounted.

'Are you hurt?' She touched the blood upon his face, checking him for injuries.

He shook his head. 'Only a few marks. But we defeated the Normans who were attacking Lionel's people. I have his vow to help us, should we ever have the need.'

Genevieve remembered Hugh's threats and felt grateful to have another ally.

'Are you going to force me to stay outside?' Bevan asked, his voice tinged with humour. 'Or will you help me to get warm?' The tenor of his voice held a double meaning that made Genevieve's skin flush.

'Come inside.' She took his hand to lead him into the fortress, but he paused, bringing her palm to his lips.

'Did you think of me?' he asked softly.

She nodded, her heart racing. He had not forgotten his promise, from the looks of it. Tonight he would bed her, and she would do her best to be a good wife to him.

But, oh, she feared the marriage bed. Though Bevan had awakened such feelings within her, she knew it would all change once he joined his body with hers. She loved it when he kissed her and touched her, but the joining would be painful. Mayhap he would get that part over with quickly. She hoped so.

'Would you like food and drink?' she asked, her nerves making her speak faster than usual. 'I could have them bring you something. Meat, or cheese, or bread?'

'*Tá,* I am hungry.' He leaned in and kissed her, his mouth leaving her no doubt as to what he was hungry for. She shivered when he released her from his embrace. 'Have a bath prepared for me. And send the food and wine above stairs. I would like your company while I eat.'

After she had left to give the orders, Bevan's body warmed with anticipation. All the time he had spent fighting he had kept the image of her in his mind. He had imagined Genevieve waiting for him, and he looked forward to teaching her the pleasures of loving. He wanted to watch her come to fulfilment with her heart in her eyes.

He was already halfway up the stairs when Ewan interrupted.

'Hugh Marstowe was here during your absence.' Ewan rested his hand atop his sword hilt. 'I sent a few men to follow him.'

'Why did he come?' Bevan remembered the way Sir Hugh had challenged him at Tara. The man wanted Rionallís, and he did not doubt that Marstowe would threaten Genevieve.

'He claimed he wanted to congratulate Genevieve on her marriage. But his eyes were hungry. He wants this place,' Ewan said. 'And he warned her of what would happen if you died.'

Norman bastard.

'Why did you let him in?'

'I didn't want to. Genevieve allowed him to enter. But I kept our men fully armed. He didn't harm her.'

Bevan was immediately suspicious of Genevieve's motives. She knew what the man was capable of. Why, then, would she endanger herself?

'How far did your men track him?' he asked Ewan.

'They were travelling towards Tara.'

To appeal to the King, no doubt. They would want to press their case again before Henry returned to England. Bevan gritted his teeth. 'You did well to inform me of this.'

He met his brother's gaze, and suddenly saw a hint of maturity there. Ewan had accepted responsibility for guarding Genevieve and he had succeeded. There was a glimpse of the man he would become.

He clapped Ewan on the shoulder. 'My thanks, brother.'

Ewan gave an embarrassed nod before returning to the others in the Great Chamber. He busied himself with eating, though Bevan saw pride in Ewan's posture. There was hope for the boy yet.

Above stairs, he stopped before the door to Genevieve's chamber. No, *their* chamber now—though he had shared it once with Fiona. Instead of the anger he'd felt when Genevieve had ordered the bed destroyed, he now felt regret. But it was better with the old bed gone, allowing nothing of the past to intrude upon them.

Opening the chamber door, he found Genevieve sitting on a bench near the fire. Her hair was undone, falling across her cream-coloured *léine*. She held her hands in her lap while she stared at a chest against the wall.

'Ewan tells me Marstowe was here,' he began.

Genevieve nodded. 'Aye.'

'Tell me what happened.' He kept his tone firm, needing to understand her reasons. 'Why did you open the gates to him?'

Genevieve met his gaze directly. 'I've been running from him for weeks now. I thought it was time to stop.'

'He could have harmed you.' Bevan caressed the side of her jaw, where the dark bruise had once been.

Genevieve held his hand to her face. 'I know it. But I wanted to face him. I wanted him to see that I will not allow my fears to rule me any more.'

'Why?' All the thoughts of what might have happened came rising up. 'Why would you put yourself in such danger?'

'Because I knew your men would keep me safe. Even without you here.'

Her trust in him was the last thing he had expected. He

didn't know what to say, so he rested his hands upon her shoulders. He massaged the tension from her neck, sliding her hair over one shoulder. She leaned back against him, closing her eyes. 'Mmm.'

He turned her to face him, and she wrapped her arms around his neck, burying her face against him. 'I missed you.'

He gripped her tightly, feeling a surge of tenderness. The faith she had placed in him made him want to give something back to her.

Cupping her face between his hands, he kissed her. She responded, meeting his lips with sweetness. Fiona had never looked at him the way Genevieve did. It made him feel powerful, knowing that he could make her feel the same passion he did. The way he never had for his former wife.

Genevieve traced a finger across the scar on his left cheek, then his right.

'Battle has taken away my good looks,' he teased.

She shook her head. 'No. The scars show your strength.' With her lips, she pressed a kiss against each one. His skin grew warm beneath her lips, his body rising to meet her.

'I have other scars,' he offered, glancing below his waist. She laughed, her cheeks flushing.

Bevan unfastened his sword belt, then removed his tunic. Bare-chested, he caught her in his arms again, pressing a kiss along her nape. 'Did you order the bath?'

'I did.'

Bevan removed the rest of his clothes, standing naked before her.

Genevieve's cheeks reddened, but she did not look away. Her heartbeat quickened with anticipation. Like a fierce warrior's, Bevan's body held numerous scars from countless battles. The skin at his shoulder wound had healed at last, a mark he would carry on her behalf.

Not an ounce of fat did he hold on his lean, muscled frame. When he sank down into the tub of water his dark hair fell about his shoulders. His green eyes beckoned to her in wordless invitation.

Genevieve picked up a cloth to wash him, and he stopped her. 'Use your hands,' he said, in a deep whisper.

She had expected to submit to him, to lie beneath him and let him do as he wished to her body. Never had she anticipated that he would ask her to take the lead. 'I can't.'

'*Tá,* you can.' He took her hand in his, soaping it and laying it atop his chest. He brought her palm over the hard planes of his chest, over the scars, and the gesture frightened her.

She wasn't any good at this. She could never please him in the same way he did her. When she tried to pull her hand away, he caught it, asking, 'What are you afraid of?'

'I'm not afraid.'

Liar, she thought. Though she tried to hide it, Bevan was not misled.

'He hurt you. And I know you're thinking of him now.'

'I'm not.' But she knew he could see through her pretence of bravery. He was partly right. She *was* remembering Hugh. But she also remembered how Bevan had turned her away the last time. What if he did so again? What if she displeased him?

He caught hold of her wrists, trapping her at the side of the tub. 'You said that you wanted to be free of him.'

'And I d-do,' she stammered. 'If you want, I'll remove my gown and lie on the bed.'

'You don't deserve to be taken like that,' Bevan said, kissing the inside of her wrist. A spiral of desire shivered through her. 'I do not want you to be afraid.' He brought her hand to his chest, dipping it below the water. 'And so I am going to let you take me.'

He stroked her hand, moving it lower down to his hips. Genevieve's eyes widened. 'But I told you—I don't know how.'

'Do what you like,' he said, 'and I'll let you touch any part of me. For tonight, I am your servant.'

She froze, hardly able to breathe. 'What if you don't like it?'

'I promise you, I'll like it.' His gaze grew compelling, his voice seductive. 'Why don't you come into the tub with me?'

'There is no room for both of us.'

'There is if you sit on my lap.' He offered a wicked grin. 'I don't think you've kissed all of my scars yet. I have a few more.'

And suddenly she realised what he was doing. He was ensuring that she would have no memories of Hugh to interfere with this. She was in command, and he would not force her to do anything she didn't want.

The heady sense of power helped her gather the fragments of her courage.

'I'll have to remove my gown,' she said.

Bevan's only answer was a smile.

Chapter Sixteen

The water spilled over the edge of the tub, and Genevieve nearly lost her balance. Bevan caught her by the waist, turning her until she sat in his lap against his chest. She could feel the hard length of his manhood pressing against her spine, and it brought the fear back.

She tensed, trying to gather her courage. This was Bevan, not Hugh. He would not hurt her.

For a moment she rested against him, her hair falling into the water. His arms wrapped around her, just above her breasts, and he kissed the top of her head.

'This is the way baths were meant to be taken,' he said.

'You don't think it's a bit crowded?'

'Not at all.' His hands wandered down, brushing against her nipples before sinking below the water. Genevieve touched his knees with her palms, running her hands over his thighs, then down to the tight calves and his feet. She explored his skin, so different from her own. His legs were strong, the muscles developed from years of riding a horse. When she reached his toes, a muffled laugh sounded from behind her.

'You're ticklish,' she accused. When he didn't answer, she tickled the bottoms of his feet, and he shook with suppressed laughter. More water sloshed onto the floor.

His laughter relaxed her. She reached for his foot again, but he captured her hands in his, placing her palms atop her breasts. The sensation of touching herself, under his guidance, made her self-conscious.

'And you?' His fingers moved her hands in a light caress over her nipples, sending a jolt of desire through her. 'Does this tickle?'

He turned her towards him, pulling her legs around his waist. He took her nipple into his mouth, and she gasped. His tongue circled the hardened tip, sucking until her blood raced within her veins. 'What about this?'

Her breathing quickened, and she felt a rush of heat between her thighs. 'My turn,' she whispered.

Emboldened by his touch, she reached into the water and took his length into her hands, stroking it. He shuddered, his face tightening with the effort to maintain control. She ran her palms over his chest, kissing each of the scars, her lips sliding lower until they touched the water.

Bevan stopped her and rose to a standing position. Beads of water slid over his body as Genevieve remained kneeling in the tub. Her mouth moved over a scar on his thigh, and he trembled.

'Do you see what you do to me?' Bevan asked in a harsh whisper.

His manhood stood erect from his stomach, and for a moment her apprehension returned. He stepped out of the tub, mindless of the dripping water, and brought a drying cloth. Genevieve rose, allowing him to wrap the cloth around her.

In a swift move he lifted her into his arms, carrying her to the bed. He laid her back, kissing her deeply, his tongue mingling with hers. He had never felt this way before with any woman, not even his wife. Why had he ever thought to deny himself the pleasure of her?

He rolled her on top of him, and she straddled his hips. Her fair skin was covered in tiny goosebumps. Her nipples were erect and damp from the water. His palms spanned her waist, caressing her hips and bottom.

She froze, watching him. He hoped she could see how much he desired her, how much he wanted this to be good for her.

'You were right,' she said. 'I am afraid.'

'Don't be.' He lifted her hips until she hovered above his manhood. A small gasp erupted from her as she slid a fraction of him inside her. Bevan forced himself to lie there, to let her make the decision whether she wanted him or not.

Lug, he didn't think he had the strength to endure such sweet torture. His body was ready to explode, and yet she moved with excruciating slowness. Deeper.

Her moist warmth tightened against his shaft. Still deeper.

His breathing was ragged, but he held her gaze, letting her continue to take the lead. She moved once more, until he could feel the barrier of her maidenhead. At long last his length was sheathed within her, and she gave a gasping cry as she was breached. He nearly spilled himself at the intense pleasure of feeling her squeeze his manhood within her depths.

She began to move, delicate penetrations that rubbed against him, making him rock-hard. Her breath came in quick gasps, her wet hair slid across his chest, and at the look of agonised pleasure on her face he could no longer bear it.

He had thought to teach her the ways of loving. Instead, she was teaching him what it meant to hold a woman in his arms who gave herself to him completely. In her eyes he saw desire and love, as she poised on the brink of fulfilment.

She needed him, as he did her. He would never let her go.

His hands clenched her hips, increasing the speed and pressure. She cried out, her back arching to take him deeper. He moved in counter-rhythm to her thrusts, pleasure filling him until there was nothing but her.

He wanted her to love him. With Fiona, he had once thought she loved him. But she had never looked at him the way Genevieve did now.

He leaned up and took her breast into his mouth, licking her nipple as she ground her hips against him. He sucked hard and she screamed. At that moment he poured himself inside her, holding her fast while the aftershocks took them both into a mindless ecstasy.

He cradled her against his chest, their bodies still joined. It felt so right having her in his arms.

And the thought frightened him.

When the morning sky turned from grey to lavender, with dawn stealing its way above the horizon, Genevieve lay snuggled against Bevan's back. She leaned over and kissed his shoulder.

'Good morn to you,' she whispered. For it *was* a fine morning—the finest she had known in a very long time.

But he said nothing, rolling over to get out of bed. His sudden coolness startled her, especially after he had loved her twice more that night. He had brought her to the edge of madness until she'd cried out in ecstasy. It was as though he'd craved watching her come undone.

'Is everything all right?' she asked, suddenly feeling uncertain. It troubled her to see him growing distant once more.

'*Tá*,' he said as he dressed. 'But I must see to my men. It is late already.'

She let the sheet slide from her body and rose from the bed.

Hoping to entice him out of his ill mood, she wrapped her arms around his waist. 'Are you hungry?'

A flicker of interest dawned in his eyes, but he shook his head. 'Not now, no.' He pulled her hands away from him and planted a distracted kiss upon her forehead. 'I will see you later.'

Genevieve forced her disappointment away. Uneasy, she pulled her shift on and donned her *léine* and overdress. The earlier contentment between them had faded. A sombre thought occurred to her—he might hold regrets about last night.

She tried to pretend as though nothing were wrong. 'I've promised Mairi that I will help her with dyeing some new wool.'

'Good.' But he did not say farewell as he left the chamber. When the door closed, her gaze travelled back to the bed. He had well and truly banished the memories of Hugh. For that she would ever be grateful.

As she straightened the room, tucking the bedcovers where they belonged, she took a deep breath.

It might be that she could never take the place of Fiona. But she felt whole again, empowered to seize the future she wanted. And though the path ahead curved in a direction she could not see, she wanted to believe that there was hope for them.

Like water that gently eroded the jagged edges of a rock, she intended to fight for her warrior's heart.

She found Mairi in one of the buildings used for dyeing wool. The malodorous scent of wet wool burned her nostrils. Bags of fleece waiting to be washed were stacked against one wall, by the heavy cauldron containing lye, which was used to soak the wool and thereby remove its natural oils. She was surprised to see Siorcha, laying out lengths of wool for more dyeing.

''Tis good to see you once more,' she remarked, recognising the older woman who had cared for young Declan at Laochre.

Siorcha's lined face managed a smile, though the woman appeared tired. Her grey hair was pulled into a tight bun, and her eyes were a dull, clouded blue.

'Rionallís has always been my home,' Siorcha said. 'Though I left when that Norman took it. I refused to work for such a monster. I am thankful to be back.'

Genevieve inwardly agreed with Siorcha's assessment of Hugh. She helped the older woman lift another pile of wool into the pot of lye to soak. She remembered how well Siorcha had cared for young Declan, treating him like a lost grandchild. 'We are glad to have you back with us.'

Siorcha stirred the pot, not replying. Genevieve greeted Mairi, who was busy preparing madder root for another pot of boiling wool. 'Can I help you with that?'

Mairi nodded in return. '*Tá*, ye can.' With a quick glance at her face, she added, 'I see he's bedded ye at last.'

Genevieve flushed. 'What do you mean?'

'Ye have a satisfied look about you. Only a MacEgan could make a woman look like that, as cold as it is today.' With a smirk, Mairi immersed the madder root in boiling water.

Genevieve started to protest, but decided it was not worth the effort. 'You were right,' she said. 'He is a fine man.'

Mairi snorted, but a moment later Genevieve released a laugh. It felt good to release the tension. As she helped Siorcha add a fixative to the dye her mind travelled ahead to the coming night, when she would share Bevan's bed again. Her body warmed at the thought, though she did not know if he would welcome her or push her away.

The pair worked long hours, assisted by Siorcha, until

they had dyed the wool a deep red with the madder roots. Another sack of wool had been dyed a rich fawn colour, with dandelion leaves and roots, while a third had become a bright orange hue from onion skins.

The Irish nobility wore every colour imaginable—some in combinations that dazzled the eye. It seemed that they believed the more colours, the better.

Later that afternoon, Genevieve stopped by the training field. Despite the freezing temperature, the men sparred against one another, practising swordplay and perfecting their aim. Bevan moved among them, challenging his men to improve their technique.

Against the far wall, Ewan observed the men. She could see him mentally performing the same exercises, watching for any flaw. The longing in his eyes to be one of them made her ache with sympathy. She knew he would go to the weaponry room long after everyone was abed, to practise alone. Genevieve prayed that one day he would learn the skills that did not come naturally to him.

Bevan seemed different today, somehow. There was an energy about him, a swiftness in the way he moved. He fought off one soldier, only to spin and catch another's sword. He moved with the grace of an experienced fighter.

He seemed to sense her stare, and lowered his weapon, stepping out of the match and nodding towards his men to continue. She could read his thoughts as he fixed his attention upon her. His hair was bound with a cord, and he wore leather armour that accentuated his muscular frame. She envisaged him plunging deep within her, his hands cupping her bottom as his mouth ravaged her throat.

Without her realising it, he had crossed the bailey and now stood before her. 'What is it?'

Genevieve blushed at the wanton thoughts clouding her

mind. 'It is naught. I should go and oversee the food preparations.'

'I'll come with you. I've finished for today.' He walked beside her, but when she reached out her hand for his, his pace increased to avoid her touch.

Startled by his rejection, she held back.

A servant brought basins, towels, and fragrant oil for foot baths. Bevan sat at a bench and removed his foot coverings. He dipped his feet into the water, but Genevieve interrupted him.

'Let me,' she said. Kneeling before him, she brought forth a linen cloth and a vial of fragrant oil. She washed his feet, massaging the soles.

At the touch of her hands upon his skin, he tensed. Ever since he had joined with her he had been able to think of little else than bedding her again.

He rebuked himself, trying to separate his mind from the needs his body demanded. He had been foolish once, letting himself love his wife. Love held no place in a marriage, and he'd not let Genevieve weaken him in such a way.

She poured the oil into her palm, using it to anoint his ankles, soles, and toes. When at last she had dried his feet, and replaced his foot coverings, he tilted her chin to look up at him. His hand threaded through her silken hair, and he captured her mouth in a fierce kiss until he needed to feel her bare skin against his.

Without speaking a word, he took her hand and led her up to their chamber. Once inside, he dropped the bolt.

Lug, but he could not contain his desire for her. He couldn't get enough—not after all this time. He loved having her in his arms, beneath him and atop him. There was none of the emptiness in her eyes when he embraced her in the darkness of their bed. Instead she looked upon him with an aching emotion, even as he closed his heart off to her.

Bevan tried to take her in his arms, but saw her attention fixed upon the hearth behind him.

There, upon the stones, lay a golden torque set with sapphires.

'What is this?' Bevan demanded.

Genevieve shook her head, her fingers pressed to her lips. 'It was a gift Hugh brought to me. I turned it away.'

The mention of the Norman knight ignited Bevan's temper. The intrusion had alerted every instinct towards potential danger. 'How did this get in our chamber?'

'I know not. He sent his first message a sennight ago.' Genevieve stared at the jewellery as though it were a living reminder of Hugh. 'It was a ribbon he had once given me. He tried to court me again.'

His hackles rose because she had not confided in him. Did she still believe him incapable of defending her from the Norman bastard?

'You should have told me of it.' He directed her from the chamber, for they both knew of the secret *souterrain* passage that led underground beyond the fortress. Whether or not Hugh himself knew of it, Bevan would not take the chance that he might be nearby.

'Ewan might know who has been seen near the chamber.'

Bevan dismissed the idea immediately. Although the boy worshipped Genevieve, and would do anything to help, he didn't want him involved in something this dangerous. 'No. I will ask some of my men to search for the answers.'

'Bevan, give him a chance. He wants so much to help. What harm can it do?' Genevieve put her hand on his shoulder, her eyes pleading. 'You can put both your men and Ewan to this task. And if he succeeds it will give him a sense of purpose. Do you not see how restless he is? How much he yearns to be one of your men?'

'Ewan is not, nor will he ever be, a good soldier. In all these years he has never shown any natural abilities.'

'But he works hard,' Genevieve argued. 'He tries.'

'Trying is not good enough in battle,' Bevan said sharply. 'A man must defeat his opponent, or he dies.' His tone softened. 'I don't want him to die, Genevieve. He should choose another path for himself.'

'This is what he wants. I do not think you can sway him. Better to keep training him until he does succeed.'

'I'll not train my brother so he can die at an enemy's hand. If he does not fight, he'll not be harmed.'

His youngest brother idolised him, he knew. And Bevan would protect him at all costs. Even if it meant causing his brother to hate him.

'Until the person who did this is found, I want you to stay here. Do not visit the tenants or leave the donjon. Remain with a guard at all times.' He started forming a plan in his mind. Which men to question first? After that, the women. He would not rest until he found out how Hugh had broken through their defences.

After being confined to the donjon for nearly three months, Genevieve was ready to scream with frustration. Ewan had discovered that a servant had been bribed to deliver the torque to their bedchamber. Even after the man had been fined for his deed, Bevan had ordered that Genevieve was never to be left alone. She had no privacy, no moments to herself.

Though she knew why he was so over-protective, her resentment at being treated like a prisoner grew stronger with each passing day. She bit her tongue each time she was barred from the gates, but she didn't know how to convince Bevan that this treatment of her was unnecessary.

Many times she had wanted to snap at him, to demand her

freedom. But then, at night, he seemed to be making up for two years of celibacy. He brought her pleasure, each time filled with intensity and passion, and he would hold her as if trying to absorb her flesh into his. In those moments she felt cherished by him.

When the day dawned, however, he turned distant, his attention ever focused on his people.

Her hopes of becoming a mother, of cradling a child in her arms had met with despair. The moon had gone through its phases two more times, and their efforts had not borne fruit.

Genevieve worked at her loom this morn, letting the mindless rhythm of weaving grant peace to her troubled thoughts. The colours blended together, creating a tapestry of lush flowers. She longed for springtime, when the snows would melt and give rise to the verdant hills and meadows.

Today was worse than usual, for a warm spell had melted some of the ice. She longed for a walk out of doors, for a momentary escape. With a glance behind her, she saw that her guard was as irritated as she, having to accompany her about her tasks. The man was a muscular, broad-shouldered fighter, with a reputation as one of Bevan's best. His skills were wasted because he was trapped in a room with her.

'I am tired of this place,' she told him. 'The day is too fine for sitting inside.'

'Bevan has given orders for you to remain within the fortress walls,' the guard reminded her.

'I am aware of his orders. But your orders are to guard me. And I intend to find him.'

She donned her cloak and *brat,* wrapping the long length of cloth around her shoulders. Outside, she inhaled the fresh air, laced with the peat smoke of small fires that gave warmth to the outbuildings. It took nearly an hour, but she found Bevan overseeing repairs to one of the inner walls. He worked alongside his men, passing them large stones that were being used to fortify the wood. Genevieve recalled his intent to replace all of the wood with stone.

'What is it?' His tone was impatient.

'I want to ride out in the meadows,' she informed him. 'The sun is shining and it is warm. I am sick unto death of this fortress.'

'No. You must remain where we may protect you.'

She clenched her fist and pushed back her indignation. Softening her tone, she said, 'I am weary of these walls. Surely I would be safe if you came with me?'

He started to refuse, but she leaned in. 'Do you not want us to spend time together, without so many eyes watching?' Her voice was seductive, filled with promise.

'I would, but—'

'Then come,' she said. 'And you may take as many weapons as you can carry, if it will make you feel better.'

When he hesitated, she knew she had him. 'It has been months, Bevan. Nothing is going to happen.' She took his gloved hand in hers. 'Let us enjoy the day together.'

He let her lead him to the stables. When the horses were readied, he swung Genevieve up into the saddle. She smiled at him, grateful to at last be free of her confinement. Her mare was a chestnut palfrey, while Bevan rode a black destrier.

His sword hung at his side, while across his tunic he wore a quiver of arrows, his bow hanging from one shoulder. A crossbow was strapped to the saddle. Genevieve had meant only to tease him about bringing as many weapons as he wished, but it seemed he had taken her seriously. Behind them, he gave orders for a party of soldiers to remain at a short distance.

They rode at a gentle pace down the hillside. The sun cast fingers of gold across the snow, and mottled patches of green veiled the landscape.

Once they were free of the outer bailey, Genevieve urged her mare into a gallop. The wind burned her ears and cheeks, but she revelled in the freedom.

Bevan caught up to her, grasping the reins of her horse. 'Stay with me, Genevieve.'

'There is nothing to fear, Bevan. No harm will come,' she protested.

'No, but I would keep you close.'

He forced her to slow the mare's pace to a walk, moving towards a copse of trees. Tall oaks and evergreens clustered around a flattened meadow, shielding them from view. With a signal for the men to remain behind at a distance, Bevan dismounted.

Lifting Genevieve down from her horse, he took her hand, guiding her towards a cluster of standing stones. The granite monoliths exposed patches of dead moss, and other fragmented stones lay upon the earth. It gave the landscape an eerie pagan look, as though it were sacred ground.

'I've never seen this place before,' Genevieve breathed. Gorse and heather surrounded the stones, and she imagined the sea of purple and yellow that would bloom come the spring.

He drew her to his side, and they walked to stand below one of the stones. It stood taller than the height of a single man, and she wondered how the ancients had created the circle.

Bevan turned her until her back rested against the stone. His eyes gleamed wickedly. 'Do you know what they say about these stones?'

She shook her head, but her body grew warm as his arms trapped her against the granite. He touched her nose with his own, nipping her lips.

'The Ancients revered these places for granting women fertility.' His hand moved down her neck, across her breasts, to rest upon her womb. Her lips parted and he kissed her, his mouth warm against the cold air.

Genevieve's heart seized at the promise of a babe, and she smiled against his mouth. 'I want to bear you a child.'

At the words, she saw the shadow of darkness in his gaze. 'Will you tell me about your daughter?' she asked.

He leaned up against the stone, a myriad of emotions crossing his countenance before he nodded.

'She was born on the Feast of St. Catherine. Fiona had longed for a son, but when I first held her in my arms I saw a babe who would grow up to be just like her mother. Beautiful.'

Genevieve laced her fingers with his, trying not to let jealousy invade her thoughts. Bevan's face turned despondent. 'Were she alive, she would be five years now.'

'What happened to her?'

'She died of a fever. I was not at Rionallís when it happened. I had gone with Patrick on a raid against the Ó Malleys. Before I left, she was laughing and running around the fortress. She hugged me and made me promise to bring her back a gift.'

His voice grew dull. 'When she grew ill, they told me that Fiona refused to let anyone see her save Siorcha. She stayed with her night and day, while Brianna suffered from the fever. Then she buried our daughter alone, with no one to help.'

Genevieve took his face in her hands. 'It was not your fault, Bevan. You could have done nothing.'

'Why wouldn't she let anyone else near?' he demanded, his voice filled with grief. 'They might have saved her.'

'I don't know.' Sensing that he no longer wished to say anything else, she offered the solace of her embrace. Leaning in, she kissed him. His response was restrained at first, but within moments it became urgent.

Shifting their position, he lifted her up, with her back

against one of the stones. His hand raised her skirts while he unlaced his trews and cupped her bottom. Within moments his body joined with hers, thrusting against her moist heat.

His eyes, shadowed with sensual promise, burned into her. He lifted her atop him as though she weighed nothing, plunging within her until she grew wet with need. Even as he brought her to exquisite pleasure, his hot mouth covering hers, never did he speak of his feelings. She wondered if he would ever think of her the way he had his first wife.

Wrapping her legs around his waist, she urged him to move faster, until the ache inside her grew to fever-pitch. She trembled, hovering on the edge of madness. With all her strength she tightened against him, arching in a way that she knew brought him incredible pleasure.

Bevan groaned, and she saw the moment of his release when he spilled himself within her. He protected her, he sheltered her. But she was afraid she would never have that which she wanted most—his heart.

Chapter Seventeen

That night, in the sanctity of the fortress, after their bodies lay joined, Bevan cuddled her against his side. With her head beneath his chin, Genevieve moved her icy feet beneath his, to warm them. Though he winced at the contact, he let her keep them there.

Her soft raven hair smelled of lavender, a fragrance he now knew she used in her bath. Though they had been wed only a few months now, their lives had blended together. She had been careful not to make more changes to Rionallís, respecting his wishes. And yet with each passing day his guilt grew stronger.

He had broken his vow of fidelity to his first wife. He had sworn never to forget Fiona, but there were times when he had trouble remembering her face. Genevieve's presence was everywhere, filling the voids in his broken memories.

She yearned to be a mother, he knew. But, though he hated himself for the thought, he was secretly glad it had not yet happened. He remembered the fragile squalling infant who had scarcely been larger than his hands cupped together. It frightened him, the thought of becoming a father again.

Though losing a child to death was common, and to be expected, he hadn't known the pain it would bring. He didn't want to lose another.

Bevan had seen the change in Genevieve recently. Though she never neglected her duties, her gaze would sometimes fall upon someone else's child. On those days she became the seductress, luring him with her body until he could no longer hold a rational thought in his mind.

It disturbed him to realise she had so much control over him. He had to put a stop to it—to the feelings she evoked within him. He had arranged a distraction for her tomorrow, one that would allow him to ease back from Genevieve, and would occupy her thoughts.

The next morn, visitors approached the gates. He watched from the inner bailey, Genevieve's hand clasped in his. When she saw who it was, her grip tightened and a smile broke over her face. She turned to Bevan, and in her eyes he saw joy.

'You brought him here for me,' she whispered, leaning up to press a kiss upon his cheek. He nodded, feeling a strange exhilaration that he had caused her such happiness.

Running towards them, Genevieve welcomed Sheela and young Declan. The woman handed Declan over to Genevieve, and she embraced the boy, hugging him tightly. He struggled to get down, and Genevieve took him by the hand, leading him to the fortress.

Sheela walked beside her, and the two women conversed together. Before she went inside, Genevieve turned back and sent Bevan a smile of thankfulness.

As the day progressed, he had difficulty keeping his attention on his responsibilities. He listened to disputes in the *Brehon* courts, offering his opinion when necessary. He inspected the construction efforts on the fortress, and spoke with several tenants about the year's harvest. But in the midst of it all he kept thinking of her smile.

'You're in love with her,' his brother Ewan declared.

Bevan sent his brother an exasperated look. 'No. I was thinking of whether to expand the fortress and outbuildings.'

'You were thinking of Genevieve.' Ewan smirked. When Bevan tried to cuff him, his brother ducked. He was not in love with Genevieve. He cared for her, but that was all.

'I am thinking that you may be in need of another lesson in swordplay,' Bevan commented. What his brother really needed was a lesson in humility.

Ewan drew his own sword and the two brothers faced off. Bevan moved forward, striking towards Ewan's left side. To his surprise, Ewan met his blade with a steady hand. Bevan changed direction, lunging forward, but again Ewan parried the blow.

'You've been practising,' he commented, trying not to let his brother see his satisfaction. It was the first time Ewan had shown any sign of improvement.

Ewan's face flushed, but he held his focus. Bevan kept up the speed, forcing Ewan to exert more effort. It was only towards the end, when he saw Ewan breathing heavily, that he ended the session. Though he could easily have defeated him, by striking when his brother had revealed his exhaustion, today he had no desire to bring down Ewan's spirits.

Lowering his weapon, he clapped his brother across the shoulders. 'Well done.'

Ewan ventured a tired grin, sheathing his weapon. He nodded. 'Genevieve has ordered the cook to prepare some of the apple pastries you like.'

'Perhaps you should go and try a few yourself?' He knew his younger brother had a fondness for the pastries.

'*Tá.*' Ewan walked alongside him. 'Bevan, may I tell you something?'

'What is it?'

'Genevieve is a good woman. She's a better wife than Fiona. There are some things you didn't know—'

He bristled at the remark. 'Do not speak of Fiona in that way.'

'But it is true,' his brother insisted. 'Fiona was never as faithful to you as you think she was.'

'Enough.' Bevan's earlier good humour vanished. 'I do not wish to speak of this again.' He returned in the direction of the inner bailey wall without sparing his brother another glance. He knew his marriage to Fiona had had its faults, but his wife had always been loyal to him. He knew it, no matter what Ewan might say. And he refused to believe otherwise.

Genevieve cuddled Declan in her lap, though the toddler was far more interested in the apple pastries she had set before him. As for herself, she had no interest in food. The thought made her slightly queasy, although she forced a smile onto her face. Ever since that morning she had felt more tired than usual.

'How has Declan fared since I saw you last?' she asked Sheela.

'He misses his parents,' Sheela said, her face darkening in sorrow. 'I heard what happened to my sister's husband. He should not have betrayed the MacEgans. Now my nephew has neither parent to comfort him.'

'I am sorry,' Genevieve said.

'Was there no justice for their deaths?'

'It is complicated,' she replied, thinking of Hugh. No one had seen or heard from him since his visit. 'But I know Bevan will see it done.'

'Good.' Sheela studied the Great Chamber, a concerned expression upon her face. 'I am glad to speak with you alone.

There is something which troubles me, and I think you need to know it.' She lowered her voice. 'My husband and I live in the north—many days' journey from here.'

Genevieve's stomach clenched again, but she closed her eyes to clear the illness away. She placed her hands upon her cheeks to cool them. 'Go on.'

Sheela hesitated. 'I know not how to say this to you, nor do I know if 'tis true. But you must find out.'

Genevieve was puzzled. 'What is it?'

'Do you remember I told you I saw Fiona MacEgan this past summer?'

Genevieve nodded. 'You had mistaken someone else for her.'

Sheela shook her head. 'No.'

Genevieve grew confused at Sheela's words. A spinning sensation gripped her stomach, but she nodded for the woman to continue.

'I discovered from others that it was she. Fiona MacEgan did not die in battle, as your husband believes. And if what I have learned is true, your marriage to Bevan is invalid.'

It was as though Genevieve's life began to unravel with Sheela's words. 'No.' She denied it, tension pounding at her temples. 'Bevan buried her himself.'

'Her body was burned. No one could know for certain,' Sheela corrected. 'They identified a woman wearing her jewels.'

Genevieve shook her head, unwilling to believe it. But she steeled herself. 'Why would you think this?'

'The Normans I spoke with say she left of her own accord. She was in love with Raymond Graham, the Baron of Somerton.'

Genevieve had heard the name. The Somerton lands were near the Welsh border, to the north of her father's. 'How do you know if their words are the truth?' she managed to ask.

Sheela's face was filled with compassion. 'Find out. I pray for your sake that it is not. But were it me I would want to know.'

Genevieve needed to lie down, to clear her thoughts. 'Please, make yourself welcome,' she told Sheela. 'I must attend some duties above stairs. We will speak of this later.'

Sheela placed her hand on Genevieve's sleeve. 'You do not look well. Shall I come with you?'

'No. I am fine,' she lied. At the moment, she didn't want anyone near. She had only Sheela's suppositions, but the possibility of its truth shook her to the core.

A terrible voice inside her questioned whether to tell Bevan. Her sense of honesty conflicted with her desire to remain with her husband. If she said nothing, her life would stay the same. But it would be a lie. She had more honour than that.

The deepening sensation of illness strengthened, so she lay down upon the bed. She would rest for a moment. And later she would tell Bevan what she had learned.

When Bevan returned at sunset, he opened the door to their chamber and found Genevieve lying upon the bed, her eyes closed. Her skin was as pale as moonlight, her breath rising and falling like the ebb of the sea. When he caressed her face, her cheeks felt fiery to the touch.

'Genevieve?' Lifting her into his arms, he stroked her hair, attempting to revive her. All at once his thoughts dwelled upon his daughter, Brianna. He had not been there for her when she had fallen ill. She'd been hardly more than a babe when he'd lost her. And still the memory of it filled him with a crushing sadness.

Genevieve opened her eyes. 'I must have fallen asleep, I fear.' She tried to muster a smile.

'I will send for Siorcha.'

'No.' Her voice sounded frail, and fear seized him once more. 'Bevan, there is something I must tell you.'

'Shh…' He held her in his arms, covering her mouth with his fingers. 'Do not speak. Rest now and regain your strength. Whatever you have to say can wait.'

She laced her fingers with his, and her hands were cold. 'Thank you for bringing Declan to me,' she whispered.

'I will summon the healer,' he insisted.

Genevieve did not protest, for she understood Siorcha's presence would reassure Bevan. When at last the healer arrived, she examined Genevieve under Bevan's watchful eyes. She gave Genevieve a powder mixed with wine to drink, to help her sleep. It was then that Genevieve remembered Siorcha had been with Fiona and Bevan's daughter when she died. It occurred to her that the healer might have the answers she sought.

Yet she did not want Bevan to witness those answers. Not until Genevieve could learn more. If Sheela's story were false, then there was no need to bring up painful memories.

'May I speak with you in private?' Genevieve asked Siorcha. To Bevan, she said, 'There are some women's questions I would ask her.'

As she'd hoped, Bevan did not object. 'I will be outside the door should you need me.'

After the door had closed behind him, Genevieve regarded the healer. She did not know precisely how to begin, but before she could say anything Siorcha spoke. 'It takes time before a woman knows if she's breeding.'

Genevieve flushed. 'I realise that. But I do not think I am.'

The older woman eased down beside Genevieve, her gnarled hands clasped in her lap. 'What do you wish to know?'

'I want to know if Fiona ever saw a man called Raymond Graham, the Baron of Somerton.'

Instantly she saw the look of alarm on the older woman's face before Siorcha shielded it. The healer shook her head.

'Do not lie to me. I know Fiona did not die in battle, as they say.' Genevieve clenched her hands to prevent them from shaking. She hoped that Siorcha would deny it.

Instead, the healer's face was haggard and wan. 'I shall tell you the answers you seek. For Bevan's sake and yours. I have seen him find peace at last, and what I did is my sin to face,' Siorcha said. 'The time has come for me to atone for it.'

'Then it is true. Fiona is still alive.' Her mouth felt dry, her lungs barely able to breathe. Closing her eyes, Genevieve knew she did not have the courage to tell Bevan herself. 'Bring my husband inside. Tell him the truth. You owe it to him if you hold any loyalty for him at all.'

Siorcha started to shake her head. 'I will be punished. I cannot.'

'Your punishment will be far worse do you hide the truth from him any longer.' Genevieve's fury was so great she no longer felt the effects of her illness. She started to rise, but Siorcha had already opened the door.

The older woman wrung her hands, tears forming in her eyes. 'I meant no harm. I loved her as a daughter.'

'What is going on?' Bevan demanded.

Genevieve gathered her resolve and took a deep breath. 'Siorcha has a confession to make. It concerns your wife Fiona.'

'The past no longer matters, Genevieve,' Bevan warned.

'It matters to me,' she said, her heart aching. 'And what she has to say affects both of us.' Tears spilled down her cheeks and she swiped them away. Bevan came to her side, to offer comfort. His presence made it more difficult.

'Tell me, then,' he said. 'If it is so important.'

Siorcha sank down onto a bench and bowed her head. 'I shall tell you the truth of what happened on the day Fiona died.'

A sense of foreboding sent a chill through him, but Bevan nodded. 'Continue.'

'When Fiona was fostered as a babe, I was her nurse. I raised her with my own daughter, and she was like my own child in all ways save her blood. I would have done anything for her. Years ago, I saw that my Fiona was unhappy. She loved her babe, Brianna, but restless she was. She would wander for hours when you were away.'

Her words made him uneasy. Bevan had suspected this, though he hadn't wanted to believe it.

'One day she met a man. And Fiona confessed to me that she was in love with him.'

The confession made Bevan feel as though he'd taken a blow to his stomach. He had given Fiona everything he had to give. And she had been unfaithful in spite of it. A dark anger formed inside of him at Siorcha's words.

'The man was a Norman. His name was Raymond Graham, Baron of Somerton.'

The red haze of anger tightened in his chest, blurring all rational thought. Dimly, he was aware that Genevieve had taken his hand. Her quiet support kept his rage in check.

Siorcha continued. 'Fiona met him when she was out alone riding one day. His soldiers were camped nearby, and the Baron found her by the stream. She loved him from the moment she saw him, and he loved her—though it was forbidden. Each time you went off to battle she sent word to him, and he came to her. I helped them meet, though it was wrong.'

Genevieve squeezed Bevan's hand, and his fingers held hers in a tight grip. Such raw grief ravaged his face. She could sense his hurt, his broken pride. He had adored Fiona, and to learn that she had betrayed him… Genevieve could only imagine his pain.

She leaned in, trying to exude the silent message that she would stand by him, no matter what else was revealed.

'When Strongbow's army planned the attack on Laochre, Raymond asked Fiona to run away with him. He intended to capture her, and for you to die in battle. But Fiona would not allow him to kill you.'

Siorcha's face softened. 'She did love you, you know. But not in the way she loved Raymond.' She took a breath. 'And so Raymond ordered you to be struck down but left alive.'

Bevan remembered his wife's screams as they had taken her away. Those screams had not been real. She had wanted to go, wanted to leave him.

'No one saw her go,' he said softly. 'I buried her body.'

'You buried her maid, Nuala. They looked alike, and Nuala traded clothes and jewels with Fiona. They meant for Nuala to be taken by the soldiers, so that all would think Fiona was captured. But Nuala's body burned inside the cottage you found that day.'

'Why did you never speak of this before now?' Bevan's voice was deadly quiet. He remembered the feeling of horror when he had found the burned body wearing the silver torque he had given his wife. There had been no question in his mind that he'd found Fiona.

'Forgive me.' Tears rolled down Siorcha's face, and she covered her eyes with her hands. 'I wanted only to help Fiona find happiness with her lover. No one was supposed to die. God has punished me for it.'

'If she did not want to be my wife any longer, why did she not ask for a divorce?' Bevan asked. 'There was no need for such a deception.'

Siorcha stared at him. 'And would you have granted it?'

She shook her head sadly. 'Fiona knew you would never let her go. You treated her as your prized possession.'

Something shifted inside him at her words. He wanted to deny it—to claim that he would have granted her a divorce if she'd asked him. But inside him he saw the brutal truth. He had loved her with every part of him. And he wouldn't have surrendered her. Especially not to a Norman.

If it had taken the rest of his life, fighting within the *Brehon* courts, never would he have let her go. His own father had refused to grant his wife a divorce. Bevan was no different. He had believed that eventually Fiona would love him as much as he loved her.

The grim reality was that he had been no different than Sir Hugh Marstowe.

'You are right,' he said softly. 'I would not have granted her the divorce.' His wife had fled him. Just as Genevieve had left Hugh. And it hurt him to know that Fiona would rather remain in hiding with another man than face him with the truth.

A terrible realisation dawned within him. His entire body grew frigid, and his breath seemed to catch in his lungs.

'Nuala is buried in that grave,' Siorcha said. 'Fiona escaped. And as far as I know she is still alive.'

Chapter Eighteen

Genevieve's eyes were heavy with unshed tears—for what was, and what was never been meant to be. Her future with Bevan was over, destroyed by a woman they had both believed to be dead.

When Genevieve had asked Bevan what he intended to do, he'd merely shaken his head. 'I wish to be alone.'

She had seen in his eyes that he didn't want her near him. The old emptiness had returned to his face, that mask of indifference. He was hurting as much as she was, and already he had begun separating himself.

If Fiona were alive, Bevan would go after her. He would mend whatever breach lay between them, and as for Genevieve—she would be discarded.

Her fear dissipated, to be replaced by anger. She felt a mind-searing fury at the woman who had taken away their second chance at happiness.

Genevieve pulled on her cloak and *brat,* needing to get away. The guards tried to block her path, but she pushed them aside. She let the rage consume her, let it fly free.

Ewan tried to stop her, but she shrugged him away.

'I overheard,' he said softly. 'Are you all right?'

'No.' She choked back the tears. 'Please, Ewan, I need to get away. Let me ride—let me have some time to mourn.'

He signalled for a horse to be brought. 'He won't want you to leave.'

'He doesn't care about me any more,' Genevieve said wearily. 'All that matters is that Fiona is alive. All he'll think about is her.'

'That isn't true. He cares for you,' Ewan said.

'He doesn't care enough,' Genevieve whispered. In her heart she believed that, given a choice, Bevan would always choose Fiona. His sense of honour would keep it so, regardless of his feelings.

Ewan helped her mount the horse, and Genevieve urged the animal forward. Ewan managed to convince the gate guards to let her go, and within moments she was galloping through the snow, her hair streaming behind her.

Icy wind chilled her to the marrow, but she did not feel the cold. She rode hard, watching the landscape blur beneath the mare's hooves. The grey sky was swollen with snowflakes, mirroring the unshed tears in her heart. The sun hid in hazy shadow, and before long it would slip below the horizon in the embrace of night.

Genevieve reached the grove of trees Bevan had shown her the previous morn. She slowed the mare and dismounted, walking towards the stone circle. With each step, her heart broke into another piece. She leaned her cheek against the largest monolith, its roughness strangely soothing.

She sank to her knees, the wet snow seeping into her gown. She wept for him, and for the years they would not spend together.

But most of all she wept because he had never even considered keeping her as his wife.

* * *

Later that night she returned, and found Bevan in their chamber. The chest belonging to Fiona lay open, and he held the scrap of linen in his hands—the one that had belonged to both his wife and daughter.

Genevieve took a step towards him. 'Bevan,' she said softly. 'What if…what if Siorcha is wrong? What if none of it is true?'

'It's true,' he said flatly. 'And I think you know it as well as I.'

'I don't understand why she left you,' she whispered. For he was the man she loved. It devastated her to see the raw pain in his eyes. She wound her arms around his neck, but he did not embrace her. His hands remained at his side.

'For the same reasons you left Hugh. You knew he would come after you, no matter what happened.' His voice sounded coarse, and his eyes were lowered. 'She fled rather than face me.'

'You are not Hugh,' she said. 'Do not even think of comparing yourself to him.'

'Am I so different?' he asked. 'I wanted to kill the men who took her from me. If I had known she loved Somerton I cannot say what I would have done to him.'

'What will become of us?' she asked quietly. She tried to take his hand, but he moved away. The rebuke made her heart crumble more.

'There is no marriage between us any more,' he said flatly. 'You should return home to your parents.'

He was giving up on her. Genevieve surrendered her pride and spoke her mind. 'If you formally divorce Fiona, we could remarry.'

Bevan shook his head slowly. 'I must find her,' he said. 'And when I do I will bring her back to Éireann.'

'And if she will not come?'

His shoulders lowered. 'I know not what she will say. It has been two years. Much has changed.'

'Do you still love her?'

He hesitated, pity filling his eyes. 'I do not know what I feel for her.'

Genevieve turned away so he would not see her tears. Why had she let herself care for him? Why did it have to hurt this much?

She took a deep breath and steadied herself. 'What of Rionallís?'

'We will live at Laochre until the issue is resolved in the courts.' He looked away for a moment. 'Perhaps your father will allow me to buy the land from him.'

Genevieve wanted to argue—but what good would it do? She closed her eyes, wishing that somehow she could undo the day's events.

'I still care for you,' she whispered. 'In spite of it all.'

Her words were a knife in his heart, for he wanted her too. But he could not have her. He was married to Fiona, and the stolen moments he'd had with Genevieve had been nothing but a sin.

He couldn't say anything. To answer her would only cause them more pain. 'It has been a long day for both of us,' he said. 'You should sleep.'

'Where?' Genevieve asked brokenly. Her gaze travelled to the bed, where only that morning they had lain in each other's arms, skin upon skin.

'It does not matter. I will sleep below stairs with the men.'

'But—' She reached out to touch him.

He stepped away. 'Don't you see, Genevieve? You are no longer my wife. It is over between us.'

Without another glance, he closed the door behind him, leaving her. He waited a few moments, and then heard the sound of her tears. His own eyes burned, but there was nothing to be done for it.

Bevan leaned with his back against the door, his head bowed. Though he shed no tears, his grief was no less than hers. The only way to atone for his sin was to bring his wife home again and try to make her happy.

And he would not see Genevieve again.

Bevan rose at dawn, packing only the barest of necessities to take with him. He broke his fast in the quiet of the morning, and stopped only to wake Ewan by nudging the sleeping boy on his pallet.

Ewan stretched, uncurling his long limbs. 'What is it?' he mumbled, yawning.

'I am leaving for England. I want you to send for Connor, and the two of you will look after Rionallís and Genevieve while I go.'

'You're going to find her, aren't you?' The look of distaste on Ewan's face revealed his feelings on the matter. 'I don't see why you won't keep Genevieve. I like her. She prepares better food.' Ewan scowled, rubbing his eyes.

Bevan shook his head in exasperation. Always thinking of his stomach, was Ewan. 'If Fiona is alive, I have to find her. She belongs here.'

'She didn't want to stay here,' Ewan pointed out.

Bevan knew it, but he would have to convince her otherwise. Guilt plagued him for dishonouring his first wife. He had allowed himself to share the intimacies of marriage with another woman. Fate had granted him his wish—to have his wife alive again. He had no choice but to bring her back.

Ewan was right, however. Bevan did not know how he would convince Fiona to return if she had left willingly.

'If I do not return within a fortnight, send Patrick to the Welsh border. He'll know what to do if I am taken captive.'

'You're going alone?' Ewan stared at him as though he'd grown a second head. 'You can't go alone!'

'I can hardly take an army with me,' Bevan said. 'The Baron will not exactly give up Fiona without a fight. And I see no reason to start a war if I can convince her to come back of her own free will. I intend to disguise myself as one of the peasants. I'll have more freedom to observe the castle.'

'It's dangerous. What if she betrays you?' Ewan asked.

Bevan donned his mantle and cloak. 'I can only hope she will not.'

But Ewan's remark left him shaken. Had Fiona betrayed them to the Normans during that first battle? They had managed to drive the enemy back, but at great cost.

Bevan knew it was a risk, but it was one he had to take. More than anything else, he had to know if she was still alive. For the past two years, he had dreamed of holding her in his arms again, of loving her.

He didn't know if he still loved her any more. Both of them had been unfaithful, though his infidelity had been unintentional. What would he say to her when he saw her again? A heaviness settled over his heart. He was supposed to be overjoyed. Instead, he felt sadness that his marriage with Genevieve had ended.

It had never been a real marriage, he knew. But it had felt like one. He had loved watching her wake up in the mornings, stretching and trying to steal the coverlet from him. He would never have that again.

Bevan cast a look up the staircase, to where Genevieve slept above. Better to leave without saying farewell. He would face the uncertain future without the memory of looking upon her one last time.

The wintry air was crisp, laced with the pungent aroma of peat smoke. His destrier was saddled and loaded with the supplies he'd requested.

'Where will you stay before the crossing?' Ewan asked.

'With the Ó Flayertys,' he replied. His brother Trahern had fostered with the family, and his mother's cousins lived in Leinster.

Somerton's lands were just beyond the Welsh border, and it would be safer to make the northern journey on their own shores before crossing the waters to England.

'What do you want me to tell Genevieve?' Ewan glanced above. 'She'll be angry with you.'

'Tell her what you like. But keep her here, whatever you do. Send for her parents to take her home again.'

'This is her home,' Ewan argued.

Bevan did not reply, but mounted his horse. Not a single flake of snow came down from the clear blue skies. The frozen ground crunched beneath his horse's hooves, iced over after a freezing rain the night before.

'God go with you,' Ewan called out.

'And with you.' Bevan urged his destrier through the gates, heading north towards Dun Laoghaire, where he would make the crossing to Holyhead. As Rionallís grew more distant behind him he tried not to think of Genevieve.

'He's going to murder me,' Ewan remarked as the Ó Flayerty lands came into view. 'I promised him I would keep you at Rionallís.'

'You promised to protect me,' Genevieve said. 'And you couldn't very well do that if I was travelling alone.'

When Genevieve had awakened to find Bevan gone, she had refused to let him leave her behind. Until she saw Fiona for herself, she would try to hold onto their marriage. Fiona might not be alive now, even if she had been last summer. And Genevieve had to cling to her hopes, for she had nothing else.

During the past several nights they had travelled north, with Ewan protesting at every mile of the journey. But he had kept her safe, and now she would face Bevan's ire for disobeying him.

Ewan greeted the men guarding the entrance to the Ó Flayerty fortress. The guards allowed them to pass, and Ewan helped Genevieve dismount. 'I'll care for the horses while you find him.'

'Coward,' Genevieve chided. But her own stomach churned. She did not know what Bevan would say when he saw her.

'*Tá*. But I shall stay clear of his fists.'

'He'd not beat you.'

'He might. For endangering you, I think he wouldn't hesitate.' Ewan glanced at the entrance to the house and gathered the reins. 'I'll leave you to him.'

Genevieve squared her shoulders. She had gone over all her arguments until she knew she could present her side with cool logic.

A rosy-cheeked woman, heavy with child, greeted her with a smile.

'I've come to see Bevan,' Genevieve said, removing her cloak.

'He is dining with my husband. I am Aoife Ó Flayerty,' the woman said. 'May I tell him your name?'

'Tell him his wife Genevieve has come.'

Aoife looked surprised, but hid it with another smile. 'You may dine with us. I'll tell Ewan to join you when he's finished with the horses.'

Genevieve followed Aoife to a crowded room where a harpist played a lilting tune. Platters of food were spread out, and torches glowed merrily from sconces set into the walls.

When Bevan saw her, Genevieve thought that Ewan might be right. He did have murder in his eyes.

Still, she faced him. She had come this far, and if nothing else he had to listen to her. Bevan spoke not a word, but took her shoulder in an iron grip. With a smile to his hosts, he half dragged her to an alcove in the corner of the room.

'You should not be here, Genevieve.'

'Neither should you,' she shot back, startling herself with the unexpected anger that rose up. 'Aye, Fiona left you. Her body does not lie next to your daughter's. But that is all you know. She may not be there with Somerton. All of this could be for naught.'

'I have to know,' he told her. 'And I will do it alone.'

'No,' she said. 'Until I see her for myself, you are still my husband.'

Gone was the timid woman he'd known, and in her place stood an indignant wife. Bevan halted the smile before it caught the corner of his mouth. 'Am I?'

'Aye, you are.' She took his hand in hers, lowering her voice to a whisper. 'And I'll not give up my last few days with you.'

Her hand touched his cheek, and lust speared through him. Lug, but he wished he did not have to make this journey. He wished he could forget Siorcha's testimony. Were it not true, he would take his wife above stairs and love her until morning dawned.

Yet, because of the revelation, he had no choice. He had broken his wedding vows, and he had no right to touch Genevieve or be with her.

But Fiona had broken their vows first.

Bevan tried to shake the argument away. He could not forsake his honour, regardless of what his wife had done. He would remain true to Fiona, despite his desire for Genevieve.

Later that evening, when they were alone, a single bed awaited them. He would take the floor and allow Genevieve to sleep on the bed.

'What are you doing?' she asked, as he prepared his cloak upon the floor.

'I intend to sleep.' He removed his boots and tried to arrange the cloak into a pallet for sleeping.

Genevieve came over and sat down beside him on the floor. 'Do not be foolish. You can share the bed with me. I promise I'll not ravish you.'

He sent her a wary look. 'You might.'

She laughed then, the tension broken. 'Bevan, for one night let us forget about the morrow. Sleep beside me. There is no sin in that.'

No, but the thought of lying beside her without being able to touch her was a torment. He ached to hold her in his arms, to taste the sweetness of her skin once more. Just one last time.

He closed his eyes, fighting the temptation. Either way, he would not sleep this night.

She made the decision for him, flipping back the coverlet and sliding to the far side. She closed her eyes, turning her back to him. He suppressed a groan at the sight of her bare skin. He slipped in beside her, still wearing his trews, the straw mattress crackling under his weight.

'Goodnight,' she whispered.

'And to you,' he whispered back. Her body lay only inches from him, and when she moved her skin brushed against him. Immediately he grew aroused, so he turned onto his back, staring at the ceiling.

He mentally counted, willing himself not to give in to his desire. Her lavender scent surrounded them, and he closed his eyes, trying to block it out.

Hours passed, and he could not stop thinking of his journey. Would Fiona want to see him again? Would she divulge his identity to the Baron? His stomach gnawed with a tension that ate at him. He admitted to himself that he didn't want to go. He wished he had never learned the truth.

He looked over to Genevieve. Her shoulders rose and fell in sleep, her dark hair spilling across the pillow.

He believed in the sanctity of marriage, believed in his vows. And it was for those vows that he would sacrifice his own happiness and return to Fiona. He had loved her once; he would learn to love her again.

His chest grew rigid at the thought of leaving Genevieve. He could not take her with him, couldn't bear to watch her sadness if he had to bring Fiona home. He knew of an abbey near Dun Laoghaire. They would say farewell there, and he would have her parents come for her.

In the darkness, she rolled over and planted her icy cold feet upon his thigh.

'Belenus,' he breathed at the contact. At first he nearly pushed her away. Then he realised that this was their last night together. He would not ever be able to touch her again.

Reaching down, he cupped her cold feet in his hands, rubbing the skin to warm them. First one, then the other. She did not stir, but as her feet warmed he pulled her close.

Wrapping his arms around her, he finally drifted off into a dreamless sleep.

Ewan bent low upon the saddle. The sun had nearly reached its zenith in the wintry sky, and his stomach rumbled. Bevan had departed at mid-morn, ordering Ewan to return home alone.

He spurred his horse onward, enjoying the speed even as he resented his brother's orders. When would his brother ever have faith in him? Ewan spent hours every day trying to become a strong fighter. He was improving, he knew. But it was never enough for Bevan.

Behind him, he heard the noise of horses approaching. Ewan scanned the horizon, but not a tree stood in sight to provide cover. Out in the open, he was a target.

He willed himself to stay calm and collected. Glancing behind him, he saw a small group of cavalry—Normans by the look of them. He recognised the armour, and when they drew nearer, it became more difficult to keep his emotions in check.

They were Sir Hugh's men. Marstowe himself rode a chestnut destrier, trimmed in elaborate armour. Ewan hoped they would ride past, but soon it became apparent that they intended to surround him.

Ewan inhaled a deep breath. He mentally recited a Latin prayer, letting the words distract him from the desire to flee. The soldiers cut in front of him and forced him to stop. Ewan lowered his head.

'The youngest MacEgan, aren't you?' Marstowe asked. He drew his horse alongside Ewan's. 'And they have sent you home.'

Ewan did not answer, but pretended Marstowe wasn't there. He tried to remember how to count in Latin, but the sword that slid to his throat made it impossible.

'Where are they going?'

Ewan remained motionless, panic clawing its way inside his throat. These men would torture him if he didn't talk. But how could he betray his own brother and Genevieve? He had failed Bevan once already, causing them both to be captured from his cowardice.

He could not allow it to happen a second time.

The sword broke through his skin and he felt the warm

wetness of his blood. A rushing noise filled his ears, and his vision swam. 'I won't tell you anything,' he said.

He prayed for courage to endure whatever Marstowe planned.

'They are travelling alone,' Marstowe remarked. 'How curious. Why would they not bring an escort? Unless they did not wish to be noticed.' The man's voice was smooth, oily in tone.

Ewan tried to reach for the sword at his side, but Marstowe twisted his arm. The knight unsheathed a dagger and ran the blade over Ewan's palm. 'Where are they going, boy?'

The MacEgans are the greatest warriors in Éireann. They never surrender. Their courage is legendary.

But as Marstowe's dagger carved through his skin, he could only manage, 'Somerton,' before darkness claimed him.

'I am not leaving you,' Genevieve said, as they reached Dun Laoghaire. 'If you believe I will stay behind in an abbey while you go after Fiona you are sorely mistaken.'

'I am not taking you with me,' he said, bringing their horses to a halt. 'And that is final.'

'If you do not, I'll follow you again.' She sat up straight in the saddle. Stubborn man. Genevieve knew that there was a strong chance Fiona was alive. But there was a slim chance of hope, too. And she intended to hold out, praying that somehow they could save their fragile marriage.

Genevieve turned her horse in the direction of the coast.

Bevan caught up to her, anger and worry lined in his face. 'Genevieve, heed my command.'

He wasn't going to let her go. She could tell. With a sigh, she stopped and faced his anger.

'Bevan, hear me.' She lowered her tone, softening it. 'Put

yourself in my place for a moment. If Hugh were still here, would you let me go alone to face him?'

'It isn't the same thing.'

'Aye, it is. You would be afraid for me because you know what he is like. Just as I fear for your safety. What makes you believe Somerton will let her go? If he catches you, he'll put you to death. At least if I am with you I can try to get help. To go alone is madness.'

She could see him beginning to consider it, so she pressed further. 'If she is alive, I'll—I'll stay only long enough to see you both safe. Then I'll leave. I promise.'

Tentacles of jealousy wrapped around her heart, for she knew Bevan would forget her as soon as he saw his wife once more. Any feelings he held towards her would evaporate like wisps of smoke when he laid eyes upon Fiona.

Genevieve wanted to fight for him, to make him love her. But her only choice was to leave, to let him go. The very thought of never seeing him again made her heart bleed.

Like as not, she had lost him already. He was determined to set her aside and find his wife. And, though it was like a blade to her soul, she would let him go if he was happier with Fiona.

She had one consolation, though. A small grain of hope. Her courses were late, and it could be that she was with child. She prayed desperately that it was so, that she would have a part of him to keep. But she could not tell him—not unless she knew for certain.

'I do not want to hurt you, *a chroí*,' he said. 'And I like it not, putting you in danger.'

'I am in more danger alone than with you,' she said. 'No harm will come to me under your protection.'

Her faith in him broke his resolve. Though he didn't want to see the sadness in her face, he understood her need to be there. It was the same as his need to see Fiona, to find out if she was still alive.

With a sigh, he nodded. 'All right. You may come with me.'

They made it to the coast to undergo the crossing. The sky was overcast with grey clouds, shadowing a sombre tint to the waters. Within a few days they would reach Somerton's castle and learn the truth.

Bevan turned his gaze to the horizon, where the coast of Wales would eventually emerge. Beyond the borders he would find the answers he sought. He cleared his mind of all thoughts, steeling himself to face whatever might come.

The Baron of Somerton's holdings were equal to Laochre in stature. The donjon stood high upon a motte, elevated above the surrounding baileys. The outbuildings were made of timber, covered in plaster save for the wooden beams that supported the structures. They surrounded the donjon in a circular pattern, and the castle boasted two palisades for protection.

Bevan had clothed himself as a peasant, and Genevieve had done likewise, wearing a brown kirtle with her head veiled. He wore his sword strapped beneath his tunic, the hilt covered behind his hood. If needed, he could reach behind his back and unsheath it. They would enter the castle behaving as servants, while Bevan searched for Fiona.

Genevieve had been unable to eat that morning. Her stomach clenched in a bundle of nerves. She prayed with every fibre of her being that Fiona was not here, that it had been a journey for naught. The fear crept into her heart that today she would lose Bevan forever.

He had eaten little himself, and his demeanour was distant. When she tried to make conversation, he answered with a single word, if at all. He had been careful not to touch her, and he behaved as if she weren't there. She knew why he was acting this way, but it didn't make the hurt less.

With each step closer to the donjon, she felt herself dying a little inside. Her eyes burned, but she kept onward, each step heavier than the last. All around them the castle buzzed with activity. Dogs barked, scampering around the inner bailey. A blacksmith worked upon armour at his forge, while the women brought steaming containers from the kitchen.

As Bevan turned to step into the donjon, Genevieve stopped. Her entire body felt like ice with the premonition that Siorcha had been right. She couldn't bear to watch another woman embrace the man she had come to love.

'What is it?' Bevan returned to her side, his face concerned.

'I am not going in.'

He pulled her away from the crowd of servants, bringing her near the outer wall. 'Tell me.'

She blinked away the hot tears. 'Go on. Find her.' She cradled her elbows, trying to keep a tenuous hold upon her feelings. 'I think you should be alone when you see her for the first time.'

He reached out and cupped her cheek. Strands of her dark hair fell against his palm. Deep inside him, he ached for her. Genevieve had healed him when all he'd wanted was to avenge Fiona's death. She had given so much of herself. And today he would have to let her go.

'I am sorry.' He brushed a kiss across her forehead, damning himself for what he must do. 'I will return for you once I have seen what I need to see.'

Genevieve nodded once, a single tear spilling over. The sight of her tears was like a knife twisting within him. But he had to go.

'Genevieve.' He breathed her name like a prayer. 'I—'

She waited as the seconds stretched between them. Bevan bowed his head. 'I am sorry. I never wanted to hurt you, *a chroí,*' he whispered.

'Do not call me that.' She couldn't bear to hear the endearment. It reminded her too much of the way he had looked at her when he'd loved her, late at night. She straightened her shoulders. 'I wish you well.' She walked away, pulling her cloak around her shoulders against the cold.

Once she saw him leave, it was as though something splintered deep within her. She had wanted so badly for him to change his mind, to choose her over his first wife. But he hadn't.

The loss of him cut her deeply, and she wished she had guarded her heart more closely. He didn't belong to her and he never would.

She stopped next to a wall, her lungs burning. With her hands on the icy timber, she grieved for the marriage she had lost. She sank down onto the snowy ground, her back against the wall. Her throat was raw and her cheeks stung. She didn't know how long she wept, but releasing the tears helped to gather what remained of her pride.

She slipped away, moving in and out of the crowd of people to ensure no one noticed her. Then she moved with another group outside the gates, until she was free. It took only moments to return to where their horses were tethered.

Spurring her horse into a gallop, she rode past the village and into the open fields, willing herself to close off the grief of losing him.

Genevieve did not know how long she rode, and in her state of numbness she did not hear the riders approaching behind her. Her mare reared as a hood was thrown over her head.

She struggled, but the men grabbed her arms, pulling her off the horse. She landed hard on the ground, and when she fought to stand, a fist struck her down. Blood trickled from her lip, and she ceased her movement. They tightened leather thongs around her wrists so she could not escape.

'Take her to the camp,' one of the men said.

'What about MacEgan?' another asked.

'He'll come when he learns we have her. Send the boy.'

Someone pulled her atop a horse. She almost wanted to laugh. Bevan would not come for her. Not any more.

If she intended to escape, the only person she could rely on was herself.

Bevan picked up a bundle of wood, following a servant into the donjon. With his head kept low, no one spoke to him.

The warmth of the donjon was a sharp contrast to the frigid air outside. Bevan deposited his wood near the hearth and hung back in the shadows. Deliberately, he kept his gaze down. If Fiona were here she would be seated upon the dais with the Baron, awaiting the noon meal.

He contemplated the rushes on the floor, suddenly wishing he had not come. He had been happy with Genevieve. She had filled up the empty pieces inside him, making him whole.

His life with her came rushing back in fleeting memories. He remembered rescuing her from Marstowe, watching her bruises fade along with her fears.

He remembered her body lying beneath his when he'd joined with her, her eyes shining with trust and something more. Even the way she would warm her freezing feet upon him in the middle of the night was something he didn't want to forget.

He felt certain she loved him, though she hadn't said it. And he wondered why he would give it up—why give her up for a woman who had left him?

Hurt and anger suffused him at the thought. He didn't want

Fiona. He didn't want to see emptiness in her eyes when he could see fulfilment in another woman's eyes. He wanted to wake beside Genevieve, to give her the children she craved. He wanted her smile, her laughter. He'd dry her tears of sorrow.

He closed his eyes, turning his back upon the dais. *Just walk away. Pretend you never came here. Let the past go.*

Bevan took a step away, convinced that this was the right thing to do. He had fallen in love with Genevieve, and she belonged with him.

Then he turned and saw her.

Chapter Nineteen

His child. His beloved daughter. Alive.

All logic and words failed him. He did not understand why or how, but it mattered not. Kneeling before her, he saw the flicker of recognition on her face.

'Do you remember me, *a iníon?*' She had grown from a baby into a young child. Her dark hair was neatly braided, and she wore a blue kirtle trimmed with gold.

'Da?' she whispered. Bevan opened his arms to her, and her small arms tightened about his neck. He could not stop the tears of thankfulness that came from his eyes.

'Brianna.' He gripped her so hard he knew he was squeezing the breath from her. But he had never expected to find her again. 'I've missed you. What happened? Why are you here?'

'Mama brought me here,' she said, hugging him tightly. He pressed a kiss against her cheek, unable to believe he was holding her once more.

Fiona had lied again. Her betrayal cut him so deeply he was almost afraid to see her. She had stolen away his own daughter. For two long years he had not seen her. His anger towards Fiona intensified.

'Where is your mother?'

Brianna shook her head. 'Mama died last autumn.'

Last autumn. It meant he was still married to Genevieve. A surge of happiness broke through him, and he envisioned Genevieve waiting for him beyond the gates. There had been no sin between them, only the sanctity of marriage. Bevan rejoiced inwardly at the thought.

Then at once he remembered that his daughter, just five years of age, grieved still for her mother. She knew nothing of Fiona's actions.

Brianna turned accusing eyes upon her father. 'I waited and waited for you, Da. Why didn't you come for me?'

'I knew not where you were. Who looks after you now?'

She pointed at the donjon. 'He does. He says he is my new father now. But you are my da, not him.'

The mixture of emotions made it hard for him to grasp what she was saying. Fiona had indeed run from him, taking her daughter with her, to this place.

'Move away from her,' a voice said.

Bevan looked up and saw an infuriated Norman lord. His grip only tightened upon his daughter.

'Fear not, *a iníon*. No one will take you from me again.'

Her captors had imprisoned Genevieve in a makeshift tent. There was no fire, and she shivered inside her cloak. Her hands were bound behind her back, and her wrists throbbed with stinging pain from the leather thongs.

Hugh Marstowe had planned a trap, intending to use her to lure Bevan. She had tried to argue that Bevan would not come, that he didn't care about her. Then she'd learned of Ewan's fate. She prayed that he lived still. Bevan would come after Hugh for vengeance, but when he did they would kill him.

She worked at her bonds, trying to free herself. They had

taken her eating knife from her, after searching her for weapons she did not have. The tent flap moved and Marstowe entered. He sat on his haunches, watching her.

'I wonder how long it will take for your husband to arrive?' he mused. He leaned in, and she shrank back. Grasping her throat, he asked, 'Would you like to watch me kill him?'

Genevieve closed her eyes, fighting the fears that rose up. She prayed that Bevan would not come for her, that he would remain safe.

A fist struck her, and pain radiated through her jaw. 'Answer me!'

When she did not, he jerked her hair back so she was forced to look at him. It made her feel as though she were reliving her past nightmare. Marstowe's hand gripped her chin. 'You gave your body to him, little whore. You let him take what belonged to me. And for touching you he will pay with his life.'

He struck her across the face, shoving her to the ground. She felt the cold earth beneath her cheek, but did not struggle against him. Fighting would only excite his anger more.

In disgust, Hugh left her alone. The icy chill of the hardened ground stung against her face, but she could see a faint light beneath the tent. Easing towards the bottom edge of the tent, she peered outside. Three men guarded her, and other soldiers stood on alert, armed and ready.

Bevan was riding into a trap. Marstowe would kill him, as he'd promised. And she would have to watch him die—unless she did something to stop him.

But what?

She bit her lip against the pain and focused on the knots. Moisture from the snow had caused them to tighten, but she worked at them with her fingertips.

Escape was her only hope of saving Bevan. At the thought

of him, her bruised heart hurt again. His handsome face, scarred from battle, rose up in her memory. She thought of his hooded eyes, the way he looked at her, hungry with desire. She remembered the way he had taken away her fears, teaching her the ways of loving.

She didn't want him to die. No matter that he had chosen Fiona, she loved him. She prayed that a child grew within her womb, that a part of him would always belong to her.

One of the knots slipped, offering a thread of hope.

'You should not have come, MacEgan.' The Baron of Somerton glared at Bevan, his sword drawn. Somerton was stocky, dark-haired, and he wore his moustache and beard trimmed close. He stood slightly shorter than Bevan, but there was no doubt the man had seen battle before, from the way he gripped his sword.

'I've come for Brianna.' Bevan would tear the man limb from limb for daring to keep her from him.

He reached behind him and unsheathed his sword to meet Somerton's weapon. The Baron had a wooden shield, whereas Bevan had nothing but his weapon. Their blades clashed as they circled one another. 'Why did you steal my wife and daughter?' Bevan demanded. 'Is it because you lacked the courage to face me yourself?'

Somerton lifted his shield to defend Bevan's strike and held his blade steady. 'That was Fiona's doing. I asked her to reveal the truth.' His features grew harsh. 'You should have died on the battlefield years ago, MacEgan. Were it not for Fiona's mercy, I would have gladly taken your life then.'

Bevan had warmed to the fight, and was now beginning to take pleasure in it.

A soldier took Brianna in his arms, to keep her from running towards the men. 'Da!' Brianna shrieked.

The sound of her voice only made Bevan fight harder. His sword collided with Somerton's shield again. The Baron struck his blade, twisting to force Bevan in a new direction. Lord Somerton was skilled—a challenge he hadn't expected.

The Baron increased the tempo of the fight. It forced Bevan to concentrate on his defence, and he realised they were evenly matched. He circled the Norman, watching for any weakness. It seemed that Somerton favoured his right side.

Bevan feinted right, and when Somerton raised his shield he changed his direction, forcing his enemy backward. Steel met steel, the blades ringing in the winter stillness. Bevan poured all his energies into the fight, releasing two years' worth of grief and rage. Sweat beaded upon Somerton's face, and his metal armour became a hindrance instead of a protection.

The Baron breathed heavily, but still he fought. Somerton sliced his sword downwards, and Bevan barely avoided the fatal strike. In response, he increased his speed, slashing until Somerton was trapped against a wall. With a final blow Bevan disarmed the Baron. He held his sword to the Baron's throat.

'I should kill you,' he said. 'For all that you have done.'

'Da?' a girlish voice whispered. 'I want to go home.'

Somerton's face softened at Brianna's plea. 'I treated her as my own daughter, you know. I wish she had been.' Lowering his shoulders in defeat, he said, 'Take her. She belongs with her father.' With a nod to the soldier, Somerton ordered the release of Brianna.

Tiny arms gripped Bevan's thigh. His left hand moved down to stroke her forehead.

'I never wanted this deception, you know,' Somerton admitted. 'I wanted Fiona to tell you the truth from the beginning. But she wanted to take Brianna with her. She swore you would never grant her a divorce, and she couldn't bear to be separated from her daughter.'

Bevan lowered his sword. 'She was right.' Even now, he could not believe the lengths she had gone to. How could she have taken his own child from him? Any feelings he had held for Fiona had now disappeared. He'd never truly known her, nor had he realised how desperate she was.

'How did she die?'

Somerton inclined his head. 'Her melancholy never left her, I fear. She grieved for the loss of her maid—the one who took her place and died in battle. Then Fiona miscarried a babe.' The Baron's face filled with regret. 'She took her life soon afterwards. I could not save her.'

Bevan lowered his sword. His wife's infidelity meant little to him any more. 'I am taking Brianna with me,' he informed the Baron.

Somerton hunched down in front of Brianna. Bevan tensed, keeping his blade ready.

'Go with your da, little poppet. Be happy,' Somerton said, his voice heavy.

Brianna's thumb tucked into her mouth and she nodded. As Somerton gave orders for an escort, Bevan's gaze searched the grounds for some sign of Genevieve.

Worry curled in his gut when he saw that she was gone.

Ewan's hands were raw, and his body was beaten and bruised, as he rode towards Lord Somerton's donjon. The gait of the horse jarred his sore muscles, and he fought to keep himself upright.

He had failed Bevan again. And Genevieve. He had told Sir Hugh everything he knew, but they had not stopped torturing him. They had carved the skin from his palms until he doubted he would ever handle a sword again. Blood seeped through the bandages on both hands, and he used his wrists to hold the reins.

At the gate, the guards would not allow him entrance. He was fortunate, for Bevan had come into the inner bailey.

'Ewan!' he called out. 'What has happened?' Bevan's face shadowed with worry.

'Marstowe,' Ewan managed. 'He's taken Genevieve.' He nodded towards the hills. 'Across the river.'

Rage blackened Bevan's face. 'Why?'

'Rionallís,' Ewan managed, before he slipped into unconsciousness.

Bevan caught his brother's body, his mind infused with guilt. He blamed himself for Ewan's wounds. At the sight of his brother's hands, he wanted to inflict the same wounds tenfold upon their enemy.

A sick dread filled him at the thought of Genevieve's fate. Bevan knew Hugh wanted him dead, and this was a means of luring him. Marstowe would take Genevieve for himself, for only through her could he gain Rionallís.

Bevan thought of asking Lord Somerton for soldiers, but he doubted if the man would help him. He held no liking for Bevan, not to mention that an entourage might inspire Marstowe to harm Genevieve.

No, he would have to go alone. If he could infiltrate Marstowe's men and get her out alive, it would be his only hope. His mind devised a strategy while he gave orders for Ewan to be looked after.

The Baron approached the pair and, seeing Ewan's wounds, sent for the healer.

'Will you keep my daughter safe for me?' Bevan asked.

Lord Somerton nodded. 'I will.'

With Brianna in the Baron's care, Bevan mounted and rode in the direction of the camp. He berated himself for letting Ewan leave by himself. He knew the boy had pride—pride that Bevan had broken many times with his words. Bevan had believed that allowing Ewan the chance to travel alone would show his faith in his youngest brother. He should have listened to his instincts. Now, because of his eagerness to find Fiona, he had endangered two of his loved ones.

A fierce need for vengeance rooted in his heart. He would find Genevieve and rescue her from Marstowe.

He could only pray that it wasn't too late.

Chapter Twenty

Ewan opened his eyes to a searing pain in his hands. He fought against crying out, and the healer pressed him back down onto the pallet. 'Hush, lad. I must clean your wounds.'

The woman gave him a bitter-tasting drink that made him feel dizzy. As she worked to tend his hands, he tried not to succumb to sleep.

'I have to help him,' he said, struggling to sit up.

'Lie down,' she urged. 'You must rest.'

No. He could not lie abed. Not while Bevan was riding to save Genevieve. Marstowe's soldiers would kill both of them, and it would be his fault.

A surge of fury welled up within him—anger at himself for his failure. Ewan used what remained of his strength to push the woman back. 'My brother's life depends upon it.'

The heaviness of sleep descended upon him from the herbal drink. Ewan went to a corner and forced himself to retch up the tea, knowing he needed his wits for survival.

Lord Somerton entered the chamber. 'What is it?'

'Marstowe's men will kill my brother when he arrives. I

need you to send reinforcements to help him. He's out there alone.'

Somerton started to shake his head. 'I do not think I should get involved in this battle.'

'He'll die if you don't!' Ewan insisted. 'Or is that what you wanted all along?' His voice shook with anger and helplessness. He had failed his brother once before, and Bevan had rescued him. If it hadn't been for his weakness, Marstowe would never have found them.

'No. Such was not my intention.'

'Then send men,' Ewan pleaded. 'After what you allowed to happen, you must help him.'

The Baron paused, deliberating. 'Where are they?'

Ewan described the whereabouts of the campsite, and after a long moment the Baron relented. 'I owe him this for what I did.' He departed to give orders.

Ewan reached out to open the door, his hands bleeding once more. He blocked out the pain, keeping his mind steady.

This time he would not fail.

Bevan dismounted from his horse when the camp came into view. He lowered himself to the ground, and the frost-laced grasses dampened his tunic. Inching over the top of the hillside on his stomach, he gazed down upon the enemy.

Not a tree or stone offered a hiding place. The soldiers awaited him in full view. In the centre of their camp was a single tent, heavily guarded. He didn't even know if Genevieve was inside.

A secret attack was not possible under the circumstances. But before he made a move he had to ensure that Genevieve was alive.

He remounted his horse, leading the destrier over the crest

of the ridge. Pulling an arrow from his quiver, he nocked it to the bowstring.

'Marstowe!' he called out.

A soldier rode towards him, his spear aimed. Bevan released his arrow, and the shaft struck its mark. The man's body fell to the ground, and Bevan readied another arrow.

'I want to see Genevieve. If she is alive, I will come down to you.'

He could not see Sir Hugh, but the guards parted the tent folds. Moments later they dragged Genevieve out. Her hands were bound behind her back; blood was trickling down her cheek.

'Bevan, go back!' she called out. 'Come no closer.'

He ignored her request, moving his horse forward but keeping out of their range. It was like a terrible dream unfolding before him.

'Let her go,' he said. 'And I will see to it you get what you want.'

Marstowe edged forward. 'All I want is to see you dead.'

Behind him, Bevan heard horses approaching. Turning, he saw soldiers coming around to flank him, cutting off his escape. He fired several arrows, but there were too many men.

When his last arrow was gone, he drew his sword. They closed in upon him.

'Bring him to me alive,' Marstowe warned the men. 'I will be the one to end his life.'

Bevan fought against his attackers, and it took six of them to disarm him. His mind raced with fear for Genevieve. The men bound him so tightly he could barely breathe from the ropes tied around his chest. His hands and feet were also tied, though he fought for his release.

Marstowe forced Bevan to look at Genevieve. Blood caked

her temple, and her hair lay dishevelled about her shoulders. Her kirtle was torn and her feet were bare.

Bevan's rage trebled at the thought of her being beaten and left to freeze. 'Don't touch her,' he warned.

'Or what?' Marstowe mocked. 'You can do nothing to stop me.'

'I swear to God, you bastard, I'll kill you if you lay a hand on her.'

'I already have,' Marstowe said. 'And for your insolence she will suffer.' Striding towards Genevieve, he struck a blow across her face.

Genevieve's head lowered for a moment. Then she stared at Marstowe, a glittering anger in her eyes. She turned to Bevan, shaking her head slightly. He wondered what she planned to do.

Marstowe stepped behind her, fitting a knife to her throat. 'She did not fight me, either.' Jerking Genevieve's head back, he rested the blade against her smooth skin.

Bevan's world fragmented at the thought of Genevieve suffering at Marstowe's hands. His muscles strained against the ropes and he threw his body at one of the guards, knocking the man down.

At that second Genevieve pushed Marstowe. She had somehow loosened the knots from her ropes enough to free herself. She leaned back and twisted against him, forcing him to the ground. The knife sank into Hugh's thigh, and he exhaled in shock. Genevieve pulled the weapon free, running to Bevan.

She began cutting his ropes, but Bevan took the dagger from her. 'Go!' he urged, and she ran towards the hillside. Genevieve's efforts had loosened the ropes enough for him to snap the remaining ones. Straining hard against his bonds, he broke free.

As the soldiers closed in on him he used the knife to defend himself. In the distance, he saw Marstowe rise from the ground, mindless of his wound. He mounted and pursued Genevieve on horseback, his sword raised to strike her down.

A cold rage descended upon Bevan, and he swung his knife like a madman, stabbing at the soldiers until he could grasp a sword. With dagger and sword, he fended them off.

Marstowe was closing in.

Bevan punched a guard, slashed at another until he could mount a horse. He spurred the animal onward, racing towards her.

Lug, keep her safe, he prayed.

She had nearly reached the top of the hill, but Marstowe charged her. Bevan raised his sword, prepared to aim it at Marstowe's back, when suddenly another horse came over the crest.

A battle cry emerged from the rider, and he saw his brother Ewan throw himself at Marstowe, knocking him off the horse. A small band of soldiers rode behind him, and they scattered to fight against Marstowe's men. Bevan breathed in relief that Genevieve was unharmed.

Marstowe rose, and in horror Bevan saw him lunge with his sword towards Ewan. His brother blocked the blade, but the tip sliced through his upper arm. Ewan cried out and stumbled to the ground.

Bevan jerked back on the reins of his mount, unsheathing his own sword. He dismounted and swung against Hugh. With all his strength Marstowe pushed back against Bevan. Bevan could see the wild fear in his eyes as Hugh wielded his sword. But his enemy's movements had slowed, his blood flowing freely from the blow Genevieve had struck.

With a fast parry Bevan moved in, his sword barely missing Marstowe's stomach. Steel clashed against steel, until Bevan's foot slipped against a patch of ice.

Marstowe pressed his advantage, but Bevan rolled away. At the last second he lifted his blade, embedding it deeply into Marstowe's chest.

His eyes froze, and Bevan met his gaze. As death closed over Marstowe, Bevan withdrew the blade and let the man's body fall to the ground.

He ran to Genevieve, crushing her in an embrace.

'Ewan—' she managed.

Bevan took her hand and they knelt beside the boy. The sword had cut him deeply across his left shoulder. Ewan's face was deathly pale, but he offered a weak smile. 'I did not fail you this time, brother,' he whispered.

Bevan clasped his hand. 'No, you did not.' He smiled back. 'I owe you our lives, young warrior.'

Ewan's smile broadened before he closed his eyes.

'Will he live?' Genevieve asked, trying to reduce the flow of blood with the hem of her kirtle.

Bevan nodded. 'We must take him back to the fortress with all haste.'

'My thanks,' Genevieve whispered. 'I am sorry for the trouble I have caused.'

Bevan pulled her into his arms. 'You have nothing to be sorry for. I am the one with regrets,' he said, his voice tinged with emotion. 'I came back to tell you Fiona no longer lives. She died long before our marriage.'

He caressed her face, mindful of Genevieve's fresh bruises. 'She hid Brianna, letting everyone believe she had died of a fever years ago. I found my daughter at Somerton's donjon.'

Genevieve's expression was brittle, but she mustered a smile. 'I am glad for you.'

'Genevieve,' he breathed, holding her tightly. 'Come back with me.'

A desperate hope welled up inside her, but she could not help the feelings of anger that shielded her love for him. He would have chosen Fiona had she been there.

And she didn't like it. Not at all.

'We must tend to Ewan's wounds,' she said, rising to her feet. 'And then I am going home to my parents.'

She saw the injured expression on his face, the surprise. He must have thought she would fall into his arms—that she would go back to Erin with him.

'I'm in love with you,' he said quietly. 'And I don't want you to go.'

Tears pricked at her eyes, but she held on to her pride. 'You made your choice, Bevan. Now I am making mine.'

Chapter Twenty-One

Imposing shadows stretched across the fortress belonging to Lord Thomas de Renalt, Earl of Longford. A solitary figure scaled the rampart and moved to the top of the battlement. Another man waited below, until a rope was lowered. He grumbled in Latin beneath his breath as he was hauled to the top.

'This is foolishness, Bevan,' Father Ó Brian remarked. 'I much prefer stairs.'

'Shh. Come.' Bevan gestured for the man to follow him across the battlement and into the donjon. 'Wait here.' The priest remained outside while Bevan searched for the right chamber.

Fortune smiled upon him, for he heard the lilting sound of Genevieve's music, alluring and haunting in its sadness. He followed the sound until he stood outside her door.

Nearly a month had passed since he'd seen her last. It had taken longer than he had anticipated to gain her father's favour, and to pay the necessary fines for the death of Sir Hugh.

He knew Genevieve was angry, but he would not accept her refusal to come home. And he didn't mind breaking a few rules. Longford had agreed to let him through the gates, but he would not grant Bevan any aid in winning Genevieve over. Which was why Bevan had resorted to bringing his own priest, and ropes to scale the walls.

He entered her chamber with stealth, motioning for the priest to await him. She sat upon a stool, the Celtic harp balanced between her knees. He'd sent her the gift, hoping to gain her forgiveness.

The top of the harp stood just above her head when she was seated. She ran her fingers across its strings, the tones rising and falling beneath her hands. Her hair remained hidden behind a veil, while her slender form was clad in a dark red kirtle.

He had practised what he intended to say, repeating the words over and again in his mind. And yet as soon as he saw her, all traces of speech fled.

At last, he interrupted her song. 'Did my gift please you?'

Her hands struck a false note, and Genevieve jerked in surprise. 'What are you doing here? If my father finds you—'

'Your father has allowed me into the castle. He knows I am here.' Bevan cocked his head to the side. 'Although I am not certain about your mother.'

'Well, I do not want you here.' She glared at him.

'You were wrong, you know,' he said, moving the harp aside. He saw her risk a glance towards the door, but he closed the distance between them. Clumsy words stumbled over his tongue. 'I wanted—no, I needed you long before I—'

Wariness haunted her eyes, and he knew he had to find the right words. 'You left before I could tell you the truth. Even if Fiona had been alive I would have come back to you. You are the one I want as my wife.'

Doubt clouded Genevieve's features. She wanted so much to believe him. 'I don't think—'

'I agree,' he said, drawing her up. He trapped her in an embrace. 'Don't think at all. Just—know that I love you.'

He meant the words. The aching intensity in his green eyes, the way he humbled himself before her, bespoke the truth.

'And I'm not leaving without you.' His arms closed around her waist while his words breached the fragile defences of her heart.

Each day without him had augmented her despair. She had missed him with a need she hadn't known. And when the Celtic harp had arrived as a gift from him, its carved wood reminding her of the days at Rionallís, she had wept with longing.

But she truly hadn't believed he would come back.

'Do you promise?' she whispered, moving her hands up the strong planes of his back.

'Do I promise what?' He lowered his face to hers, poised to meet her lips.

'Do you promise to carry me off like the Irish barbarian you are?'

He smiled against her mouth. 'As long as I am allowed to ravish you a time or two.'

'Or three,' she whispered, even as his mouth came down to claim hers.

His hands removed the veil, twining in her hair and clinging to her in an embrace that made her whole again.

'I love you,' she said, claiming him as her husband.

His hands moved over her body in thanksgiving. Then he stepped back, a look of startled wonder on his face. His hand moved down to the hardened curve of her stomach.

'Genevieve?' He breathed the question. At her nod, he embraced her again, and Genevieve wrapped her arms around his neck, needing his closeness.

A soft knock sounded at the door. Bevan tilted her chin to look at him. 'That will be Father Ó Brian, I believe.'

'What do you mean?'

'I brought the priest with me.' Kissing her lightly, he called out, 'You may enter, Father.'

Genevieve's throat closed up with emotion, and a desperate laugh bubbled forth. 'You can't possibly mean to do this.'

Moments later, Father Ó Brian cleared his throat. 'This is not proper, Bevan. I have never blessed a marriage ceremony like this one.'

'Sometimes stronger measures are called for when it comes to stubborn women. Continue, Father.'

Father Ó Brian began the Latin words of the marriage rite, while Genevieve took his hand. His thumb caressed her palm as he gave his vow, promising himself to her.

'I've made my choice, Genevieve. And for ever and always that choice is you.' Bevan gazed down upon her, and she saw the depth of emotion in his eyes. 'I love you, and I want you as my bride.'

The priest awaited her response.

'I will take you for my husband again,' she whispered.

His face spread into a magnificent smile, and the priest continued with the marriage rite, giving his final blessing.

The kiss Bevan gave her afterwards removed every shred of doubt she might have had.

'Leave us, Father. I've a marriage to consummate.'

Genevieve blushed, even as her body warmed to his words. As the moon rose to illuminate their chamber, Bevan lifted her into his arms. His hands slid across her ribs, stroking every inch of her. When he reached her stomach, his hand rested over the manifestation of their loving.

'I love you,' Bevan whispered, 'and I would wed you a thousand times if I could.' He cupped her face in his hands, and she marvelled that he belonged to her at last. 'Is that what you want?'

The pleasure building within her rushed in a flood of desire for him. 'No.' She slid her arms around his waist, pressing her cheek to his chest. Her heart swelled with love. 'All I've ever wanted is you.'

Epilogue

'You have a son,' Isabel said, presenting him with a tiny swaddled infant. The boy's hand curled about Bevan's thumb, and he could not describe the magnitude of the love that filled him.

He was a father again. He touched the boy's cheek, offering up a silent prayer of thanks.

When his sister-in-law opened the door to their chamber, he saw the tired face of his wife. Never was any face more dear to him than hers. He sat beside Genevieve, nestling their son between them.

'We've a fine son, *a ghrá*.'

'Aye, we do.' She leaned her head against his shoulder. 'Brianna will be eager to see her new brother. Though I know she wanted a sister.'

Bevan stroked her hair. 'What shall we name him?'

A head poked around the doorframe. 'Ewan is a good name.'

Bevan grinned at his brother's suggestion. 'I thought you were preparing for your travels to England.'

Genevieve's father had offered to continue Ewan's training, now that his hands had healed. Each day Ewan practised with the sword, and Bevan had seen a new confidence in him.

Ewan would always be the greatest of warriors in Bevan's eyes, for he owed Genevieve's life to him. And he hoped that one day his younger brother would gain the skills he so desired.

'I wanted to see my nephew before I left,' he said. 'Good wishes to you both.'

Genevieve embraced him, and Bevan did likewise. 'Safe journey to you. Send us word when you arrive.'

'What was your father's name?' Genevieve asked Bevan, after Ewan had left.

Startled, he answered, 'Duncan.'

'I like it,' she said, kissing his cheek.

'I love you, Genevieve,' he said, capturing her lips for a deeper kiss. Though he said it often, he wondered if she truly understood how much he meant it. Each day with her was a blessing.

'And I love you.'

With their child cradled beside them, Bevan felt a profound sense of goodness. For out of his greatest sorrow had come his greatest joy.

* * * * *

Mediterranean Nights

Join the guests and crew of Alexandra's Dream,
*the newest luxury ship to set sail on the
romantic Mediterranean, as they experience
the glamorous world of cruising.*

*A new Harlequin continuity series
begins in June 2007 with*
FROM RUSSIA, WITH LOVE
by Ingrid Weaver

*Marina Artamova books a cabin on the
luxurious cruise ship* Alexandra's Dream,
*when she finds out that her orphaned nephew
and his adoptive father are aboard.
She's determined to be reunited with the boy...
but the romantic ambience of the ship
and her undeniable attraction to a man she considers
her enemy are about to interfere with her quest!*

Turn the page for a sneak preview!

Piraeus, Greece

"There she is, Stefan. *Alexandra's Dream*." David Anderson squatted beside his new son and pointed at the dark blue hull that towered above the pier. The cruise ship was a majestic sight, twelve decks high and as long as a city block. A circle of silver and gold stars, the logo of the Liberty Cruise Line, gleamed from the swept-back smokestack. Like some legendary sea creature born for the water, the ship emanated power from every sleek curve—even at rest it held the promise of motion. "That's going to be our home for the next ten days."

The child beside him remained silent, his cheeks working in and out as he sucked furiously on his thumb. Hair so blond it appeared white ruffled against his forehead in the harbor breeze. The baby-sweet scent unique to the very young mingled with the tang of the sea.

"Ship," David said. "Uh, *parakhod*."

From beneath his bangs, Stefan looked at the *Alexandra's Dream*. Although he didn't release his thumb, the corners of his mouth tightened with the beginning of a smile.

David grinned. That was Stefan's first smile this afternoon, one of only two since they had left the orphanage yesterday. It was probably because of the boat—according to the orphanage staff, the boy loved boats, which was the main reason David had decided to book this cruise. Then again, there was a strong possibility the smile could have been a reaction to David's attempt at pocket-dictionary Russian. Whatever the cause, it was a good start.

The liaison from the adoption agency had claimed that Stefan had been taught some English, but David had yet to see evidence of it. David continued to speak, positive his son would understand his tone even if he couldn't grasp the words. "This is her maiden voyage. Her first trip, just like this is our first trip, and that makes it special." He motioned toward the stage that had been set up on the pier beneath the ship's bow. "That's why everyone's celebrating."

The ship's official christening ceremony had been held the day before and had been a closed affair, with only the cruise-line executives and VIP guests invited, but the stage hadn't yet been disassembled. Banners bearing the blue and white of the Greek flag of the ship's owner, as well as the Liberty circle of stars logo, draped the edges of the platform. In the center, a group of musicians and a dance troupe dressed in traditional white folk costumes performed for the benefit of the *Alexandra's Dream*'s first passengers. Their audience was in a festive mood, snapping their fingers in time to the music while the dancers twirled and wove through their steps.

David bobbed his head to the rhythm of the mandolins. They were playing a folk tune that seemed vaguely familiar, possibly from a movie he'd seen. He hummed a few notes. "Catchy melody, isn't it?"

Stefan turned his gaze on David. His eyes were a striking shade of blue, as cool and pale as a winter horizon and far too solemn for a child not yet five. Still, the smile that hovered at the corners of his mouth persisted. He moved his head with the music, mirroring David's motion.

David gave a silent cheer at the interaction. Hopefully, this cruise would provide countless opportunities for more. "Hey, good for you," he said. "Do you like the music?"

The child's eyes sparked. He withdrew his thumb with a pop. *"Moozika!"*

"Music. Right!" David held out his hand. "Come on, let's go closer so we can watch the dancers."

Stefan grasped David's hand quickly, as if he feared it would be withdrawn. In an instant his budding smile was replaced by a look close to panic.

Did he remember the car accident that had killed his parents? It would be a mercy if he didn't. As far as David knew, Stefan had never spoken of it to anyone. Whatever he had seen had made him run so far from the crash that the police hadn't found him until the next day. The event had traumatized him to the extent that he hadn't uttered a word until his fifth week at the orphanage. Even now he seldom talked.

David sat back on his heels and brushed the hair from Stefan's forehead. That solemn, too-old gaze locked with his, and for an instant, David felt as if he looked back in time at an image of himself thirty years ago.

He didn't need to speak the same language to understand exactly how this boy felt. He knew what it meant to be alone and powerless among strangers, trying to be brave and tough but wishing with every fiber of his being for a place to belong, to be safe, and most of all for someone to love him....

He knew in his heart he would be a good parent to Stefan. It was why he had never considered halting the adoption process after Ellie had left him. He hadn't balked when he'd learned of the recent claim by Stefan's spinster aunt, either; the absentee relative had shown up too late for her case to be considered. The adoption was meant to be. He and this child already shared a bond that went deeper than paperwork or legalities.

A seagull screeched overhead, making Stefan start and press closer to David.

"That's my boy," David murmured. He swallowed hard, struck by the simple truth of what he had just said.

That's my *boy.*

"I can't be patient, Rudolph. I'm not going to stand by and watch my nephew get ripped from his country and his roots to live on the other side of the world."

Rudolph hissed out a slow breath. "Marina, I don't like the sound of that. What are you planning?"

"I'm going to talk some sense into this American kidnapper."

"No. Absolutely not. No offence, but diplomacy is not your strong suit."

"Diplomacy be damned. Their ship's due to sail at five o'clock."

"Then you wouldn't have an opportunity to speak with him even if his lawyer agreed to a meeting."

"I'll have ten days of opportunities, Rudolph, since I plan to be on board that ship."

* * * * *

Follow Marina and David as they join forces to uncover the reason behind little Stefan's unusual silence, and the secret behind the death of his parents....

Look for FROM RUSSIA, WITH LOVE by Ingrid Weaver in stores June 2007.

HARLEQUIN®

Mediterranean NIGHTS™

Tycoon Elias Stamos is launching his newest luxury cruise ship from his home port in Greece. But someone from his past is eager to expose old secrets and to see the Stamos empire crumble.

Mediterranean Nights
launches in June 2007 with...

FROM RUSSIA, WITH LOVE
by *Ingrid Weaver*

Join the guests
and crew of
Alexandra's Dream
as they are drawn
into a world of
glamour, romance
and intrigue
in this new
12-book series.

MN1

REQUEST YOUR FREE BOOKS!

Harlequin® Historical
Historical Romantic Adventure!

2 FREE NOVELS PLUS 2 FREE GIFTS!

COMING NEXT MONTH FROM

HARLEQUIN®
HISTORICAL

- **THE PREACHER'S DAUGHTER**
  by **Cheryl St. John**
  (Western)
  Lorabeth Holdridge is a bright butterfly, struggling to break out of
  her suffocating cocoon—will Benjamin be the man to help her?

- **McCAVETT'S BRIDE**
  by **Carol Finch**
  (Western)
  Ex-lawman Jack wanted a quiet life and a restful companion, so
  he sent for a mail-order bride. What he got was Pru—heiress,
  suffragette and all-around firebrand!

- **ROGUE'S WIDOW, GENTLEMAN'S WIFE**
  by **Helen Dickson**
  (Victorian)
  Christopher Claybourne is back—for his title, his revenge and,
  most importantly, for his bride!

- **TEMPTED BY INNOCENCE**
  by **Lyn Randal**
  (Tudor)
  Diego Castillo had vowed his life to God, but Celeste's purity
  could be his downfall....

HHCNM0507